The Mighty Heart of Sunny St. James

Ashley Herring Blake

LITTLE, BROWN AND COMPANY

New York Boston

Copyright © 2019 by Ashley Herring Blake
Excerpt from *Ivy Aberdeen's Letter to the World* copyright © 2018 by Ashley
Herring Blake
Cover art copyright © 2019 by Good Wives and Warriors
Cover design by Angela Taldone
Cover copyright © 2019 by Hachette Book Group, Inc.

Hachette Book Group supports the right to free expression and the value
of copyright. The purpose of copyright is to encourage writers and
artists to produce the creative works that enrich our culture.

The scanning, uploading, and distribution of this book without
permission is a theft of the author's intellectual property. If you would
like permission to use material from the book (other than for review
purposes), please contact permissions@hbgusa.com. Thank you for
your support of the author's rights.

Little, Brown and Company
Hachette Book Group
1290 Avenue of the Americas, New York, NY 10104
Visit us at LBYR.com

Originally published in hardcover and ebook by Little, Brown and
Company in March 2019
First Trade Paperback Edition: March 2020

Little, Brown and Company is a division of Hachette Book Group, Inc.
The Little, Brown name and logo are trademarks of Hachette Book
Group, Inc.

The publisher is not responsible for websites (or their content) that are
not owned by the publisher.

The Library of Congress has cataloged the hardcover edition as follows:
Names: Blake, Ashley Herring, author.
Title: The mighty heart of Sunny St. James / Ashley Herring Blake.
Description: First edition. | New York ; Boston : Little, Brown and
Company, 2019. | Summary: "Twelve-year-old Sunny St. James must
navigate heart surgery, reconnection with a lost mother, the betrayal
of a former best friend, first kisses, and emerging feelings for
another girl." —Provided by publisher.
Identifiers: LCCN 2018017613| ISBN 9780316515535 (hardcover) | ISBN
9780316515504 (ebook) | ISBN 9780316515511 (library edition ebook)
Subjects: | CYAC: Mothers and daughters—Fiction. | Heart—
Transplantation—Fiction. | Friendship—Fiction. | Sexual
orientation—Fiction.
Classification: LCC PZ7.1.B58 Mig 2019 | DDC [Fic]—dc23
LC record available at https://lccn.loc.gov/2018017613

ISBNs: 978-0-316-51554-2 (pbk.), 978-0-316-51550-4 (ebook)

Printed in the United States of America

LSC-C

10 9 8 7 6 5 4 3 2 1

For Rebecca Podos

If it is true that there are as many minds as there are heads,
then there are as many kinds of love as there are hearts.

—LEO TOLSTOY

CHAPTER

1

I'm going to die today.

Definitely for a few minutes and maybe forever. Kate keeps telling me no way, nohow is it going to be forever, but she isn't the one who's about to have her most important internal organ switched out like a new swimsuit at the start of the summer.

I've imagined this moment a lot. I mean, a lot. Day in and day out, while Kate biked back and forth from our house to the bookstore she owns downtown about a million times a day to check on me, I would weave together this very moment in full color. And my imagination is fierce. One of the best on Juniper Island, if I had to guess. When you've spent most of the past two years on your couch watching the sun tick across the sky like I have, you've got a bunch of time to work on your thoughts.

There's usually a lot of blood involved. Of course there is. It's my heart, after all, puny as it may be, the lousy blood-bringer to all my other top-notch organs. The color is pretty, bright red against my pale skin and the white and steel operating room.

Then there are the noises and smells. A lot of people leave out noises and smells when they let their imaginations ramble, but not me. The scalpel zips down my sternum, and my body squelches and squishes as gloved hands dip into my open chest.

I know, I know. I've made my own stomach twist more than once, but this kind of stuff is not for the faint of heart.

Or actually, I guess it is.

"You're doing it again," Kate says. She sits on the edge of the pea-green pleather chair that doubles as a bed in my hospital room. There's a book open on her lap, but I know she's not reading it. She's too busy watching me, watching the tubes hooked into my arms and nose, watching that machine *beep-beep-beep*, proving I'm still alive. Which I am.

For now.

My eyelids close heavily. They've been doing that a lot lately, dropping like an iron door every time I blink. I pry them open again. "Doing what?"

"Picturing things," she says.

"We could play Frisbee instead. Did you bring a Frisbee?"

She smiles and shakes her head at me. "Just picture good things, okay?"

"Like running and going to the beach with—"

I cut myself off, but we both know who I was about to say. My official FBF—aka Former Best Friend. Even after four months of not having her in my life, she's still a habit. A bad one.

"Like running and going to the beach this summer," Kate finishes for me, conveniently leaving Margot Banks out of it.

"I called Suzette, just so you know," Kate says.

"What? Why?" Suzette is Margot's mom, who I've known since I was four, when Kate brought me from Nashville to Juniper Island, just off the coast of South Carolina.

"Because she loves you," Kate says.

I roll my eyes, even though I know it's true. But Suzette was never the problem.

"I told her we got the call and the surgery was today," Kate goes on. "She said she was sending you all her good thoughts and she'd let Margot know what was going on."

I wait for Kate to tell me more, that Margot had a message for me, even if it's just a simple hello and, you know, *good luck with that whole new-heart thing, and, while I'm at it, I confess I'm pretty much the worst friend ever,* but Kate just sits there, her eyes going all misty on me again.

"Kate."

"What?"

"You're crying."

"Well, yeah, I'm allowed to cry."

She stands up, her book sliding to the floor, but she doesn't bend to pick it up. Usually, Kate's a neat freak—everything in our house and the bookstore is just so. Before Margot's debacle of a birthday party back in January, she and I used to play this game where we'd move something small, like a candle from the living room to the kitchen or a picture frame from one side of a shelf to the other, and see how long it took Kate to notice.

The longest she ever went was forty-seven minutes, and for twenty-one of those minutes, she'd been at the bookstore.

Now her book is facedown on the germ-filled floor, the pages all crinkled up, and she doesn't even care. It's a hardcover too. It's because of me. I sucked the care right out of her. I'm ready to stop doing that.

She lies down next to me and tucks my hair behind my ear, then rubs circles into my temple over and over again the way she does when I can't sleep.

I look at the machine next to my bed, my heart rate pulsing 62 ... 63 ... 64 ... 62.

"Are you scared?" Kate asks.

"What, about dying? Meh."

"Sunny St. James."

"What?

"You're not going to die," she says.

"But I am. For a few minutes after they snip the bad heart out—"

"Hey, I love that heart."

"It's still bad, right?"

She doesn't say anything to that. Two years ago, when I was ten, I fainted during recess at school. Just totally face-planted in the rubber mulch. A day later, I was diagnosed with cardiomyopathy, which pretty much means my heart is bad. A total failure.

"And after they cut it out," I say, continuing my morbid lesson, "I'll be dead. Like, actually dead while they put the new heart in and attach all the blood vessels and arteries and stuff."

Kate sighs and rubs her forehead. "I shouldn't have asked."

I nudge Kate with my shoulder as hard as I can, which has about as much force behind it as a gnat smacking against a window.

"I wonder if death is like being underwater," I say. "You know, like when you go really deep and then look up and everything is all dark and hazy and flowy. Doesn't sound too bad, does it?"

Kate groans.

"Maybe death is like getting a big hug from the ocean."

"Sunny!"

I smile and snuggle against her as much as the tiny bed and all the tubes will let me.

The truth is, I'm pretty scared. But I'm excited too. I think you can be both at the same time. I'm tired of being sick. I'm tired of thinking about Margot and her swim team friends and how much cooler they are than me because they can, you know, do more than just lie on a couch. I'm tired of seeing the ocean but not being able to dive under the waves. I'm tired of thinking about death too, even though I talk about it so much, Kate probably believes it's my favorite thing.

But I don't want to die. I want to turn thirteen. I've never even been inside Juniper Island Middle School and I'm technically supposed to start seventh grade this fall. I want to do amazing and awesome things I never thought I'd get to do, like bungee jumping and skydiving and water skiing. I want to go to an overnight camp and make myself sick on junk food with a best friend.

I want to have a best friend again.

And I really, really, really want to kiss a boy. Like, I want to kiss a boy so bad, my lips itch all the time. I don't mean the kind of kiss that Kate pops onto my forehead every night or the way Dave kisses my hand sometimes when he's being silly. I mean a real kiss. The kind that Margot has already had with Sam Blanchard and

Henry Lee. The kind of kiss that could change my whole life.

Okay, fine, yes, I know kissing doesn't seem like such a huge deal when my heart is gasping its last breath, but if I die without ever being really and truly kissed, I'm going to be so mad.

71 ... 72 ... 73 ...

Kate holds me closer. She always knows when my mind gets going because I get really quiet, and quiet isn't exactly my usual thing. She pats my head like she's trying to calm it down, then circles her thumb on my temple while she stares at me. Kate's an excellent starer. When Margot and I would stay up too late during sleepovers, making all sorts of noise way past midnight, she'd open my door and stare at us. She didn't even have to say anything. We knew she meant business and we shut up really fast.

This is a different kind of stare, though. I'm not in trouble, I know that, but she keeps looking at me, like her eyes are thirsty and I'm a cup of cold water.

"What's wrong?" I ask. Which, yeah, might be a silly question considering where we are and what's about to happen, but it's more than that. I can tell. For the past few months, Kate's been my number one best friend. We're all each other has, aside from Dave, so I know her pretty well. I also know that wrinkle between her eyebrows means she wants to talk about my mom.

"You're in love with Dave, aren't you?" I say to throw her off her game.

Her eyes widen. I try to keep a straight face, but a grin tugs at my mouth. Dave's her best friend from high school and everyone's favorite person ever. He's a musician with muscular arms, curly black hair, and dark brown skin and, true to his artistic nature, wears plaid shirts and black-framed glasses three hundred and sixty-five days a year. Even I think he's cute and he's about a million years old. It's obvious to everyone but Kate that all the tortured love songs he writes are about her.

"Sunny, for goodness' sake," she says, but her cheeks are red. "No."

"Uh-huh, sure."

She takes a deep breath and her smile flattens out again. "Sunshine."

My weak little heart kicks up a notch. I tell it to calm down, but, like always, it doesn't listen to me.

"I don't want to talk about her, okay?" I say.

Kate sighs and that wrinkle disappears. Whenever she tries to bring up my mom—which happens every year on my birthday, every major holiday, and the first day of school like clockwork—I can never figure out if she's relieved or sad when I shut her down. Either way, she's always telling me it's okay to have questions and I'm always telling her I don't have any.

I was born in Nashville. My mother's name is Lena and she was a musician, like Dave. My dad, whose name was Ethan, died in a motorcycle accident right after I was born. Then, when I was four, Lena couldn't take care of me anymore, so she gave me to her best friend, Kate, because Kate was all she had. Kate had just bought Cherry Picked Books on Juniper Island, so she moved me down here with her. Kate, who's been there every day of my life since. Kate, who cried a bunch when I got sick, but didn't freak out and didn't leave me, even when things were really bad. Kate, who's here right now.

That's all I need to know, right?

Right.

"Sunny," Kate says. "Your mom—"

"Kate, come on. I'm about to kick the bucket. Let's talk about puppies and rainbows."

"Or how death is like an ocean hug?" Kate says, rolling her eyes.

"Yes, exactly." I take the deepest breath I can and shove Lena right out of my head. "Now, do you think it'll be cold or hot? Or maybe it'll just be a whole bunch of nothingness, like before being born? That would be disappointing, wouldn't it? I hope death is *something*."

Kate groans again but smiles and presses her nose against my cheek. "I love you, Sunshine."

Her voice sounds funny, even though she's smiling.

Before I can tell her I love her too, Dr. Ahmed comes into the room, her dark hair pulled into a tight bun. She doesn't have her white coat on. Instead, she's covered in green scrubs from head to toe. Behind her, two orderlies wheel in a gurney, maneuvering it right next to my bed.

Dr. Ahmed smiles down at me. She's been my doctor for two years. She was the one to tell Kate and me that a transplant was the only thing that would save me. That was a year and a half ago.

Last night, the pager the United Network of Organ Sharing gave us went off in the middle of dinner. We were sitting on the porch so I could smell the sea, eating grilled cheese and talking about how maybe, if I wasn't too tired, we'd go down to the beach later and dip our toes in the cool, early-May ocean. But we never got a chance because suddenly the pager that Kate always kept clipped to her front pocket started beeping at us. It had never gone off before and it could only mean one thing.

"We're ready for you, Sunny," Dr. Ahmed says now, placing a cool hand on my forehead after checking my vitals. "New life awaits."

"Maybe," I say.

She cracks a smile, used to my realism by now.

"I'll do my best to make that a *definitely*, all right?"

I give her a thumbs-up and then she nods to the order-lies hovering around me. Kate inhales a shaky breath and kisses my cheek. She kisses it so hard, it almost hurts, but I'm glad. I can really feel that kiss. Remember it.

"I'll be here when you get back," Kate says as she gets up from the bed. "I'll be right here, Sunshine." Tears are already falling down her face, and her voice is thick, like she's talking around a mouthful of peanut butter.

"One, two, three," one of the orderlies says, and then they lift me up, like I'm a plank of wood, and set me gently on the wheeled gurney.

I can't think of anything super-awesome or emotional to say as they start rolling me out of the room, so I just hold up my pinkie. Kate's face is red and soaking wet and she's making these soft whimpering noises that make my throat feel all thick. She wraps her little finger around mine and gives it a wiggle.

Then the scene changes. Kate's gone and I'm zooming down the white-walled hallway, fluorescent lights bright overhead. We turn this way and that until they wheel me into a cold room. It smells exactly like I thought it would—almost like nothing, like a slate wiped clean.

Another doctor, with glasses, appears and puts a clear mask over my face. Dr. Ahmed is just behind him, her own mask in place. Nurses are everywhere, IV bags full of clear liquid and blood ready to go, all their faces covered up so they don't sneeze or breathe on me.

"Count down from ten for me, Sunny," the glasses doctor

says. I nod, the good little patient, but my stomach is going crazy, like there are a million ants in there.

Ten . . . nine . . .

I let my eyes close.

Eight . . . seven . . .

I feel floaty, like there really is water underneath me. I'll have to remember to tell Kate, but I'm not sure if I will because six . . . five . . .

I only make it to four before the ocean swallows me whole.

CHAPTER

2

It turns out that being dead is a lot like dreaming.

The world feels soft and gauzy and slow, as though I'm underwater. In fact, I think I am underwater. Everything is blue. All sorts of blue—navy and cerulean, aqua and royal, all swirling together like a kaleidoscope.

Way off in the distance, I see a dark shape moving toward me. It gets closer and closer, bigger and bigger, and soon, I can tell it's a person.

A woman. She has a graceful tail instead of legs and her hair is long and inky, just like mine.

She moves closer and closer, her hands scooping away the deep blue to get to me. I hear my name, thick and bright at the same time, and I know exactly who the mermaid is.

I know because the mermaid's face is the same face

that's in this picture in my nightstand at home. Kate gave it to me when I was super-little. She thinks I threw it away a long time ago—because that's what I told her—but instead I take it out every night after Kate goes to bed and think about how the face inside the photo looks just like mine, only older.

When I was seven years old, and eight and nine, and okay, maybe even ten, I would look and look at that picture and tell myself the lady inside was a mermaid. She was a mermaid and that was why she was gone. She was a beautiful, iridescent-tailed mermaid with long black hair who didn't know what to do with a two-legged human girl. After a few years of pulling me up from the deepest parts of the ocean to gulp at the salty sea air, she finally decided that I fit better on land and left me nestled in Juniper Island's sun-white sand for Kate to find. Then she disappeared into the great big blue, never to be seen again.

But now I'm in the sea with her. We're together, so I know something's off. Something about this isn't real, so maybe I really am dead. I pump my human arms and legs to swim toward the mermaid. And the closer I get, the happier I feel, but my eyes sting with a whole bunch of sad tears that shouldn't even be able to fall if I was really underwater.

Soon she's right in front of me. Our hair flows together, jet-black against the glowing aqua sea. Her amber-brown eyes stare into my amber-brown eyes. Freckles spill across her nose and onto her cheeks.

"I didn't know you had those," I say.

"I knew you had those," she says back. She smiles and reaches out a fingertip, touching the dots on my own nose and cheeks. "We match."

She says it like it's a good thing, like it matters. I don't know if it matters or not, so I stay quiet, floating, floating, floating in the middle of all the blue.

"Oh, Sunshine, I'm so sorry," she finally says. Underwater tears fill up her eyes.

"Only Kate and Dave call me Sunshine," I say.

"They call you that because I did."

I shake my head, and my hair breaks away from hers, lacy and flowy like jellyfish tentacles. She looks so sad and her mouth is still moving, but I can't hear her anymore. She's getting smaller and smaller because the ocean is pulling me away from her, pushing me up to the surface. My mermaid reaches out both of her arms, her tail flapping wildly to get to me, but it's no use. I've got legs, lungs that need air, and for the second time in my life, the ocean spits me back up on land.

CHAPTER

3

I guess *land* is a hospital bed.

The mermaid from my dream sits by my side in a pea-green pleather chair.

Her tail is covered up with a pair of torn jeans, and she's wearing a gauzy black tank top. She has dark tattoos all over her bare arms, from her shoulders to her wrists. My eyes are all fuzzy, but I can see a million suns scattered over her skin, peeking out from between flowers and stars and trees. Her hair is black and her eyes are amber, just like mine, just like my dead-dream mermaid. She leans forward. There are freckles on her nose and a silver ring looped around her bottom lip, which is painted a pretty plum purple, just like a mermaid's would be.

"Sunshine," she says. Her eyes are shiny with tears. I squeeze my own shut and pop them open again. I must still be dreaming. Or maybe I really am dead and this is the afterlife. She takes my hand and I can feel the warmth. That smell that seems to soak into all hospital walls—pee and bleach and baked chicken—fills my nose, and I can hear the *beep-beep-beep* of my heart monitor.

My heart.

No, not mine. Someone else's.

"Sunny, you're okay," the mermaid says. I shake my head, because no, no, no, I'm not okay. I'm dead. I don't have a new heart. They didn't bring me back to life.

I yank my hand out of hers and tug at my hospital gown. It's scratchy and smells like sleep, like I've been lying here for years and years. You'd think I'd get better clothes if I was dead. You'd think the sea would've just kept me.

The *beep-beep-beep* gets faster and faster. I pull on my gown and see a white bandage on my chest. It goes all the way down to right above my belly button. I have a tube in my arm, one in my nose. I pull, claw, because the mermaid is still here. She's standing now, trying to grab my hands. She has legs.

"Sunny, calm down. Sunny!"

I thrash like a seal.

Beepbeepbeepbeepbeep.

People in green and blue scrubs swell into the room like an ocean wave. I see Kate and no, no, no, she can't be here. She can't be dead too.

17

"Sunny, sweetie, it's okay," she says, taking my face between her hands. A nurse jabs a needle into some clear thing attached to the tube in my arm. Heat spreads into my chest like I swallowed warm water.

"Katie, what can I do?" my mermaid asks.

"I gave you ten minutes, Lena," Kate says, her hands still on my face. "That's enough for today."

"There are way too many people in here anyway," the nurse snaps. "One visitor at a time." She presses a stethoscope to my chest, then checks the big white bandage. It hurts. It feels like I've been cut in two and sewn back up again.

"Katie," my mermaid says, but Kate shakes her head.

"I knew this was too soon. You need to go."

The mermaid's face crumples. I think her name is Lena. I think she might be...I think she's...

But my whole body is warm now, the *beep-beep-beep* steady as the tide, and the ocean takes me back again.

CHAPTER

4

I wake up feeling like I've swallowed gallons of salty seawater and then promptly puked it all up. I'm floaty and fuzzy, and I guess I keep mumbling about mermaids and being in the ocean, because someone—judging by the snippy sound of her voice, an overtired nurse—keeps telling me I'm in Port Hope Children's Hospital, which is solidly on dry land and a good half hour from Juniper Island.

When the fog clears a little, I have no clue what day it is. I'm sore all over, still have a tube up my nose and a needle in my arm, and can only see Kate for a few minutes at a time while I'm in the cardiac ICU. My chest feels weird—part numb, part oh-wow-that-hurts, and part... well, just weird. A bright red line crisscrossed with stitches runs from just below my throat to right above my belly button, a scar I'll have for the rest of my life.

As it turns out, I'm not dead. But it sure was weird when I was.

✸

"You weren't dead, Sunny," Kate tells me as she fluffs the unfluffable pillows on my bed. It's now been about a week since the surgery and I'm well enough to move out of the ICU and into my own room.

"But I was. I kept dreaming about…mermaids. In the ocean and then in my hospital room. The ocean part was nice, but I could do without hospital room dreams, thanks very much."

I don't want to tell her that the mermaid was my mom. If I did, Kate would sit down and sigh and ask me if I want to talk about it, the answer to which is and always will be a ginormous *Nope*.

So I keep my mouth shut, but Kate rubs her eyes and sits down on the edge of my bed anyway, breathing out my name like it weighs a gazillion tons.

"Wow, you sure know how to put the clouds in Sunshine," I say.

That gets a smile out of her and she runs a hand over my hair. "You're still you. That's good."

I nod, but it gets me thinking. Am I? I don't care what Kate says. I *died*. The old Sunny is gone. Forever. I have a whole new heart underneath my scar. Like, it's not the heart I was born with. I put my finger on my neck, then right below my thumb, then press my palm to my chest. I feel the same thrum-thrum-thrum every time. It's in there, doing its job. It hasn't rebelled against me yet.

I can't stop thinking about whose heart I have now. What their name was, if they ever got to kiss anyone. It had to be a kid, because I'm a kid and you can't just stick any old heart in a kid's chest. Whoever it was had to die. Whoever it was is dead-dead, not just dream-dead. And I'm alive because of them.

But with heart transplants, you never really know what will happen the next minute, the next second, even. My body can just up and say, "Um, no thanks," to the new heart. Organ rejection, Dr. Ahmed calls it, meaning my body thinks the heart is an enemy combatant and starts attacking it. Death is pretty much a guarantee if that happens, so I have to take a bunch of pills and stay in the hospital for a long time so the doctors can poke and prod me a billion times a day.

So, yeah, I'm alive. For now. But now is long enough to start my *New Life* plan. Whenever I think about my *New Life*, I always see the words capitalized and in italics, like the title of an amazing music album or book. I've been cooking this plan up for months, just in case I ever did get a new heart. Now here I am and everything is going to be different.

But first, I've got to get out of this hospital, and to do

that, I need to get stronger. So I don't even complain when a lady named Viv comes to my room and makes me get out of bed. Then she makes me walk. Even with one of those old-people walkers, it takes me about five hundred hours to shuffle down the hall, but I get it done. And, aside from the fact that I'm sore everywhere and have to drink my food, I do feel better. I'm not short of breath and my ankles don't swell up. When I get tired, it's a good tired, the kind of tired I remember feeling after swimming hard or running down the beach with Margot.

My new heart hasn't abandoned me yet. I'm getting stronger every day and soon, I'll be able to go home. And then . . . Sunny St. James takes over the world.

Or, at least, my own little corner of it.

☀

About three weeks after my surgery, I'm scarfing down some pudding. Butterscotch, to be precise. I used to hate pudding. The consistency freaked me out, and what in the world is butterscotch anyway? Now, though, it's the nectar of the gods. It's cool and smooth and doesn't hurt my throat, which is still sensitive from having a tube shoved down it for hours and hours during the surgery.

Kate walks into the room with a vase of wildflowers the Cherry Picked employees sent over. Then, when she sets it down on the table next to my bed, she clears her throat and sighs. Sighing is what Kate does best, but something about this sigh makes Dave stop playing his guitar and sit up. He's on the chair that turns into a really uncomfortable-looking couch, which Kate has been sleeping on every night. They share a look. They don't think I catch these things, but they're way wrong. I could write a whole book about all the looks Kate and Dave pass between them. I wish they'd just go on a date already.

"Are you guys gonna leave me here so you can go kiss?" Their eyes go wide and yep, there it is. Kate's face turns into a bright red tomato, while Dave rubs his forehead over and over again.

"What? No...no!" Kate splutters. Dave fiddles with his guitar's tuning pegs. "For goodness' sake, Sunny."

"Sing the kissing song, Dave!"

"Sunny St. James," Kate says, her hands on her hips.

I grin. It's weird, but I'm totally in love with Dave's music. I pretty much hated it before my surgery, but now I'm obsessed with it.

He used to play guitar in this rock band, Truth Lies Low, and they were actually kind of famous. A couple of years ago, the band broke up and he moved to Juniper Island. Now he helps Kate run Cherry Picked Books, but he still plays at coffee shops and tiny venues in Port Hope, which is on the mainland, and people just eat up his super-moody songs. I used to call it Whiny Boy Music just to make Kate laugh. Now I make Dave play all the whiniest songs for me over and over and over. I had Kate add all of Truth Lies Low's albums to my phone and I've been falling asleep with earbuds stuck in my ears every night while I've been in the hospital.

My favorite is this song called "Out of Orbit." It's all about how this boy finally kisses the girl of his dreams and the whole world pretty much implodes. In a good way.

That's why I want to kiss someone so bad. Because love and kissing inspire the greatest songs and poems and books. Honestly, the idea of pressing my mouth to someone else's kind of freaks me out. Because, wow, you really have to like someone to do that, right? And they really have to like you. I say, if you mash mouths with someone, you'll never forget that person. And they'll never forget you.

In fact, I love Dave's mushy songs so much, I'm trying to write my own. Sort of. I mean, other than my checkups and physical therapy, there's not all that much to do. I just sit here in my hospital bed, day after drab day, and music makes me *feel*, you know?

I've never really wanted to write stuff before, but now I'm a brand-new Sunny. I have all these thoughts. Not that I didn't have them before, but it's a whole new ball game now that I know I get to keep all these thoughts and get a bunch of new ones every day. I've been working on my own ode to kissing, but I can never get any of the words to rhyme. My brain just wants to spill all my thoughts out on the paper. I mean, there are only so many words that rhyme with kiss.

Miss.

Bliss.

Hiss.

And who wants hissing mixing up with kissing? Not me. I've been writing a whole lot of song-ish-type things since my surgery, but none of them feel like a song yet. They just feel like...the ramblings of a girl who really wants to smooch someone.

"Sunny," Kate says as I shove another spork full of caramel-colored goo into my mouth. "Can you put the pudding down? I need to talk to you."

"Now, Kate?" Dave asks.

"She's here," Kate says back, real low like she thinks I can't hear her. "I told her three weeks and it's been three weeks."

"Who?" I ask.

"You don't owe her anything," Dave says.

"Yes, I do," Kate says. She's got tears in her voice. She even swipes at her face and sinks down onto my bed. She picks up the potted blue violets that Suzette sent—Margot's name was also on the card, which I promptly ripped to shreds and trashed—and runs her thumb over the thick velvety leaves.

"What's going on?" I ask. I finally set down my pudding, which now feels like a rock in my belly.

Kate takes a deep breath while she puts her hand on my cheek. She only does that when something's wrong.

"Sunny, it's okay," she says. "I promise."

"What is? What's okay?" I pull her hand off my face. Other than still being sore and kind of weak, I feel okay. My new ticker's still in there, doing its thing, but who knows? I'm a kid. Grown-ups don't tell kids anything, even stuff about their own bodies. When I was diagnosed with cardiomyopathy, Kate took two days to tell me that meant I could actually die. Which is just messed up, in my opinion. "Is it my heart?"

Kate's face goes super-white and she leans close to me, her forehead on mine. "No, sweetie, it's not. Your heart is perfect."

Easy for her to say.

"Then what? Just tell me."

Kate nods against my head. She keeps nodding and Dave's just sitting there with his arms hanging over his guitar and I'm about to scream.

"When you were in the ICU," Kate starts, "you had a visitor."

My stomach turns into a coil of snakes. There's only

one person who Kate would be all nervous telling me about. After all, Kate was the one who came and picked me up from the slumber party from H-E-double-hockey-sticks this past January. I fold my arms and glare. Or I try to. Really, my lower lip keeps bumping around and my eyes sting.

"She's here again and would like to see you," Kate says.

"What, her dumb violets weren't enough?"

Kate frowns. "What?"

"I don't want to see her." I spit the words. Not actual spit, but I really force them out, all mean and stuff.

"Do...do you remember when she was here?" Kate asks.

"No. And I don't want to remember now either. Margot can just get over it."

Kate blinks at me. Dave blinks at me. They blink at each other.

"Sunshine," Kate says softly. "Margot...it's not—"

Someone clears their throat in my doorway. My head pops up and my heart drops down to my feet, which is not an excellent place for a newly attached heart to be. But when I see my visitor, my heart goes all rogue on me.

Because Kate's right. Margot, it is not.

CHAPTER

5

It's my mermaid.

She has a normal human body covered in torn jeans and black stomping boots and a slouchy black T-shirt with some band name on it. Her hair is black too, and her makeup is...well, it's amazing. Light purple lips and darker purple eyeshadow that somehow all works together to look totally subtle and perfect. On top of all that, she has a bunch of tattoos. Familiar ones. Ones I know I've seen before. A million suns. Flowers. Stars.

"Hi," she says.

Her voice is familiar too. Velvety and soft.

"I asked you to wait outside," Kate says.

"I did."

"You're not."

"Katie," Dave says.

I think he motions toward me. I think Kate grabs my hand. I think a lot of things, but I'm not sure about any of them, because there's a mermaid in my room. And this time, I'm pretty positive I'm not dead.

"Sunny," Kate says. "This is Lena. She's... she's—"

"My mermaid," I say out loud.

Lena lifts her dark eyebrows and smiles. "I've always wanted to be a mermaid."

"Well, yeah. Who wouldn't?" I say.

Lena smiles at that, but I don't smile back.

"Are you okay?" Kate asks me, glancing at my monitor.

Okay seems like a silly word right now, so I don't answer.

"Lena called me about a month ago," Kate says. "It had been a long time since I'd heard from her. Years. The last number I had for her was disconnected every time I tried."

"When did you try calling her?" I ask.

Kate winces. "A few times, after you got sick."

The mermaid... or whoever... doesn't say anything to that. She doesn't even look down. She just stares right at me, totally still like a statue. I don't think she's even breathing.

"She wanted to see you," Kate went on, "but you were so sick, baby. I couldn't do that to you. Or her. I just couldn't risk the stress on you and..."

Dave gets up and puts his hand on Kate's shoulder. Tears run down her face, and I know I should hug her or something, but all I can hear is *a month ago* and *called* and *Lena*.

"I was trying to figure out how to handle it all when we found out you got a heart," Kate says. "I called Lena when you went into surgery. I knew I had to."

"I didn't know you were sick." Lena takes another step into the room. Her voice sounds so . . . real. "I never knew. I'm so sorry, Sunshine."

Oh, Sunshine, I'm so sorry.

My dead-dream floats back to me. Lena, reaching out to touch my freckles, our matching jet-black hair. Matching eyes. Matching eyebrows. Matching mouths with the bottom lip just a little bigger than the top.

"I can go, Sunny," Lena says. "If you're uncomfortable at all, I can leave right now."

I stare at her, still trying to piece together if this is all really happening. Whenever I think of Lena, looking at her picture night after night, she's always just this story that never had an ending. A question mark instead of a period.

Lena and Kate used to be best friends. I know they grew up together in Mexico Beach, Florida. Kate brought me to Juniper Island after Lena gave me up.

I was in first grade when I started wondering why I was never allowed to call Kate Mom. I had foggy pictures in my head of a black-haired lady who used to sing a lot, but I could never really figure out if she was real or just some dream I had once. But I knew she wasn't Kate and I knew Kate wasn't my mom. Margot had a mom. All my friends had moms, but I didn't. I just had a Kate, with her white-blond hair and blue eyes that looked nothing like mine.

One day I came home and asked Kate if I could call her Mom. I remember she set down the knife she was using to spread peanut butter over apple slices.

"No, Sunny, you can't," she said.

"Why not?"

"Because I'm not your mom."

"You are, though. You make me take baths and you bought me my favorite unicorn pajamas."

She smiled at me, but her chin wobbled like she was trying not to cry. "That's true."

I scrunched up my brows, because nothing she was saying made sense. Moms took care of kids. Moms bought awesome and amazing pajamas. "Do I have one?"

"A mom? Of course you do. And a dad."

"But he died."

She ran her hand over my hair and nodded.

"But my mom didn't?" I asked.

"No, sweetie. She didn't. She was very sad, though,

31

and she didn't know how to get through it. She didn't handle everything very well."

"What everything?"

"Being sad. And trying to do the best job she could with you."

"She didn't do a good job?"

Kate sighed and handed me my plate of apples. Then she grabbed an old book off her bookshelf and we went onto the porch. She pulled me into her lap on the swing. It creaked as we swayed in the salty air, and the ocean whispered a soothing hush-hush just over the rocks, like a lullaby.

Kate opened the book and took out a picture of a pregnant lady with long dark hair and bright, light brown eyes. My mouth fell open as my fingers closed around the glossy photo.

"She looks like me," I said.

"She does. That's your mom and that's you inside her stomach. Her name is Lena and she loves you so much."

"If she loves me so much, where is she?" I ask.

"She couldn't take care of you anymore."

"Why not?"

"She's sick."

"Like with a cold?"

"Not that kind of sick," Kate said. "She's an alcoholic."

"What's that?"

"She drinks alcohol too much and it's not good for her. It makes her do things she shouldn't."

"Like leaving me at the grocery store?" In that tiny moment, my six-year-old brain flashed to a dingy tile floor and a blue-vested cashier asking me where my parents were while I wailed.

"Oh, Sunny girl," Kate said, kissing my hair.

"So she gave me to you?" I asked.

"Sort of. Yeah."

"She left me?"

"She'll be back for you. She loves you. She's getting help and she'll be back."

Kate pressed her face into my black hair, her arms so tight around me it almost hurt. We sat there in the swing for a long time, watching the ocean swirl while I stared at the picture of Lena. She was so pretty. I wanted to know her, but I wanted Kate too. I ran my fingers over my mom's face and thought about what would happen to Kate when my mom came back.

Well, I never had to find out. I waited, year after year, for my mom to get better and come back, but she never did. I stare at that picture every single night so I'd know her the second I saw her, but it never mattered. So I made up my own ending to the story. Like I said, I've always had a killer imagination, even before my heart flaked out on me, and about a year after Kate gave me the picture, I decided that Lena was a mermaid. That she had to leave me because we were too different and she was too mysterious and exotic for a human girl.

I never asked Kate about my mom again. I knew she wasn't actually a mermaid, but I didn't want to know who she really was either. Because whatever the answers were, they all ended up being about the same thing—my mom left me when I was four and I didn't hear from her for eight whole years.

And now, here she is. After all that nothing. After the heart she gave me shriveled up and got yanked out and replaced with a new one. Suddenly, my question-mark mom is a big old exclamation point.

My brain gets that it's her. My brain gets that she was sick too.

But my heart doesn't.

At least, not this one.

Because she could've called. She could've written. She could've visited, even if she had to leave again. And she never did.

I want to ask her why. I want to know. And I don't want to know. It's weird, wanting something so bad for so long and not wanting it at the same time. It makes me feel dizzy, makes my breath come too fast and shaky.

I scrunch down in my bed and roll over so my back is to my mermaid, to everyone. It hurts, the incision on my chest fiery and sharp, but I don't care. My fingers itch for a pen and paper, because, wow, do I have some thoughts that I need to get out of my head, thoughts that would probably make a great whiny song if I could get the words to rhyme the right way. My brain fills up with all sorts of words like remember and lost and left and I grab on to all of them, holding super-tight so I don't start crying right in front of everyone. No way I want to do that.

No one says anything. Eventually, Kate kisses me on the forehead and gets up from the bed. Dave follows her, because Dave always follows her, and then she starts whispering to my mermaid.

I stick my fingers in my ears and push until it hurts, until all I can hear is my brand-new heart pushing blood around my body, just like a heart should.

You're nothing like I remember.
Maybe that's because
I don't remember much.
It's all blurry,
like we lived underwater
before you left,
and you've just now come up for air.

How did it feel,
when I turned my back today?
Did your heart get stuck in your throat?
Mine beat strong, mine beat sure.
It doesn't know you anyway.

CHAPTER 6

"Sunny, will you please hold still?" Kate says as she rubs a glob of SPF 4,000 onto my back. Okay, fine, it's SPF 70, but it's so thick, it might as well be a bulletproof vest.

Hold still, she says. Like I could possibly sit still on a day like today.

"You need to finish your Ensure," Kate says, nodding to the half-empty can of chocolate yuck nestled in the sand.

"I'd rather never touch the ocean again," I say.

"I doubt that. I'm not letting you dip a toe in that water until you drink your nutrition shake."

"How about a toenail?"

She turns me around and stares her wicked stare, her eyebrows reaching for her blond hairline. I huff loudly and give in, bending over to snatch my Ensure from the sand. Kate winces. She's been doing that a lot lately. Anytime I, you know, *move*.

It's been two weeks since Dr. Ahmed said my heart was ticking along all right and sent me home from the hospital, which means I've had a new heart for six whole weeks. Even though I'm still going strong, Kate watches me like I'm a bomb about to explode. Then again, maybe I am. Sometimes I get real quiet and still and push my hand to my heart. I listen to it work, feel it pump blood under my palm. It's like any minute, I expect it to just... stop.

I guess Kate feels the same because sometimes, she sleeps in my room in a sleeping bag on the floor, like I'm a newborn baby who might suffocate in my blankets. On top of all that, I have to take a mountain of pills every day, go back to the hospital three times a week for checkups, and do all this physical therapy so I can lift stuff and walk around like a normal person.

But today. Oh, beautiful, amazing, cloudy-but-I-don't-even-care today. Today is the day I've been waiting for ever since Dr. Ahmed spoke the words *dilated cardiomyopathy*.

Oh, yes.

Today I am going into the ocean.

And looking for a boy to kiss, but one thing at a time. I have a three-step plan for my *New Life* and I can't really do them out of order.

Step One: Do awesome amazing things I could never do before. Okay, no, getting in the ocean doesn't seem all that amazing and awesome and, okay, yes, I've done it before. But not for a couple of years, I haven't. Not to actually *swim* and have fun without huffing and puffing. Not without Kate risking her own heart attack.

Step Two: Find a new best friend. I may have missed out on the past two years of kid-hood, but I know that I do not want to enter the halls of middle school without a best friend.

Step Three: Find a boy and kiss him. Because kisses. Also handholding and maybe cuddling while watching movies. I'd really like to hug someone who's not a parent figure and thirty-four years old. I *used* to think about kissing girls too, but not anymore. No way. Boys only from here on out. Plus, I like boys, so it might as well be a boy.

I've still been trying to write my own kissing song to go with my New Life plan, but every time my head gets all crowded with song-ish thoughts, I end up writing about something else.

Like Lena. I try not to, but your long-lost mom showing up after eight years is hard to forget, and writing stuff helps me get the words out of my head. None of the songs rhyme, but I like the way they sound when I read them back to myself.

Now, my new heart is so excited about my New Life,

it *thrum-thrums* in my chest. I press a hand to my sternum and give it a little high five. Then I say a thank-you to whoever gave me their heart. I don't know their name and I never will. Some donors want to stay anonymous and mine does. Or, their family does. All I could do was send them a letter that had to go through the United Network of Organ Sharing. I sent it right when I got home from the hospital and, thinking back on it, it seems so silly. *Thank you* is such a silly thing to say for a heart, isn't it?

So I wrote them a song instead. A nonrhyming song, but still. I'm alive because they're dead. That's not something I can ever forget. I wonder what their name was and what their favorite color was and if they liked soccer or if they liked to read.

Look, it's the sea, I whisper to them in my head. *Isn't it beautiful?*

The beach is pretty scarce for a Friday in the middle of June, but that's mostly because it's super-early in the morning and it's cloudy. Still, the pastel beach houses that line the coast are already filling up with vacationers, so any second now, this beach will probably be crawling with people.

I look around for Former Best Friend, my heart pumping out a big old beat of relief when I don't see her. I don't need Margot ruining Step Two. She's really good at ruining best friend things. And kissing things, for that matter.

Kate finishes slathering me with a second skin and I take my last chalky sip of Ensure.

"Okay," she says, capping the sunscreen and tossing it in her enormous beach bag. "I think we're all set."

I give her some side-eye as I carefully, oh so carefully, get my towel out of my bag and ball it up in my arms. "We?"

She takes off her tank top to reveal her black one-piece. "It's your first time back in the water and Dr. Ahmed said—"

"That I'm fine."

"Yes. Fine to swim around a little, not race yourself to the sandbar and back."

"I'm not going to—"

But Kate does her staring thing and I shut up. She knows me too well. The sandbar is a good two hundred yards from the shore and I'm itching to move, move, move.

"Kate, come on. Let me go by myself. I want to do this alone."

"Why?"

I shake my head and gaze out at the water. Honestly, I don't really know. I usually love swimming with whoever, anyone, the more the merrier. But it's my first time back out there. In a lot of ways, the ocean feels like my first friend and I never have to worry that we'll grow apart. It's always there, ready whenever I am. I just want a minute to get to know the water again.

There's a reason why it's Step One of my *New Life*.

"Sunny—"

But whatever Kate was going to say is cut off by her phone's blaring ringtone. This time, it's blasting "Yellow Submarine" by the Beatles.

"Ugh, David Alexander," Kate mutters, digging into her bag for her phone. She only uses Dave's full first and middle name when she's really annoyed. I can't help but laugh. Every time Dave sees Kate—which is all the time, either at our house or at the bookstore—he steals her phone and changes her ringtone. She's tried putting a passcode on it, but he usually figures it out. It's pretty funny.

Kate finds her phone and grapples for the side button to silence the song. She huffs again, but there's a little smile on her face. Yup. Totally in love with Dave.

She looks at the phone and that smile drops like a shell in the sand.

I know what that means.

"It's her, isn't it?" I ask.

Kate sighs and rubs her forehead. She doesn't even have to nod for me to know the answer is yes. Lena's been calling a lot over the past few weeks and every time, Kate's smile falls on the floor, she sighs and rubs her forehead, and then she disappears into her room or wherever so she can talk to Lena in private. Kate never asks if I want to talk to her. She knows I'd just say no. And I would. I would totally say no.

My excitement about my New Life plan fizzles and pops like a soda going flat.

"What does she want?" I ask, and Kate's eyes widen on me. I'm still pretty ticked at Kate for not telling me that Lena had called her while I was sick. Not that I would've talked to her even if I'd known, but still. It's the principle of the thing. If someone's mom comes calling, you tell them, right? So, this is the first time I've even acknowledged the fact that Lena calls, that she's back, that she... exists. My heart jumps all over the place. I press a hand to my chest, trying to get it to calm down.

"She wants to see you," Kate says. "Talk to you."

I nod, but I have no clue what to do with that. Lena is most definitely not part of my New Life plan.

"You don't have to, sweetie," Kate says.

"Yeah, I know."

"But..." Kate takes a big breath and presses her mouth flat, her eyes closed like she's trying to calm herself down.

"But what?"

She opens her eyes and tugs on the end of my hair, a tiny sad smile on her lips. "But you can if you want. Whatever you want to do is okay with me. I'll support you."

"I don't want to." It comes out automatically, a habit.

My heart is a closed hand against my ribs, knocking super-soft.

Kate nods. "I get it. You're angry and you should be. I just don't want you to regret anything. She's still your mom."

I shake my head and chew on my lip to keep it from wobbling. "No, she's not. You are."

Kate cups my cheeks then. "Sunshine."

"Kathryn."

She smiles a little at that, then opens her mouth to say something else, probably about how things with Lena are *complicated* and *when you're an adult, you'll understand.* Blah, blah, blah.

But she never has a chance, because her phone belts out another round of "We all live in a yellow submarine!" and cuts off whatever she was going to say.

She sighs, but this time, I can tell she's going to answer it.

"All right," she says as her thumb hovers over the screen. "Go ahead, okay? I'll watch from here."

"Really?"

She nods. "I trust you. Don't overdo it, all right?"

She tucks a flyaway strand of hair behind my ear and then plops down into the sand, her phone clutched between her hands. She looks dazed and a little upset, but hey, she's letting me go swimming by myself and I'm not about to waste one second of this glorious freedom.

"Thanks Kate love you bye!" I say all in one breath, then

take off toward the water before I can hear her say hello to Lena, careful not to squish my towel under my arm.

"Walk!" she calls after me, but I cannot be stopped. I need to get away from Lena and her phone calls. I need my *New Life* plan and I need it now. My feet *shh-shh* over the dry white sand and it's the most delicious sound I've ever heard. Well, aside from the *hush-hush* of the waves and the wind whipping through my hair and around my arms and legs. A stripe of sunlight escapes from the clouds and falls right on my shoulders, warm and perfect.

Behind me, I hear Kate's voice rising and falling. Talking to Lena. Talking to my mermaid. I go faster until they both fade away.

I stop when I hit wet sand. I place my towel on the ground and unwrap it, making sure I keep it out of Kate's view. Then I take out a clear bottle that used to be full of root beer. Now it's got the song I wrote for my donor inside, scrawled on a rolled-up piece of paper. I found an old cork from a bottle of wine Dave and Kate drank in celebration of the night I came home from the hospital and stuffed it in the opening, sealing the poem inside. I hold it with both hands as I move closer to the water and feel the sand under my feet.

It's amazing.

Of course, I've walked on the beach in the past two years. I've felt the water, but today seems different. I inch forward and stop again, letting the waves come to me. The water slides over my feet and ankles and I nearly squeal. It's cold. Really cold. Beautifully cold. I take another step and the sea greets me again, this time swirling around my calves like a little hello.

I think I cry a little and, hey, no shame here. You'd cry too if you had someone else's heart in your chest and were now looking at the big ocean, feeling small and gigantic all at the same time.

The water gets it, though. I push forward and it rises up and hugs me. The waves are gentle today, as if the sea knew I'd be here and wants to take it easy on me. I go deeper and deeper, the water curling around my hips, then my chest, then my chin, until my hair floats around me. I wait for Kate to call me back, but she doesn't. It's just me and the sea and when I let it pull me under, the world goes quiet.

I stay still for a few seconds, testing out my lungs, feeling my heart do its job in my chest. The water presses me on all sides and it's like I'm home. I never used to like opening my eyes under the ocean. The salt stings something fierce and it's not like I could really see all that much. This time, though, I can't stop myself. It burns for a second, but then my vision clears and everything is dark blue and hazy.

It looks sort of like my dead-dream. I half expect a mermaid to swim up to me, but she doesn't.

She's not in the sea anymore.

I come up and take a breath. The sun peeks at me from behind the clouds, bright and happy, warming my shoulders. I plunge back under, the bottle still gripped tight in my hands. I go as deep as I can, my tippy-toes just barely brushing the sandy bottom, and then...I let my song go.

I watch the bottle swirl and sway in the current until I can't see it anymore. Maybe it'll just end up back on the shore. But maybe not. Maybe the waves will carry it far, far away and someone will read it.

I got the idea last night when I finished writing the song for my donor. I didn't want to send it to their family—I wanted to send it to them. Obviously, I know I can't. I know they won't ever be able to read it, but sending my song out into the ocean feels like they will. It's cosmic and hopeful and maybe, just maybe, my song will make its way around the world and a million people will read it. And if they all read it, they'll all know that I'm alive because of a super-brave kid who died way too soon.

And that's enough for now.

I swim up and take another breath before diving back underwater. I feel all achy, like I need to cry, but I press my feet together and pump my legs like a dolphin, sending my body this way and that. My chest burns a little, but I don't want to go to the surface yet. I used to be able to hold my breath for almost three minutes, way longer than Margot ever could.

"Maybe you really are a mermaid," she'd say, and I'd smile, puff my cheeks full of air, and dive back under. She'd follow me and we'd dolphin-kick out to the sandbar at low tide, pretending it was our secret perch where we'd come up from the deep to rest and spy on the humans.

I push myself up for a gulp of air and plunge back down. The less time I spend on the surface, the better. Kate will just make me get out of the water to smear on more sunscreen.

Or worse, talk to Lena.

I've just grabbed another swallow of air and escaped back underwater when I see a dark silhouette swimming toward me from the deeper part of the sea. It's fuzzy, but I definitely see some flowy hair and a pair of arms cutting through the water. I float, watching as it gets closer and closer, just like my dead-dream. My heart picks up speed, knocking against my chest like it's trying to get out. I swim backward a little, but whoever it is keeps coming.

It's a girl, around my age. She stops right in front of me and we stare at each other, the ocean deep enough to keep us both covered. Her legs circle just like mine, treading water, and I'll admit I'm a little disappointed that she doesn't have a colorful fin instead of legs.

But I don't have time to think about that for too long because, hello, there's a girl I've never seen before staring at me under the ocean. She smiles and lifts a hand to wave.

I wave back, my hand slow through the water. Her hair looks...blue, but maybe that's just the water. Maybe my hair looks blue too, which would be totally awesome.

She holds up a finger and then swims backward a bit before doing a double somersault. I smile and do the same, but I add a twist at the end that takes my body to the side. She makes a slow clapping motion, then stretches her body out—she's wearing a bikini way cooler than my new practical, scar-hiding one-piece—and spins like an ice skater twirling in the air.

I'm about to do the same—adding my own special flourish, of course—when I realize my lungs are screaming for air. I don't want to be the one to stop our game, but I can't wait any longer. If I drown in the ocean after all we've been through, Kate'll kill me herself.

I kick and kick and my head breaks the surface. I gulp at the air, my legs still treading because I'm way farther from the shore than I meant to be. The girl pops up right next to me, taking big swallows of salty air too.

"You're hair really is blue," I say between huffs, and

then wish I hadn't. Of course she knows what color her hair is.

But she laughs and runs a hand over her wet head. "Yup. My mom lets me dye it whatever color I want."

"It looks so cool." And it so does. It's not neon blue or anything, but more blue-black, with the tips brighter than the rest of her hair and streaks of blue all over.

"What color should I do next?" the girl asks.

I tilt my head and narrow my eyes, thinking. She's pretty and has dark eyes, with smooth brown skin covered in water droplets. And, of course, the super-cool bikini, which is grass green with little pink lollipops all over it.

"Purple, for sure," I finally say.

"Yeah?"

"Maybe lilac or lavender."

She grins. "That'll take a lot of bleach. You'll have to do it with me."

"Me? I don't think so."

"Why not?"

I open my mouth to say no way again, but nothing comes out. I've never really thought about dyeing my hair before. About a year ago, when Margot and I still talked every single day, she dyed her curly hair, but it was only to a natural-looking red. I remember because the dye left red trails in the pool. Margot said it looked like blood.

But me? Nope. Kids with heart disease don't dye their hair. They don't do anything fun at all. But now it seems like the best idea in the world.

"Um...maybe?" I say.

She narrows her eyes at me. "You should definitely go blue. Like, aquamarine."

I'm about to tell her that's my favorite color when my chest starts to ache. We're still treading water and I'm breathing hard. I really wish I hadn't swum out so far.

"You okay?" the girl asks.

I nod but start paddling toward the shore. The girl comes with me. She slides through the water like a seal, while I suddenly feel like a flopping fish. My heart yells at me, pounding hard. I whimper a little and the girl puts her arm around my waist, helping me swim, so now not only am I possibly dying, I'm blushing as red as a maraschino cherry from embarrassment. I can't believe Kate hasn't called in the coast guard yet.

As I get closer to the beach, I see why.

She's still on the phone. She's not even looking at me. Instead, she's walking around in circles with that little worry wrinkle between her eyes, yammering away.

Part of me is super-annoyed. Lately, she's been sitting on the closed toilet lid while I take a shower to make sure I don't pass out and crack my head open. She cuts up my food like I'm a baby, just to make sure I swallow it all okay.

Then, the moment I feel like my heart might really be freaking out, she chooses to take a break.

The other part of me thinks...well, let's just say I'd rather not get into the whole I *have another person's heart in my chest* Thing with this new girl right now. Or ever. And Kate? If Kate saw me huffing and puffing, she'd definitely make it a Thing. A very loud Thing.

My feet finally scrape at the shore, shallower and shallower, until I collapse facefirst into the wet sand. So tired. So...tired.

"Are you sure you're all right?" the girl asks, glancing toward Kate. "Is that your mom over there? Should I get her?"

I roll over and shake my head, but I can't talk yet. Still, the ache is getting duller and duller, my breathing steadier. I just overdid it. I'm not dying. My heart still likes me.

I tell myself all of these things over and over while my body calms down. And also while this girl sits down next to me and waits, her teeth chewing on her bottom lip.

After a few minutes, I sit up. I press my hand to my chest—thrum-thrum-thrum, slower and slower until it settles into a nice, healthy rhythm. I glance behind me and Kate is still on the phone. She's not talking anymore, though. Now she's listening.

"Sorry," I say to the girl, and leave it at that.

She shrugs. "That's okay. I like saving the day."

"You did *not* save the day."

"I so did."

"Look, I'm a great swimmer." I turn so I'm facing her. The sand scratches at my legs. "Give me a week and I'll kick your butt in a race."

"Oh, you're so on. I'm a great swimmer too."

I stick out my hand and she grabs it, pumping it over and over. Pretty soon we're doing all sorts of handshakes—hooking our fingers, fist-bumping, slapping the backs of our palms together. We bust up laughing when we try to high-five and it sends a sand shower down on our heads.

"I'm Quinn Ríos Rivera," she says, rolling her Rs.

"Wow, that's really pretty."

"Right? I love it. Ríos was my dad's last name and Rivera is my mom's last name. My grandparents were born in Puerto Rico. A lot of people there use both names."

"Okay, Quinn Ríos Rivera."

I don't say it as pretty as she does, but she doesn't seem to mind.

"What's your name?" she asks.

"I'm...Sunny." I kind of mumble, heart ticking up into my throat while I wait for some eye-widening or wincing or, even worse, an *oh you poor thing* frown. I've never seen Quinn before, so she has to be a visitor or super-new to the island, but still. Our town is the size of a Mason jar and people just love talking good and loud about tragic stories. Like, say, the one about a motherless twelve-year-old who needs a heart transplant. And it's not like my name is super-common.

But Quinn just smiles and shakes sand out of her hair. My heart relaxes into a rhythm. I can't remember the last time I talked to someone who didn't already know who I was.

"Do you live here?" she asks.

"Yeah."

"Wish I did. I'm only here for the summer. I got here a week ago with my mom. She's an underwater photographer and she has to get a whole bunch of photos of dolphins for National Geographic."

"Whoa. Cool."

She sighs and starts digging a hole in the sand. "I guess."

"Does she just, like, jump in the water with her camera?"

"Pretty much. A boat takes her out really far and she scuba dives."

My skin breaks out in goose bumps. I can't imagine going that deep in the ocean, so deep the sun barely lights the way. I bet there really are mermaids down there.

"Do you ever get to go with her?" I ask.

"She won't let me dive with her on shoots, but I get to go on the boat sometimes. The water near Australia is really cool. She took me snorkeling around the Great Barrier Reef."

"No way."

She nods and pulls up a nautilus shell, all cream and brown swirled together. "A lot of the reefs there are dying because of global warming. That's what she was there to photograph, so it was kind of sad. But still really amazing. I guess it was both."

Amazing and sad at the same time—I know what that's like, but all I can get out is a super-smart "Yeah."

"It's just me and my mom," Quinn goes on. "She travels all over the world for work. I've been to every continent except Antarctica."

"Whoa," I say again. I'm in awe. Literal, heart-thumping awe. But Quinn shrugs her shoulders while she picks sand out of the shell, as if she just told me water is wet.

"Hey, do you want to go with me to the beach movie tonight?" she asks. Now her eyes light up and her mouth curls into a big old smile. The beach movie is pretty fun, but I don't know if it's better than the Great Barrier Reef or deep-sea diving.

Every Friday in the summer, the island shows really old films, mostly in black-and-white. I love them, though, and almost all of them have at least one good kissing scene in them.

Margot and I used to go to the beach movie all the time

back in elementary school. We'd drag Kate and Suzette with us, bags full of buttery popcorn with dark chocolate M&M's mixed in, so it's basically the best stuff on earth.

I haven't been to one of those movies in a long time. Kate tried to take me a few times after I got sick, just me and her, but I'd always fall asleep before the sun went down all the way, right there on a towel for the whole island to see. It wasn't even close to fun.

But Quinn...she's not Kate or Margot. She's not a Juniper Islander. She's the first person I've ever really met. I've known all my friends—well, Margot—pretty much forever. The whole island knows that my mom took off before I even started kindergarten. When I got sick, they all knew. When I stopped going to school, they all knew why. I've never told my story to anyone. I've never had to.

Until now, I guess, but I don't want to tell the same old story. This is my New Life, after all. I got a whole new heart. I should at least get to be a whole new Sunny to go along with it, right?

"Yeah, I'll go," I say.

Quinn smiles so big, my stomach flutters. I did that. I made someone smile instead of frown or fake-smile with worry.

"It's going to be amazing," she says. "Meet me here around six?"

I nod and then she squeals happily before pulling me into a search for an auger shell, one of those that look like a unicorn horn. My heart ticks along, good and excited. I could be anyone with Quinn. Kate could be my birth mom. My heart was never broken. My best friend never promised to be there for me no matter what and then committed the worst betrayal that betrayers ever dared to betray.

"Got one!" Quinn yells triumphantly, holding up a white and brown auger, spiraling like a soft-serve ice cream cone. She runs over to where I'm digging in the wet sand and presses the shell into my hand. "You keep it."

"What?" I say. "These are pretty rare. I can't keep it."

She shakes her head. "You can give it back to me when I beat you to the sandbar and back."

"Oh, so you mean, I get to keep it forever?"

"You wish," she says, but she's grinning. I grin back.

Step One: Completed.

Step Two: In progress.

I totally forget about Kate and her dumb phone
call until Quinn says she has to meet her mom for lunch
and runs off down the beach. I watch her blue hair flapping like a curly kite and try to remember what it was like
to run that long, that hard.

When I turn back around to where Kate had been pacing, Dave is there too—in jeans, because I've never seen
him wear anything but skinny rock star jeans, even on the
beach—and they're sitting in the sand.

He's got his arm around her shoulders, and she's
wiping at her face like she's been crying. My stomach
knots up, wondering what she and Lena talked about that
made her cry, but I don't want to think about that or how
a million questions are trying to jump out of my mouth

right now. I want to think about the auger shell in my hand.

The auger shell and a new heart that didn't go kaput in the ocean.

The auger shell, a happy heart, *and* an invitation from Quinn to go to the movie on the beach tonight.

When Kate sees me, she scrambles to her feet, grabbing Dave's hand and pulling him up with her. Then she drops his hand super-fast, because she's weird and won't admit she's madly in love with him.

"Sunny, sweetie, how'd it go?" she asks.

"It's a miracle, I'm alive!" I singsong, doing a little skip and a hop and flourishing my arms.

"Not funny," she says.

"Kind of funny," Dave says, winking at me.

She elbows him in the stomach.

"You guys stop flirting," I say, and they both turn candy-apple red. It's just too easy.

"Do you feel okay?" Kate asks. "Seriously. Any dizziness or shortness of breath?"

I tap my chest lightly. "Good as gold in here."

Kate nods and then shoots Dave a look. "Listen, honey, Lena—"

"Can I go to the movie tonight?"

Kate blinks at me and I hold my breath. If she pushes

me too much about Lena, I know I'll cave like an empty Coke can. I feel all jittery, and I can't decide if it's from the ocean or Quinn or hearing the name Lena spoken out loud way too many times in the past few weeks. Probably all three. I squeeze the auger shell in my hand.

"The beach movie?" Kate finally says, and I let blood back into my fingers.

"Yeah, I met this girl just now and I really, really, really want to go."

"The girl with blue hair you were talking to?"

"Her name is Quinn. She's very nice and healthy and probably knows how to administer CPR."

Kate cracks a smile, but it fades quick. "Oh, honey, I don't know..."

I groan, but it's not like I'm surprised. Kate goes into total Mama Bear mode whenever I want to leave the house lately. And leave the house without her? Double the freak-out.

"Kate, come on," I say. "I did fine just now. And you weren't even with me!"

"We could go and spy on her like really horrible grown-ups," Dave says to Kate.

"No, you could not," I say.

"I'll wear my Speedo," Dave says.

"Kate, chain him in the basement."

Kate tries to hide her laugh, but she can't. She always goes all squishy around Dave, because love.

"Can we make a big old batch of buttery popcorn?" I ask. "With M&M's? Oh, and can we go shopping? I need some new clothes. All my old ones suck."

"Language, Sunny."

"But they do!" I need a *New Life* wardrobe, stat.

"Your clothes are adorable. They're so you."

Which is exactly the problem, but I'm on the hunt for a yes right now, and getting all existential about my new heart isn't the way to do it.

"Please, please, please!" I clasp my hands and bounce on my feet. Kate wants to press my shoulders down to keep me on the ground, I can tell.

"Fine," she finally says. "But no butter."

"Katie," Dave says. "For real?"

"Whine at her for me, Dave," I say.

His back straightens and he pushes up his sleeves.

"Oh, no," Kate says. Her voice still sounds kind of watery, but she's smiling. She backs up toward the dunes and waves her finger at him. "No, no."

Dave rolls his shoulders back and clears his throat.

"Get her, Dave, get her," I say.

Kate groans, but Dave cannot be stopped. He starts singing, loudly, one of Truth Lies Low's most famous songs, "You're the Sky." There's more people on the beach by now and most of them turn their heads to listen.

You gotta let me cry.
You gotta let me try.
You gotta let me tell you that you're the sun and you're
*   the sky.*

See? Super-whiny. Dave's voice is really nice, though, all velvety with a little growl on the end, which he plays up big-time whenever he sings to Kate. She hates it. But she really doesn't hate it, because soon she's laughing and says, "Fine, fine, you can have a little butter on the pop-corn. But no shopping today. I have to go by Cherry Picked for a couple of hours. And only if you take a nap before the movie. And be sure to take your phone. And charge it fully before you go."

Well, it's not all my wildest dreams come true, but I'll take it.

When we get back to our house, Kate and Dave hang out on the porch while I bolt inside.

"Slow down, Sunny!" Kate calls after me, but I'm already down the hall and turning into my bedroom. Our house isn't very big. It's actually the old lighthouse and used to guide ships into the harbor with a lightbulb the size of a small city. Kate grew up in Mexico Beach, Florida, but she inherited this house from her great-aunt, who used to be the for-real lighthouse keeper. It doesn't function now, because Juniper Island's not a big trading port anymore. All the ships and boats go into Port Hope, and our island just has the usual speedboats and pontoons. The entrance to the tower is all boarded up—not that Kate would let me climb up there in a million, billion years—but still, it's pretty neat.

The house part is a two-bedroom that's mostly all open, with big windows that show a blue blip of ocean from all sides. I love it.

I also love my room, which I affectionately named the Reef when I was sick. I spent so much time in here, so Kate tried to make it really awesome. She built a seat under my window, full of bright pillows and flanked by sheer white curtains. Little white lights wrap around the frame like a vine. My bed is a tiny twin, but it's covered in lots of aqua, turquoise, and sea-green pillows.

I press my back against my bedroom door and breathe-breathe-breathe. I'm going out. Without Kate. With an actual human person who's my age. I can't keep the smile off my face as I set my auger shell on my nightstand and then throw open my closet.

Red V-neck, green tank top, blue T-shirt, shorts, jeans,

more shorts. A whole bunch of boring solid colors that Kate picked out and that remind me of being sick. I don't care what Kate says—nothing in here looks like *New Life Sunny*.

I shut my closet and poke my head out my bedroom door. Kate and Dave are still on the porch. They're talking low and serious, probably about me. Or worse—Lena.

I tiptoe down the hall, careful to avoid the floorboards that squeak, and slip into Kate's super-neat room. It has light blue walls and white linens, dark wood bookshelves filled to the brim and arranged alphabetically by author. I don't even bother opening her closet, though, because I know exactly what's in it—a whole lot of the same kind of blah that's in mine.

Instead, I head straight for the cedar chest at the end of her bed and lift the heavy lid. Inside is another world. Big tan envelopes filled with pictures; lots of jewelry I can't imagine Kate ever wearing; and a pair of black stomping boots from her college days, which are exactly what I'm after.

I take a big breath and grab the boots. I shuck off my flip-flops and plop them onto Kate's floor. The boots are super-heavy, lace halfway up my calves, and are very un-Sunny.

Which, of course, means they're perfect.

I hook my flip-flops on my thumb and close the chest, which sends a puff of cedar and old rubber up my nose.

Back in my room, I stash the boots in my closet and flop onto my bed. I promised Kate I'd take a nap, and I'd be lying if I said I wasn't a little wiped out after all that swimming. I turn onto my side and wrap myself around my pillow, waiting for sleep to come.

The sun is too bright, though, and my brain is all revved up. I roll over and open my nightstand drawer, taking out the picture of Lena that I hide under a bunch of sticky-note pads and pens. She looks the same as she always does—tangly dark hair, amber eyes soft as she looks out the window of whatever room she's in, long fingers splayed on her big pregnant belly. It's an artistic kind of picture. Something I might frame so the whole world can see her, so I can say, "Look at my mom, isn't she amazing?"

But the thing is, I don't know if she's amazing. I don't know anything about her at all. She's just a question. A hard one. A mad one. That question is always what makes me start crying and stuff the picture back into my drawer. And the next night, that same question is always what makes me take the picture out again and stare at her until my eyes blur and I can't see her anymore.

CHAPTER

8

As soon as I see Quinn, I feel totally ridiculous. We meet near the pier for the movie and she runs toward me, waving and calling my name.

"Hey," I say, cool as a cucumber when she reaches my side. Her hair has dried curly, with blue-black spirals everywhere. She's wearing cute white flip-flops and a pair of cute black shorts with a cute white tank top with little red kiss prints all over it and she's basically the cutest thing I've ever seen.

And me? I'm in frayed cutoff shorts, a boring old navy blue T-shirt with a neck that might as well be up to my forehead so it covers my scar, and Kate's boots, which I now realize are the stupidest choice of all choices for a night on the beach.

"Hey, awesome boots," Quinn says, looking me up and down.

My shoulders let go of my neck. "Yeah?"

"Yeah, totally love them. They're like rock star boots."

My face warms and heats. I finally understand what it means to *beam*—I am a human lightbulb right now.

"You ready?" she asks. "My mom gave me some money, so our tickets are on me."

"Awesome, thanks. And I'm so ready," I say.

Then Quinn loops her arm with mine and my heart feels like a whirligig in my chest. In a good way. It's been so long since my heart did something that felt this right.

After Quinn gets our tickets, we find a spot as close as we can get to the water without getting wet. She brought a big blanket and we spread it out over the cool, dry sand. A huge screen and a bunch of speakers are set up by the dunes, so we have to turn our backs to the water to see the movie. But I can still hear the ocean, whispering softly to me like a friend.

I pull the popcorn out of my bag.

"Want some?" I ask, and offer the gallon-sized Ziploc to Quinn.

"Oh, yeah, thanks." She digs in, grabbing a big old handful of popcorn and chocolate and stuffing it into her mouth.

I appreciate a gal who eats with gusto. I grin and do the same. The salty butter and dark chocolate are perfect together. I've missed tasty food so much.

"So are you excited to be here for the whole summer?" I ask.

Quinn is chomping on a mouthful of popcorn, so she doesn't answer right away. She holds up a finger and chews and chews while the movie screen flickers to life. Finally, she nods.

"I love it here. These shoots my mom does take months sometimes," she says. "She has to do about a million shots from a bunch of different depths, and some days, whatever she's taking pictures of won't cooperate. There are a lot of bottlenose dolphins off the coast here, but you never know where they are. We're going out tomorrow morning to see what we can find."

I nod, entranced. "What's the coolest animal she's ever photographed?" I ask.

Quinn scrunches up her face in thought. "Probably an octopus. Or the immortal jellyfish. It's super-tiny and can start its own life cycle over again. They're so weird-looking. It's like they shouldn't exist, because what in the world are they, but they do and they're really amazing."

"Wow. Did you get to see them?"

She shakes her head. "It was too deep for me to dive, but I saw the photos. And my mom's really good."

"I'd love just to be on the boat."

"Yeah, it's pretty cool, when you're that far out in the middle of the ocean. It's really quiet. Like, freaky quiet."

"What's your favorite place you've lived?"

She tosses a single piece of popcorn in the air and catches it on her tongue. Margot and I used to do the same thing all the time, except we'd throw the popcorn at each other.

"I wouldn't call it *lived*," Quinn says. "But, I guess, maybe..." She trails off and then shrugs. "I don't know. Alaska was cool."

"Alaska? You've lived in Alaska?"

"Yeah. Right before coming here."

"Wow. The only cool thing about where I live is that it used to be a lighthouse."

Quinn's eyes go wide. "You *live* there? That lighthouse is amazing. It's so pretty, with the red and white stripes."

I wave a hand. Lighthouse shmighthouse. *Alaska.* If I'd been to Alaska, I'd talk and talk and talk about it and never shut up, but Quinn doesn't seem too interested. Still, my curiosity eats at me until another question spills out.

"Did you make a lot of friends in Alaska?"

She doesn't answer for a second. I'm about to say, hey, whoa, you don't have to spill your best friend history to me or anything, but finally, she glances at me.

"One. This girl named Sadie whose mom was a

fisherman. Fisherwoman? Fisherperson. She had a big boat and we'd go out on it every week. She was..."

Quinn trails off and squints toward the movie. Her throat bobbles with a hard swallow.

"You okay?"

"Yeah, sure." She shrugs and takes a deep breath. "I had to leave without saying goodbye to Sadie. It was hard, because I, well, I thought we were friends. Maybe even..." She blows out a breath through puffed cheeks. "Anyway, I never talked to her again."

"Did she have your number?"

Quinn nods and shrugs again. "It's whatever."

"Did you call her?"

"Nah. What's the point, right? It's not like I'll ever see her again. Plus, she was friends with all these mean girls and..."

More trailing off, more shrugging. But hey, I know about mean girls. Every time Kate brings up how I haven't seen Margot in a long time, I trail off and shrug too.

"I don't get to keep many friends," Quinn says. "I've never even had a best friend. Never stick around long enough. Can you believe that?"

No. No, I really can't, because Quinn is so cool and interesting and pretty and smart. But I guess moving around would be really hard on best friend–hood. Just like being sick. Just like thinking you can trust someone when you really can't.

"I don't have a best friend either," I say.

Her eyes go wide. "No way."

"Major way."

She sits up straight and grabs some more popcorn. "We should try it out. You know, the whole best friend thing."

I grin so big my face hurts. "For real? You want to? With me?"

"Of course with you."

"What if you..." *Don't like me*, is what I almost say, but that sounds like *Old Life* Sunny. *New Life* Sunny is cool and calm and confident. So instead, I make my mouth say, "I think we'd be really awesome best friends."

She nods and smiles and my heart zings and zips around my body.

"So totally would. What should we do first?" she asks.

"First?"

"Yeah, like, our first best friend adventure."

"Oh..." I look up at the movie screen, where this dark-haired actress is riding her bike around Rome. "I guess a movie and greasy popcorn isn't much of an adventure."

"It's a start," she says. "Now we just need something... exciting." She pops up onto her knees and looks around with her hands on her hips, as though something exciting is going to wave its arms above the crowd and yell, *Hey, I'm exciting!*

Then it hits me.

Step Two is completed. Quinn is my best friend. At least, we're going to *act* like we are, which will probably lead to being really real best friends. I like her. I like her a lot and she doesn't seem to think I'm a big old stick-in-the-mud like Margot did, so I think Step Two is totally done.

On to *Step Three: Find a boy and kiss him.*

"I've got something we could do," I say.

CHAPTER

9

Quinn and I face each other, our knees pulled up to our chests. My toes just barely touch hers. Pink and orange streak across the sky as the sun sinks lower and lower and the movie goes on behind us, but we don't hear a word. There's only us. There's only... Step Three, which I've now spilled out between us and it's just hovering there, waiting to see what Quinn thinks.

"I've never kissed anyone before," I say.

"Me neither," she says. "I got close, once. At least, I think I did, but... well, it didn't work out."

"Was he your boyfriend?"

Her nose wrinkles and she glances down. "Nope."

"Well, this way, we can do it together."

My face heats up and I know it's cinnamon-candy red. "I mean, not *together* together."

"No, no, I know that's not what you meant," Quinn says. She's not looking at me and keeps picking at her nails.

"We look for the boys together, help each other figure out what to do. That kind of stuff."

"Right. Boys," Quinn says, and I relax a bit. My stomach, though. It's full of bees. Bluebirds. No, eagles. Something huge and screechy.

"We don't have to," I say. "Only if you want."

She takes a deep breath and crisscrosses her legs. Then she grabs both of my hands and looks me right in the eye.

"No, I totally want to," she says, so serious I almost laugh. But I don't. Because it's not funny at all. It's Major Best Friend Business.

"Really?" I ask.

"Really really."

I grin and squeeze her fingers. She squeezes back and then I release a squeal that's been hiding in my chest since . . . well, since I met her, if I'm being honest.

"Oh my god, we're really going to do this?" I say. "We're going to have our first kisses."

"We're going to kiss so good, they won't know what hit them!"

"How do we kiss good?"

"I have no idea."

We crack up, leaning close to each other and giggling with our hands over our mouths.

Just then, a boy about our age in red board shorts walks by with a giant bag of puffy pink cotton candy. I don't know him, so he must be a vacationer, but when Quinn and I see him, our eyes go all big and round and we bust up again. He looks at us funny, but it's super-worth it, just to laugh with Quinn.

"Hey, guys."

The voice behind me makes me choke on the laugh. For real, it's like a dry cracker stuck in my throat.

I turn and look up, hoping I'm hallucinating, but nope. There she is, in all her Former Best Friend glory. I don't smile. I don't even blink. I probably look like a robot or something, but my heart has different plans. It works hard, as though it's trying to jump right out of my chest and hop into Margot's arms. She looks just like she always did—wavy hair back to its natural brown, green eyes, slim arms and legs.

Margot stuffs her hands in her shorts pockets and smiles at me. Like it's just any other day. Like she didn't do what she did.

I would ignore her. I totally would. I'd loop my arm with Quinn's and stomp us both off into the sunset, except Quinn says, "Hey, Margot," and I nearly swallow my tongue.

"Hey," Margot says back.

They know each other? How? Why? And if they do, does Quinn know about...about...

I shake my head, trying to clear it so I can figure out what in the world is happening right now.

"What were you two laughing at?" Margot asks.

"Nothing," I say. Or, rather, snarl.

Margot frowns at me.

"It was just this boy," Quinn says, grinning at me. I try to grin back, but I think my mouth is broken. Margot, Breaker of Smiles. "He walked by right after we—"

"Decided to get a funnel cake," I say, standing up. "I want something super-greasy. Don't you, Quinn?"

Quinn blinks at me. "Um...what?"

"Funnel cakes are my favorite thing ever in the whole wide world."

Margot snorts a laugh. "You hate funnel cakes. You said they're like sponges soaked in grease."

I glare my best glare at her. She's right, but I don't care. She shouldn't be talking about all the stuff I like and don't like as if she's still my friend. As if she still knows me.

Margot clears her throat and looks down. "Plus, are you sure you should be eating...um...fried stuff?"

"Should anyone?" I shoot back.

Margot and Quinn both wrinkle their brows at me. I plop back down on the blanket.

"So...you guys know each other, huh?" Quinn asks.

"Yeah," says Margot, sitting down so close to Quinn their knees touch. "Since we were four. She'd just moved here and my mom forgot to send me to preschool with a snack. Sunny shared her peanut butter and graham crackers." She smiles at me, but she drops it real quick when I just stare at her.

"Wow," Quinn says. "I can't imagine knowing someone for that long. Other than my mom."

"Your mom is so cool," Margot says.

Quinn shrugs and rolls her eyes. "Everyone says that."

"It's true!" Margot says, grabbing my bag of popcorn. I frown at her total cluelessness. "Her hair is blue. I mean, how many moms do you know with blue hair?"

"She's only doing it to bond with me or whatever."

"So annoying. My mom started painting her nails the same color as mine." Margot brandishes her fuchsia fingers. "Like, what?"

"Totally."

"Hang on," I say, because they really do know each other. Are they friends? My stomach goes all wobbly with nerves. "How...how did you two meet?"

"Quinn and her mom are renting Sandy Dunes," Margot says, munching on popcorn. Her dad owns a vacation rental company and has a bunch of cute little white beach houses all over the island. One time, for Margot's ninth birthday, we got to spend the night in Sandy Dunes, which was always our favorite house because it had its own pool shaped like a kidney bean in the backyard and a screened-in porch with two big hammocks full of fluffy pillows we could sleep in. There're few things better than a sleeping porch on the beach in the winter.

"It's the cutest house," Quinn says. "Margot and her mom helped us unpack."

I nod and swallow hard, trying not to panic. Quinn smiles at me. I wait for her to roll her eyes at me or something, but she doesn't. She's the same Quinn. Still, I didn't plan on her knowing Margot. The whole thing is making my stomach hurt.

Quinn stands up and brushes the sand off her shorts. "I'm going to go get a Coke. You guys want one?"

"Sure," Margot says.

"I'll come with," I say. I'd rather sleep in a sandpaper sleeping bag than stay here alone with Margot, but Quinn waves me off, already weaving through the moviegoers.

"So," Margot says.

I say nothing.

"Sunny."

Nope.

"Look, I've been meaning to come over," Margot says to my back. "My mom told me your surgery went well. I just wasn't sure—"

"Don't worry about it," I snap. Then I try to watch the movie while Margot watches me. I can feel her eyes boring into me. She's probably trying to catch a glimpse of my scar. Heart transplants fascinate people. Or freak them out.

"Stop," I say.

She flinches. "Stop what?"

"Staring. It's rude. I have a new heart. I'm not, like, half robot or something."

She huffs and tucks her hair behind her ears. We sit in the quiet for a few seconds and it's weird. Since January, we haven't been alone together. We haven't been together at all. Juniper Island might be small, but it's easy to avoid someone when you're sick and pretty much homebound and really good at screening your calls and texts.

Still, I can't help but think about the last time she was at my house, just me and her, before that terrible slumber party, before everything changed.

※

"I can't wait to have my first kiss," I said, tucking my pillow under my head.

"It's so amaaaaazing," Margot said. She lay on her stomach across my bed and flipped her hair off her shoulder. "Do you like anyone?"

"You'd know if I liked someone." Although, even as I said it, I wasn't so sure that was true anymore. Margot hadn't slept over in a month. Tonight was the first night she'd even been to my house in like two weeks. A whole lot of stuff could happen in two weeks. At least, it could happen to Margot.

But then she smiled at me and nudged my foot and said, "I'd better know," and everything felt like it always did.

"Well, it's kind of hard to like someone like this." I waved a sluggish hand at the oxygen tank hanging out next to my bed, a clear tube snaking over the covers and straight up my nose.

"Please," Margot said, flicking my leg. "I think it's cool. You look like a superhero."

"Yeah, right."

"For real! Henry just told me the other day that he thought you were cute."

"Aw, you're lying to make me feel better. You're the bestest best friend ever."

Margot laughed. "I'm serious. You should ask him out."

"Oh, sure. Hey, Henry, want to go to a movie? It'll just be me and you . . . and Kate with a suitcase full of pills, Dr. Ahmed if Kate has her way, and of course, Raspy."

"Raspy?"

I patted the oxygen tank. "I named her Raspy."

She rolled her eyes at me, but then she got all serious, her brows scrunched in the middle. She scooted up so she was lying right next to me and wrapped her arm around my waist, hugging me tight. I let out a happy sigh and forgot all about Margot's new friends or how they could race down a beach, laughing and splashing in the waves, and I couldn't.

"It won't always be like this," Margot said. "You'll get a new heart, I know you will. And then you'll get to kiss whoever you want. You can even leave Raspy at home."

I smiled, but my throat got all achy. I hoped she was right. I could tell she believed it. She'd always believed I'd get better. She'd always believed anything was possible, from the moment I told her I was sick.

"Well, I won't want to kiss Henry Lee, I can tell you that right now."

Margot nudged my shoulder. "Why not? He's nice! Very soft lips."

"Oh my god." I covered my face and cracked up, as much as I could crack up without popping a lung. She laughed with me and then we got super-quiet. She laid her head on my shoulder and my mind went a mile a minute, thinking about kissing. A year ago, I'd never really thought about it all that much, but lately, I could hardly think about anything else. Every night, I went to bed scared I wouldn't wake up. That my heart would just go kaput in the middle of the night and I'd never get to kiss anyone.

"Have you ever wondered what it would be like to kiss a girl?"

The question flowed out of my mouth, like a big old exhale after holding your breath for a long time.

Margot didn't answer right away, but her body went all tense next to mine. Right away, I wished I could take the question back. Stuff it into my oxygen tank.

"Never mind," I said, but Margot never did like to let stuff go.

"Um . . . wait . . . you think about kissing girls?" She pushed herself up to her knees and I sat up, my stomach clenching. "Are you serious?"

"You've . . . never thought about that?"

"Um. No."

I tried to take a deep breath, but I wasn't too good at those lately. "I want to kiss a boy too. I just wonder sometimes, that's all."

"But . . . why?"

"I just do. I don't know." Tears stung my eyes, but I managed to keep them from falling down my face. My mind started going in circles, trying to think of a way I could play this off as a joke, but everything I could think of to say sounded stupid.

Plus, it wasn't a joke. And Margot should get that. She was my best friend. She didn't laugh at me when she found out I secretly sucked my thumb at night until third grade. She never made me feel weird for having a mom who took off on me when I was four years old. She'd gone to a bunch of doctor appointments with me, even the ones where they had to draw my blood, and Margot hated blood. She helped me pick out young adult novels from Kate's shelves at home and read the best kissing scenes with me over and over again. She loved me no matter what. I know she did.

"Hey," I said, keeping my voice light. "It's not a big deal. It's just like wondering about boys."

"Except they're not boys."

"So what?"

"I don't know." She wouldn't look at me. "I was just surprised. I didn't know you thought about girls like that."

"I don't know what I think yet. I'm just . . . wondering."

"Yeah, you said that."

"Well, it's true."

My oxygen tank puffed and huffed and I wished I could erase the last five minutes. For real, a time machine would be really awesome right now.

"Don't tell anyone, okay?" I asked when she just sat there, picking at the peeling turquoise nail polish on her fingers. My nails matched. She'd painted them for me just the day before.

"I won't," she said, finally looking at me. "Of course I won't."

"Pinkie promise?"

She reached out and wrapped her pinkie around mine. "Pinkie promise."

✺

I pull my knees to my chest and replay that conversation with Margot over and over. If I'd never said anything about kissing girls, I wouldn't be sitting in the sand right now with my stomach all knotted up and my shoulders shoved up to my ears next to Former Best Friend. I'd be telling Margot all about Step Three. I'd be grinning at how excited she'd be that I was going to get my first kiss. I'd be tugging on her arm, blushing but laughing, when she called out to some floppy-haired tourist boy that I thought was cute.

My eyes start stinging, my throat aching.

"Hey, Sunny?" Margot asks.

I sniff in response, making sure there aren't any tears leaking out.

"Are you okay?" she asks.

"Like you care."

She sucks in a breath. "How can you say that? Why . . . why wouldn't I care?"

I just shake my head. My eyes are aching super-bad now. I blink-blink-blink to keep the tears back.

"Why did you stop talking to me?" she asks when I don't say anything else.

Her voice sounds super-soft. And sad. Maybe even hurt. It makes my heart feel all tender, like a finger poking at a fresh bruise. She would think our eight-year-long friendship totally falling apart was my choice. Nothing's ever her fault.

She doesn't know I heard her talking to her swim team friends the night of her twelfth-birthday-party sleepover, two weeks after I told her my biggest secret. They were all cozied up on her bed together while I was supposed to be in the bathroom.

I don't even know why she invited them. I mean, I know she's friends with them, but birthdays were usually only a Margot and me thing. Just like everything was only Margot and me for years and years. Sleepovers almost every Friday, sharing school lunches—half of my peanut butter and honey for half of her ham and provolone—picking out what clothes we'd wear on the first day of school every year.

Sixth grade had been different, though. By the start of school, I was pretty sick, so Kate and Dr. Ahmed decided home study would be the best thing for me. Margot and I didn't pick out any first-day outfits. We didn't bike to school together. We didn't scope out the cafeteria and pick the best lunch table, we didn't have lockers next to each other, we didn't share a homeroom. I wasn't there at all. It was the worst thing that could've happened to two best friends.

And Margot barely even noticed.

She joined the swim team and didn't seem to care that I couldn't join with her. Even if I had still been at school, there was no way I could hold my breath underwater for ten seconds, much less huff it down a whole pool lane. I thought it would be fine, because, you know, BFFs and stuff. When she didn't have practice, Margot still came over all the time and slept over on weekends.

But then, every weekend turned into every other weekend, which turned into once a month. Margot started hanging out with all the swim team girls more and more. I still saw her, but it was always at my house, watching movies or talking while swinging on the front porch swing. With her new friends, she could go to the mall and to school dances and to Adventure Cove, the little amusement park over in Port Hope. She could do all the stuff there was no way Kate would let me do, especially after I got my oxygen tank.

I couldn't compete with them. No way. The swim team girls were popular and talked about boys and wore lip gloss and had fully functioning hearts. It was Margot and me less and less. I knew it was because I was boring, because I couldn't do much of anything other than walk on the beach really slow or watch movies on my couch. I wanted my best friend back, so I told her about my secret. I told her I wondered about girls sometimes. I told her, because I knew, I just knew, that she'd be happy that I'd talked to her about it and she'd remember that it was her and me. I knew that she'd get it, that she'd help me figure it all out, that she'd let me wonder to my heart's content and never, ever judge me for it.

Well. Clearly, that didn't go the way I thought it would.

When her birthday rolled around and she told me she'd invited half her swim team, I wasn't all that surprised. It still hurt, though. The swim team girls never talked to me very much, so I knew I was getting left behind. I just didn't know Margot would betray me the way she did.

Now, my heart starts pounding, thinking about what I heard her say the night of her party, standing in the hallway outside her bedroom.

I didn't want to invite her, she said.

My mom made me, she said.

It's so weird, I don't know what to say to her anymore, she said.

You don't think she'll die in her sleep, do you? she said.

And then she laughed. *Laughed.* And all the other girls laughed too. Bri and Xiomara, Eliza and Alexa and Annabel. Even Iris, who I'd always thought didn't have a mean bone in her body. They all laughed at my broken heart, like it was a joke.

But that wasn't even the worst part. The worst part, the worst of worse things ever, was when Alexa said, *She hardly talks to any of us except you, Margot,* and then Eliza, the swim team captain and most popular girl in the whole school, said, *Um, yeah, it's like she has a crush on you or something,* and then Margot didn't say anything for a second and I peeked through the crack in the door, because what Eliza said was just so ridiculous, I didn't understand why

Margot hadn't stuck up for me, and then I saw Margot lean forward, all secretive and stuff, the other girls pulled toward her like magnets, and then she said, *You guys, she might. Because guess what she said to me a couple weeks ago? I went over to her house because, you know, she can't go anywhere, and she told me she thinks about kissing boys and girls.*

Eliza wrinkled up her nose and said *Ewwww*, but all the other girls totally lost it. Xiomara even fell off the bed because she was laughing so hard.

After that, I went back to the bathroom and tried to cry, but I couldn't because I was so mad. Then I left, saying I didn't feel good, which wasn't even a lie. I swear Margot looked relieved. I wasn't even supposed to go to the party anyway. I was pretty sick by that point and Kate was freaking out, but I'd been having a good week and Dave had convinced her that I needed to feel normal. I needed to feel like a kid.

Well, all I ended up feeling was that, apparently, my first and only best friend was a jerk who didn't care about me one bit. Margot texted me a few times after that, but I wouldn't respond.

Eventually, Kate noticed that Margot was never at our house anymore and I wasn't glued to my phone, texting my best friend all the time. Kate freaked out about that too, because Margot was pretty much my only friend, but I wouldn't tell Kate what had happened. I was too embarrassed. Plus, I never, ever wanted Kate to worry about me more than she already did.

After a few weeks, Margot stopped trying to talk to me, Kate stopped asking why, and everything went quiet.

For a while, I tried giving up my kissing dream too, but then I got super-mad at Margot for yanking that away from me. Especially when she knew I was only thinking out loud about kissing girls that night in my bedroom two weeks before her stupid party, which is what you're supposed to be able to do with a best friend.

No way, nohow was Margot going to ruin kissing for me. So I started sneaking Kate's young adult novels into my room and reading the kissing scenes again. But I only read the boy-girl scenes. I'd read some girl-girl kissing scenes before and I liked them. I liked them so much, a few of them even made me cry, but I was done with all that. Thinking about kissing girls was too scary, and I had enough scary things in my life, thanks very much. So I was going to kiss only boys. If I ever got the chance, I was going to kiss so many boys, Margot would end up asking me for kissing advice. In fact, all those girls would. Xiomara and Eliza and Alexa—every seventh-grade girl at my school would bow down to me as the Kissing Queen of Juniper Island.

And now, I have my new heart and my *New Life* and I don't have to do it all alone. Quinn's on a mission too. With me.

Margot drags her hand through the sand and huffs a breath. "I just don't get it, Sunny. Did I do something wrong?"

I shake my head and hug my knees even tighter to my body. I don't look at her. If I look at her, I'll end up telling her everything, and if I tell her everything, she'll just laugh at me again.

"Fine," she snaps, demolishing the little sand pyramid she was building. "You know, I hope whoever gave you your new heart was a lot nicer than you are. Maybe it'll rub off."

I whip my head toward her, my mouth hanging wide open. She looks pretty surprised herself, but before she can say sorry or spit in my eye or whatever else she was going to do, I see Quinn standing there with three cans of Coke in her hands, looking at me like I've got snakes for hair.

"New heart?" she asks. "What are you talking about?"

My face goes nuclear and my heart isn't doing much better. It feels like it's about to bust right out of my chest and answer Quinn's question itself.

"Um, you didn't tell her?" Margot asks. Her jaw is in the sand. I want to yank it back up and tape it shut.

"Tell me what?" Quinn asks. "Are you okay, Sunny?"

She looks so concerned that it makes me want to hug her. And I would, if I wasn't melting into a puddle of embarrassment right now. It's not like I wasn't going to tell Quinn my whole deal—we're best friends, after all—but for today, I liked not being the Heart Disease Girl. I liked that Quinn didn't know. I liked that she looked at me and smiled a real smile instead of that fake, pitying-worried-nosy smile everyone else uses whenever they're around me.

"I'm fine," I say.

Quinn still looks terrified, her knuckles white on the soda cans.

"She's okay now," Margot says. "But she had a heart—"

"Will you shut up?" I snap.

"You had a heart *what*?" Quinn asks. "What happened?"

I shake my head. I know I should just say it—*I had a heart transplant*—but the words get all stuck in my throat. Because my heart is gone. The heart I was born with doesn't even exist anymore. It's in some medical waste dump or has been incinerated or something. I don't even know what happened to it. How could I not have asked Dr. Ahmed what they did with my heart?

Every now and then—like right now, thanks a heap, Margot—everything that's happened since we got that call about my donor heart really hits me and I don't know what it all means. My head swims and my non-Sunny heart pounds and I wonder if I'm still me and wondering just gets me laughed at and I just want to go home. I want to lay my head in Kate's lap and watch a cheesy movie while she weaves little braids into my hair and calls me Sunshine.

"Sunny?" Quinn says.

"Sunny?" Margot says.

Sunny? my heart says.

"Look, I'm sorry," Margot says. "I didn't think—"

"I've got to go." I stand up and grab my bag. Then I push myself through the sand before I can hear either of them call my name again.

You shook my heart up in a cup
and poured it over the bed,
like you were rolling dice in a game.
When I left
Your footsteps didn't follow me.
I knew that wasn't what love was about.
But I didn't know a question could
take away part of my heart
and leave a friend-shaped hole behind.

CHAPTER

10

I sit on a bench and write my song about Margot on the playing card–sized notebook I've thrown in my bag. Then, I'm not sure why I do it, but I tear out the paper and roll it up before sticking it between the wooden slats for someone to find. I've never let anyone read my songs, but it felt really amazing sending my donor's song into the ocean earlier today. It felt...big. Like it mattered. The song about her doesn't have any names on it, but I sure hope someone finds it and thinks, *Wow, this person is a horrible friend.* I even smile a little, thinking about it.

After that, I wander around town for a while. Juniper Island's downtown area is all cobblestone sidewalks, salty air, and round-globed streetlights. There are a lot of people around, everyone piling into Sea Salts, the frozen yogurt shop, and walking around town with their friends.

I think I spot Eliza and Iris inside Sea Salts, laughing at a bright blue table, but I speed past before I can really be sure. I keep my head down so no one spots me, walking and walking until it's dark, thinking and thinking.

When I first got sick, Margot spent every weekend night at my house. Every single one. Sometimes, her mom would let her stay on a school night, as long as Margot promised to do all her homework and stuff. Margot pretty much lived with us for half the week. She slept on my floor and kept an extra toothbrush in my bathroom.

It's still there, that toothbrush. It's all crusty and gross, stuffed into the back of a drawer. Even after everything Margot did, I haven't been able to throw it away. I don't know why. Maybe, somewhere in the back of my too-trusting brain, I thought she might come around and apologize. That maybe, because we were BFFs for so long, she'd feel it in her soul, how upset I was, and she'd immediately know why and she'd come groveling for forgiveness. Then, being the merciful friend that I am, I'd forgive her and then she'd listen to all my wonderings about kissing, I mean really listen, and she'd hold my hand and say it was okay to wonder about stuff like that and then she'd use that dumb old toothbrush again.

I walk down the sidewalk that winds along the coastline. It's almost totally dark now, just a bit of purple twilight still fighting the moon, and I can see the white tower of my lighthouse reaching for the sky. It's on the south end of the island, away from all the hustle and bustle of the vacationers, which I kind of like. I can still walk anywhere, Juniper Island being about the size of a teacup, but it's quiet down here on the tip of our little world, perfect for thinking and planning.

I'm cooking up all sorts of ways to finally destroy Margot's toothbrush—snapping the blue plastic in half over my knee, setting fire to it—when I realize it's past eight o'clock and I'm sure Kate's freaking out that I'm not back yet. The beach movie is always over by now.

Except, when I get home, Kate isn't waiting for me on the porch swing. Before I got sick, Kate always waited for me on the porch swing whenever I walked to Margot's or the beach, so she should definitely be waiting for me now.

Suddenly, I want to see Kate so bad, my heart hurts. Like, really hurts. I want her to make me some mint tea while she rubs my temples and tells me how much Margot is missing out on because she's not my best friend anymore.

I'm climbing the porch steps, really ready to cry now, when Dave comes out the front door with his guitar.

"Hey, Sunshine."

"Hey." My voice cracks a little and I clear my throat. "Where's Kate?"

He frowns at me, worry all over his face. "You okay?"

I nod and shrug all at the same time. "Is Kate here?"

"Gee, way to make a guy feel welcome."

"Dave, don't be a dumb-butt."

"A dumb-butt?"

"That's what I said."

He sighs and settles onto the porch swing, patting the spot next to him. I set my bag down and sit.

"Kate's with Lena," Dave says, and my shoulders curl around my neck. "And she asked me to come over so you wouldn't be here by yourself and worry."

I blow out a big breath and try to relax, but my fingers ache from balling them up so tightly.

"She's just trying to figure out how to help you both," Dave says.

"Why does Lena need help? I'm the abandoned child."

Dave chuckles at that. I can always count on him to laugh at super-serious stuff. Not in a mean way, though.

"Lena needs help, trust me," he says.

"You don't like her, do you?"

Dave frowns. "I like her, Sunny. I even love her. We were all friends, you know. Way back when we all lived in Nashville. I opened for one of her concerts."

"You opened for her?"

"Lena Marks was the real deal. Still is, probably."

Marks was Lena's name before she married my dad, and she did all her music stuff as Lena Marks.

"So what happened?" I ask.

Dave presses his mouth flat. "She lost her way, that's all. But she's trying to find it. I hope."

"Well, I'm not lost, so she doesn't need to come looking for me."

"We're all a little lost, Sunshine."

"Ugh, go write a whiny song."

He laughs long and hard at that.

"Speaking of, sing me something whiny," I say, resting my head on his shoulder. He smells like paper and spruce, which is the kind of wood on the top of his guitar. The back is Brazilian rosewood, which is this really pretty copper-colored wood, and it sounds like angels are plucking the strings whenever Dave plays.

"What is it with you and my music lately?" he asks. "You used to hate it."

"I didn't hate it. I just—"

"You hated it."

"Okay, I hated it. You're so whiny, Dave."

He laughs again and I like the way his laugh vibrates against my cheek.

"Why do you like it so much now?" he asks.

I shrug. "You write about feelings and stuff."

"Whiny feelings, apparently."

I poke him in the arm. "Yeah, but still. I just...want to get to feel all those feelings, you know?"

He lays his cheek on top of my head. "You will, Sunny girl."

"Will you sing my favorite song?"

"Again?"

I lift my head and make my eyes super-big as I look at him.

"Fine," he says.

I smile and lay my head down again. Dave never could resist my wide-eyed-wonder look. He starts finger-picking the strings, the beat slow and easy, the key nice and moody. Then the chorus really gets going, dramatic, but still soft and needy, like all the best love songs.

I wonder what you're thinking
Standing here in the snow
We both should be sleeping
But there's nowhere else to go
Your kiss, my kiss, our kiss tonight
The earth is out of orbit
The dark sky is made of light

I sigh against Dave's shoulder. I sigh so loud and so wistful, he stops playing and looks at me.

"Penny for your thoughts?" he asks.

"You'd need to fork over a lot more than a penny."

Dave laughs and starts the song again. I sing under my

breath. Then I sing a little louder because it sounds nice with Dave's voice and it make me feel better. Emptier, but fuller, all at the same time.

"Hey," Dave says, still strumming, "you're pretty good."

"Whatever."

"No, you are. I don't think I've ever heard you sing before."

"Well, I hated your music before, remember?"

He nudges my shoulder. "Sing the chorus with me again."

I roll my eyes but do what he asks. My notes don't match Dave's, but he seems to like it.

"That's a killer harmony, Sunshine."

He launches into the chorus again and this time, I sing a little louder. I sing all the way through the end of the song, my heart aching a little from all the feelings. It's a nice ache, though. The sort that makes me wonder if that's why people write love songs and poetry. For that ache.

"Do you ever get scared when people listen to your songs?" I ask.

He sets his guitar down next to him. "What do you mean?"

I shrug. "Just . . . your songs are really personal, right?"

He nods.

"And, like, having other people listen to them . . . isn't that scary?"

"Ah." He sighs and scrubs his hand through his hair. "Yeah. It's really scary. But it's also exhilarating, knowing that other people connect to something I wrote, you know? Knowing it means something to them. It sort of connects us all, is the way I look at it. Artists don't just make art for ourselves. We make it for others too."

I nod and snuggle closer to him, thinking about my donor song floating in the sea, about my Margot song flapping in the sea air on that bench. It is scary, thinking about someone else reading my songs, even though no one who found them would know it was me. But it's just like Dave said too. Exhilarating. My words are out there now. Me.

"Thanks for singing with me, Sunshine," Dave says, kissing the top of my head.

"Don't expect me to start whining with you all the time now," I say.

He cracks up again. I make Dave laugh more than any other person in the world and I pretty much love it. Laughing is cool and all, but making someone else laugh, making them happy for that tiny second, is even cooler. I used to make Margot laugh a lot. Before I got sick and life got all *serious* and then I went and *wondered* out loud and then she was laughing at me.

"Oh, hey, I almost forgot," Dave says, getting up and

stretching his arms like a cat. "Someone came by looking for you."

I sit up quick. "What? Who?"

"That girl from the beach earlier today. Super-cool blue hair."

"Quinn?" I stand up so fast, the guitar comes with me, clattering to the ground with a loud twang.

"Sorry, sorry," I say, scooping it up carefully.

"It's been through worse, trust me," Dave says, taking it from me.

"Um, Quinn came by?" I ask. "You're just now telling me?"

"Hey, man, we got lost in the music."

I roll my eyes. "What did she want?"

"She left you a note." He starts patting his pockets and looking around. "She seemed kind of worried. You were at the movie together, right?"

"Oh, yeah...I left a little early."

"If you left early, how come she beat you here?" Dave stops his search and lifts his dark eyebrows so high, they arch above his glasses.

"Um...well...I was just walking around."

"Alone? You know Kate would totally lose it if she knew that."

"I know, I know. But I'm fine, see?" I hold out my

arms. "I just needed some time. To think. Being back in the land of the living is weird, you know."

Dave deflates at that, just like I knew he would. Mention my ticker or my near death, or, hey, my just-for-a-few-minutes death, and he caves like an airless soccer ball.

"Sorry, Sunshine," he says, ruffling my hair. "I can't imagine—"

"Back to Quinn," I say, batting his hand away. I need answers and I need them now. "Where's the note? Was she alone? Was Margot with her?"

"Just Quinn." He checks his jacket, which is slung over the back of the swing. Then he looks under the swing. Then—I kid you not—he looks inside his guitar. Like, right in the sound hole. Meanwhile, I'm about to have a real-life heart attack.

"Dave!"

"I'm sorry, I'm sorry," he says, still hunting on his hands and knees. "She came by right after Lena picked Kate up. It was a lot of things at once."

"Wait, Lena was here?"

"Aha!" Dave says. He stands up, a piece of paper folded into a secure little square in his hands. "It was in my guitar case."

"Of course it was."

He grins and hands over the note, which I promptly rip open, trying to ignore the weird feeling in my stomach

102

at the thought of Lena being at my house. Quinn's neat handwriting spilling down the page is a good distraction.

Hey Sunny, I hope you're ok. I was really worried when you took off like that. I was going to go after you, but Margot said I should let you cool off and she seems to know you pretty well, but I still felt so bad. I hope it's ok I came by your lighthouse. I hope you're not mad at me. Because I think you're amazing and I still really want to do our First Kiss You-Know-What Adventure. If you're in, meet me at the docks tomorrow morning at eight. My mom said you could come on the boat with us on her dolphin shoot. And I have a surprise for you. A mega-awesome surprise. Text me if you can come.
        Your BFF,
        Quinn

She thinks I'm amazing. Me. Sad Sack Sunny. And she wrote her phone number at the bottom of the page, so I can text her whenever I want. I stifle a squeal and smack a kiss on Dave's cheek before rushing inside. I head straight for my room and try to breathe. My heart thrum-thrum-thrums.

First, I text Quinn. Of course.

I can come!

Then I realize she has no idea who the "I" might be in that text, so I text her again.

It's Sunny by the way.

Then I pace around my room for the longest two minutes of my entire life—seriously, it feels longer than waiting for a heart—before I see those three beautiful, magnificent dots pop up on my message window.

Yes! So excited.

Then she texts a heart-eyes emoji and I text her back a boat emoji with a kissy face emoji and just when I'm panicking that she'll take my kissy face emoji all wrong and think I'm weird, she texts back five pink kiss mark emojis and my heart starts beating again.

I throw open my closet door and grab a black tank top and a pair of cutoff shorts—as close to *New Life* Sunny as I'm going to get when a bathing suit must be involved. I fold them on top of my dresser and stare at them, wondering if I need to change now so I'll be ready to go in the morning. No, that's silly. But I do need a notebook and some pens to plan our kissing...mission? Quest? I need a name for it. I need some flavored lip gloss and some fruity perfume and maybe a bra.

Do I need a bra to plan a Kissing Quest? To do the actual kissing?

I need to Google it. Oh, wait, I don't need a bra because I'll have on a bathing suit. I need to find my bathing suit and make sure it's not full of sand. I need to calm down is what I need to do. I roam the house in a daze, trying to breathe, tossing stuff in my bag as I go. I don't even know what I take. I'm so excited, so relieved that Quinn is still in this with me, that I really think I might pass out.

I hide my bag under my bed and stuff myself into bed before my body has the chance.

I'm still wide awake, too pumped about Quinn's surprise to fall asleep, when I hear a car door slam outside. I sit up in my dark room and glance at my clock.

Way past midnight.

I crawl out of bed and peer out the window. There's an old truck in the driveway, its headlights beaming onto our front porch while Kate and Lena talk by the steps.

My stomach clenches like a fist. I press my hand to the cool glass. Lena has her arms crossed and she's staring down at her big stomping boots, nodding at something Kate is saying. She wipes at her eyes. Then Kate wipes her eyes too and shakes her head. I wish I could hear what they're saying. I wish I could just fling the window open and ask them. More than that, though, I wish I didn't care what they're saying at all.

CHAPTER

11

I slam a bottle of SPF 40.000 onto the kitchen table, rattling the dishes.

"Sunny, what in the world—"

"Slather me down!" I say. Then I crack open a can of Ensure I already grabbed from the fridge in preparation and sip dutifully. "Ah, delicious."

"What are you doing?" Kate asks. She wipes up a few droplets of coffee spilled by my exuberance. She looks exhausted. Her hair is in a messy bun and there are mascara flakes under her eyes.

After Lena drove off last night in her old truck, I didn't sleep super-great. I kept staring at Lena's photograph, wondering when she'll just give up on trying to see me. And then I thought about Quinn and going out on her boat today before circling right back around to Lena. Sleep was totally impossible.

"I'm willing to endure all manner of sun- and sea-related precautions, just know that," I say to Kate. She and Dave share yet another look. He stayed late last night until Kate got home and then he came over early this morning to walk with her to the bookstore.

"What are you talking about?" Kate asks.

I take a deep breath and let loose. "My friend Quinn wants me to meet her at the beach"—my face burns fluorescent red because I'm a terrible liar—"and I can totally go by myself and I won't swim out to the sandbar and you can stay home and relax because you look way tired."

I inhale dramatically and Dave smirks while he sprinkles a little shredded cheese and dill on the sunny-side-up eggs he's cooking at the stove. Kate only likes eggs when he cooks them. Kate says this isn't true, but I made her some truly magnificent scrambled eggs one time for her birthday, just like Dave taught me, and she nearly puked. And she says she's not in love with him. Yeah, right.

"Gee, thanks," Kate says, then eyes me over her cup. "The beach, huh?"

I nod, my breath held tight in my lungs. "And I'll be with Quinn, which means she'll be there to call 9-1-1 if I drop dead."

"Not helping your case there, Sunshine," Dave says as he adds some toast to his and Kate's plates, but he's still smiling.

"I'm just saying, I won't be alone."

Kate shakes her head, but she's smiling too. She doesn't notice my bright red liar face, I guess. The docks are part of the beach, technically. Just less...beachy.

"You did okay yesterday, I guess," Kate says.

"I so did."

"But that doesn't mean you should overdo it."

"I will underdo it, I promise."

She sighs and that dratted wrinkle between her brows sinks in real deep and I know what's coming and it's not permission to go to the beach.

"Sweetie, I've been talking to Lena a lot and I—"

"Kate," I say. "For real?"

"I just worry you'll regret not talking to her. I don't want that for you. She wanted to come by today if you're up for it and..."

She trails off as my face scrunches up tighter and tighter. Dave clears his throat and shoves some eggs into his mouth. Kate sighs again. She's made of sighs.

"Okay, sweetie," she says. "One step at a time."

Try zero steps. "Can I go with Quinn?"

"Yes, you can go to the beach with Quinn, but I want to meet this girl. Soon."

"Deal. No problem." I knock back the rest of my Ensure and grab my bag, which is heavy with I don't even remember what, my heart already skipping happily. "Love you bye!" I kiss Kate on the cheek and bolt.

"Sunny St. James, get back here."

When I turn around, Kate's heading straight for me, already popping the cap off the SPF 400,000.

So close.

☀

When Quinn sees me wandering up the dock—probably looking totally lost until I see a flash of her blue hair—she climbs over the side of a white dive boat named *Adeline*, and waves at me.

"You're here!" she yells as I get closer. She's wearing her grass-green bikini top with the pink lollipop print and cutoff shorts, her blue hair piled on top of her head, curls everywhere.

"I'm here," I say, breathless from my excited-nervous walk over here.

"Are you okay?" she asks.

"Yeah, why wouldn't I be?"

She shrugs, but I know. Heart transplantee starts huffing and puffing and everyone freaks out. Her eyes dart down to my chest, where I know my high-necked bathing suit covers up my scar one hundred percent.

"I'm not mad at you for how you reacted," I say. Because it's not like we can ignore the fact that she knows and I know that she knows. "I freaked out, that's all. I wanted to tell you myself."

She takes a step closer to me and her arm brushes mine. "I get that. It just surprised me. I mean...a heart transplant. That's...wow."

"Yeah. It was pretty wow for me too."

"I can't imagine what that was like. Margot said it was really rough."

I fight back a massive eye roll. I don't want to get into Margot with Quinn. Ever.

"It pretty much stunk," I say.

She smiles nice and soft. "Well, I think you're amazing and brave."

"Not really. It's not like I had a choice. It was either die or don't die, you know?"

"I never thought of it like that."

"I've thought about it a lot of ways."

"Yeah. Well, I still think you're amazing."

My face gets all warm and I shrug. "Thanks."

She smiles at me. "And we don't ever have to talk about it unless you want to."

"You don't have a million questions you're dying to ask?"

"Oh, I do. But I can wait until you're ready to tell me."

"You're a pretty great best friend."

She giggles and it's the cutest sound. "I'm about to be even greater. Guess what?"

"Oh, yeah, my surprise." I look around for something amazing, but all I see is a bunch of people in bathing suits walking around the dock and untying boats to cast off. "It's not the boat?"

She grins. "Nope."

"We get to go diving?"

"I wish."

"Ride a dolphin? Please tell me we get to ride a dolphin."

She laughs and shakes her head. "Come and put your bag down."

I follow her onto the boat, which is small and has a thick navy stripe running down the side. There's a low platform in the back where divers jump into the water, and a silver ladder descends into the aqua depths. In the wheel-house, a lady with brown skin, dark brown eyes, and the same blue-black hair as Quinn sits surrounded by a bunch of camera equipment. She has on a wet suit and looks super-smart and official.

"That's my mom," Quinn says, flapping her hand at the lady, but she doesn't introduce me. Instead, Quinn stands up on her tippy-toes and shades her eyes with her hand while she looks down the dock.

"Hey, you must be Sunny," the lady says. She stops twisting what I think is a big old lens onto a big old camera and smiles at me. "I'm Marisol."

I hear the faintest trace of her Puerto Rican accent. I wave at her. "Hi. Thanks for letting me come."

"Of course. Hopefully the dolphins will cooperate and you and Quinn can catch a glimpse."

"That'd be amazing."

Marisol winks at me and then goes back to her camera. I'm about to ask how it all works—diving, breathing underwater, how the camera gets a clear shot under the ocean—when Quinn yanks on my arm.

"Whoa, hey," I say, but Quinn just keeps pulling me until I collide with the boat's rail.

"Here's your surprise," she says, smiling so big I can hear it in her voice.

"What is—" But I don't get the rest of the question out because I see what it is very clearly.

What *he* is.

A boy our age with super-tan skin and floppy, sun-lightened hair is striding down the dock with an older guy. They both have on flowered board shorts, white T-shirts, and sunglasses.

"Oh."

Quinn giggles and then covers her mouth to stop the giggling.

"Who is he?" I whisper-yell, but Quinn just shakes her head. Then she rolls her shoulders back and clears her throat as the guys—the men? the boy and the man?—get closer.

"Ladies," the older guy says, nodding at me and Quinn as he steps onto the boat. "Hey, Marisol."

Marisol stands and shakes his hand. "Hey, Nathan. I think I'm all set."

"Good weather for it today."

She nods and squints at the clear sky. "Let's hope the dolphins agree. Hey, Sam, how are you? You remember my daughter, Quinn, right? And that's her friend Sunny."

Sam squints at me and I squint back.

Oh, no. Oh, no, no, no. That isn't just any old Sam. That's Sam Blanchard. I haven't seen him in over a year, but it's definitely him. He was in my kindergarten, second-grade, and third-grade classes. His favorite color in elementary school was pea green and he was obsessed with fish. Or maybe it was squid. Could've been sharks. Point being, he likes ocean life and hardly ever talked about anything else.

He's also the first boy Margot ever kissed.

"Hey..." he says, still squinting. He flicks his perfect hair off his forehead. "Sunny St. James, right?"

I nod and wave while Quinn chokes on another giggle.

"How's your...uh, you know..." Sam drags his eyes to—I kid you not—my *chest* area and back up again.

"Good," I say. "I'm great."

"Oh, good. Margot told me you had, like...well, you know." He waves his hand back and forth. Quinn stops giggling.

"A heart transplant?" I say. "Yeah...I know I had one of those."

Sam nods, his face going tomato red. "Right. So...glad you're okay."

"Yep. I'm fine. Everything's fine." I grab Quinn by the arm and drag her to the diving platform. We pretend to watch the dock fill up with vacationers carrying fishing poles and coolers. Really, I see nothing. Just Sam's short, bronze-colored hair and that awful pitying look in his eye.

"So, I guess you know him, huh?" Quinn asks after a couple of seconds of silence.

"It's Juniper Island. I know everyone, pretty much. How do you know him?"

"His dad owns this boat and is taking my mom out on her dives this week. The first time we went out, a couple of days ago, Sam was there too. I figured you could try with Sam, since it was your idea."

"Try...what?" I squeak out, even though I know. But I need to be sure Quinn and I are talking about the same thing here.

"K-I-S-S-I-N-G," she singsongs, a giggle sliding through the letters.

I grab my stomach, which has grown fingers and is yanking my heart down to my feet. "I can't kiss Sam."

"Why not?"

"I just...I can't. I want a boy I don't remember eating glue in kindergarten."

Quinn cracks up. "Did he actually eat glue?"

"I don't know. I just can't." He was Margot's first. He will not be my first too. "You should kiss him. He's perfect for you."

Quinn's eyes get really big. "Um, no way."

"What? Why not?"

"Because this was your idea, Sunny. You should go first."

I crane my neck to get a look at Sam in the wheelhouse; he's chugging water from a neon-green Nalgene bottle. "I don't know if I can do this."

"You can. For sure. I'll help you," Quinn says.

"You will?"

"BFFs, right?"

I nod. "Holy mermaids, are we really doing this?"

"Do you still want to?" she asks.

"Yes!" I say it loud, and Sam glances at us while filling a cooler with ice. I slap my hands over my big mouth. I do want to. Super-want to. I'm all about the kissing, I am. I just didn't realize the wanting was going to turn into doing quite this fast. But New Life Sunny is nothing if not spontaneous and fun and ready for anything.

"Okay," Quinn says. "So what do we do?"

"We need a plan. The best plan that was ever planned." I open my bag and look through the supplies I collected last night. Notebook and pens for said plan, coconut-flavored lip balm that Margot left at my house over a year ago that I can't bring myself to throw away because I really like coconut, a lone flip-flop that has no clear purpose, and—

Oh. My. God.

In my frenzy last night, I actually put a bra in my bag. A real-life bra. It's black and lacy and definitely belongs to Kate. It also wouldn't fit me if I stuffed it with a whole drawerful of socks.

I clamp my bag closed with my arm. "Um. Well—"

"You girls take a seat," Marisol calls at us from the wheelhouse. "We need to cast off."

Quinn and I glance at each other, our eyes as big as full moons.

"Here we go," she says, swallowing so hard I hear the gulp.

"Here we go," I say. Then I slick on some coconut lip balm.

CHAPTER 12

We head to open sea. I stretch my arm over the side of the boat and watch my shadow flicker over the blue water. There's so much under there. A whole universe.

Quinn and I stand at the front of the boat—pardon me, the *bow*—and lean on the railing as it speeds over the waves. Quinn used some of my lip balm, so she smells like coconut and her mouth is super-shiny, which makes me want to bust up laughing and makes my stomach flip and flop all at the same time. I can't believe I might get my first kiss today.

Quinn tosses another look over her shoulder at Sam, who's standing with his dad in the wheelhouse. Marisol is still snapping and clicking camera stuff. Quinn and I have decided to play it cool with Sam. Act totally uninterested.

That's what I remember Margot doing and it seemed to work. We flip our hair a lot. Or, at least, I do. Quinn doesn't need to try too hard to act cool and pretty.

"Do you ever wish mermaids were real?" I ask her.

"Totally," she says. "Wouldn't that be amazing?"

"Maybe they are. There's no way we can know everything that's out there, right?" I sweep my hand over the ocean.

"I guess not. When I was little, I used to believe there were people in the water. I called them the Water People."

"Clever."

She nudges my shoulder and laughs. "Shut up. I was, like, four. Plus, I was on boats a lot, because of what my mom does, and it got pretty lonely. I made up friends, that's all."

"Mermaid friends?"

She shrugs.

"I used to tell myself that my mom was a mermaid," I say.

Quinn laughs.

"No, really." Then I tell her the whole story. How Lena left me with Kate when I was four and never came back, so I made up this whole tale about how she was a mermaid. And since I was a human girl, with legs and all, she decided that I fit better on land than in the water with her.

Quinn doesn't say anything for a couple of seconds. When I finally glance at her, she's looking at me with her eyes all sad.

"It's okay," I say. "I know she's not really a mermaid."

"No, I know," Quinn says, her voice super-soft. "So . . . that lady on the beach yesterday. She's not your mom?"

I shake my head. "She's my Kate."

"Your Kate."

"A Kate is better than a mom."

Quinn nods, like that makes complete sense, and I think I like her even more.

"I don't have a dad," she says. "Well, I do, but he died."

"Oh. Wow, I'm sorry."

She shrugs. "It was before I was born."

"How?"

"Cancer."

I wince and press my hand to my chest, feeling that my heart is still in there. Then I reach out and slip my fingers between hers. She jolts a little, her eyes widening on our hands. I'm about to yank my arm away when she squeezes my palm. I squeeze back.

"My dad died too," I say. "Right after I was born."

She squeezes my hand even harder. "How?"

"Motorcycle accident."

"That's sad."

"Yeah." I don't think about my dad very much. Kate

119

doesn't even have any pictures to show me. He was never like Lena, where I had to figure out how to fit in my brain somehow the fact that she was alive and chose to live without me. My dad never even had the chance.

"Do you know why your mom really left?" Quinn asks. "Do you think it was because of your dad dying?" She scoots closer to me so our shoulders touch. Her hand is warm in mine, as balmy as the sea air.

"No way." I stick out one flip-flopped foot and wiggle my toes. "It was because I don't have a mermaid tail."

Quinn laughs and I laugh, but my stomach knots up. I want to tell Quinn the truth, that Lena is an alcoholic and couldn't take care of me, but suddenly, I feel embarrassed. Like, why couldn't Lena just stop drinking? If she really loved me, couldn't she stop? Even if she had to leave me for a while, why did she stay gone for so long? Eight years. That's two-thirds of my whole life. I've never talked about it with Kate, but I've thought about this stuff a lot over the past few years. Like maybe Lena knew. She knew there was something wrong with me, with my *heart*, which is the most important part of a person ever, and that's why she stayed away.

And now that I'm all fixed, she's back, looking all cool with tattoos, tugging at all the questions I'd knotted up in my secret heart of hearts for years and years.

I press my other hand to my chest and take a few quiet

breaths. But before I can think on it all too much, Quinn yanks her fingers out of mine and grabs my arm.

"Ow, what—"

"Hey," Sam says as he joins us at the rail.

Ah, that's what.

"Hey," I say.

"Hey," Quinn says.

The boat's motor rumbles to a stop and we slow until we're bobbing up and down, up and down. There's so much blue, everywhere, all the shades. I can almost taste it, clean and bright and a little tangy.

"We're stopping," Sam says.

"Oh, are we?" Quinn asks, even though it's pretty obvious we are. Her voice is like a thousand-watt bulb. She glances at me and grimaces and I have to swallow a laugh.

Sam and I follow her to the back of the boat—the *stern* for the seafaring folk—and over to where her mom is fitting a mask over her face. Nathan checks all these tubes that sprout from the big tank strapped to Marisol's back and then lowers the dive platform. Quinn helps her mom pick up a camera that, honestly, looks like a giant insect. There's a big lens in the middle, along with two handholds on either side. Two lights stick out from the sides like antennae. It looks like it weighs a thousand pounds.

Marisol sticks a big rubber mouthpiece between her teeth and gives Quinn a thumbs-up. Then she just falls off the boat, back first. It's pretty much the coolest thing I've ever seen.

"Keep an eye out, kids," Nathan says as he checks some official-looking gauge on some official-looking instrument in the wheelhouse. "Dolphins love to play in this area and show off."

"Did you know that the killer whale is actually a type of dolphin?" Sam asks as we head back to the bow and sit on the padded benches that border the boat. Quinn stuffs me between her and Sam, and the wind keeps snapping pieces of her blue hair in my face.

"No, I didn't know that," I say.

"They can live up to twenty-nine years."

"Wow. Killer."

He blinks at me.

"You know...killer...like cool, but killer because it's a killer whale."

"Oh." He frowns at me. "Yeah."

I clear my throat. Maybe I shouldn't get my adjectives from a retired rock star. "I bet Quinn knew that, though, right, Quinn?"

"Huh?" she says, trying to corral her hair. She let her bun down for optimum hair flipping, but the wind pulls at it like fingers. The ocean is really choppy, taking my stomach on a roller coaster.

"Um, yeah, I totally knew that," she says. "And striped dolphins can live up to sixty years."

"Whoa, really?" Sam asks.

Quinn nods and Sam grins at her. Quinn smiles back, but it looks weird on her face, and the second he looks away she nods her head toward him and mouths something I don't understand. Does she just want me to lay one on him right here?

"Hey, Quinn," I say, searching my brain for a question that might interest Sam. Then I've got it. "Could you die if you got stung by an immortal jellyfish?"

"Immortal jellyfish?" Sam asks. "That's a thing?"

"Yeah," Quinn says. "But I'd rather talk about... um...Sunny, what are you really good at?"

"What am I what?"

"Good at. Like, you know, art or music or running. You have long legs. I bet you'd be a good runner. Don't you think, Sam?"

"Well, um, I can't run," I say. "At least, not for longer than about thirty seconds before Kate would call an ambulance."

Her eyes go as big as planets. "Oh, god, Sunny, I'm sorry. I totally forgot."

"It's okay."

"No, I just...I was..."

123

I nudge her arm and give her a chill the heck out kind of look.

"Um...what's an immortal jellyfish?" Sam asks, scratching the back of his head.

"Oh," Quinn says. "It's a really tiny jellyfish. So, Sunny—"

"Wait, why is it immortal?" Sam asks.

"It can start its whole life cycle over again," Quinn says, huffing a breath. "After they reproduce, they turn themselves back into their polyp state."

Sam's mouth drops open. "For real?"

Quinn barrels onward, a total rock star. You can tell she likes talking about this stuff. "Their tentacles retract, their bodies shrink up, and they sink to the bottom of the ocean and pretty much become a baby jellyfish again."

"That's the coolest thing I've ever heard," Sam says. "What else do you know?"

"Um...a shrimp's heart is in its head."

Sam laughs. "Gross."

"Totally. Good thing we don't eat that part," Quinn says.

"I don't eat them anyway. They're like water roaches," Sam says.

"Ugh. I've never thought of them like that before." Quinn makes a face and shudders. "Thanks a lot."

Sam smirks. "No problem."

I watch the conversation like a tennis match. Sam's definitely flirting with her. He's grinning like a doofus and watching Quinn from under his lashes.

Quinn flicks her eyes to me and I shoot her a quick thumbs-up. She frowns and shrugs and I waggle my eyebrows at her while Sam takes a few more gulps from his water bottle.

"Sam!" Nathan calls from the wheelhouse. "Come help me check this equipment for Marisol's next dive."

Sam groans but stands up. He tosses Quinn a tiny smile before he leaves, then heads into the wheelhouse.

"Wow," I say when he's gone. "That was a thing of beauty. You're an expert flirter."

Her eyes go big and round. "I am? I was just...talking."

"If by talking you mean sweeping Sam off his feet, okay."

"No, no, no. Sam is kissing you, remember?" she says.

"But he likes you," I say, turning so I'm facing her.

"He totally doesn't."

"He does."

"Well, I don't like him," she says.

"Well, I don't like him either."

"So what are we doing?"

"You're going to kiss Sam," I say.

"Sunny, I don't *want* to."

I stare at her for a second, because she kind of yelled

it. Not loud, just . . . snappy. "Okay. You don't have to. I just thought—"

"And you don't have to either, you know. This whole thing is stupid."

I sit back against the bench, my heart a weak little putter in my chest.

"I'm sorry," she says. "I didn't mean that. I just—"

"Hey," Sam says, "check out the dolph—"

But he doesn't finish whatever he was going to say, because he lays a hand on my shoulder and it scares me half to death. I'm already all tense, so I jerk to my feet and whirl around, arm flailing, and my elbow catches Sam right in the nose.

Hard.

Blood squirts everywhere. And I mean, everywhere. Sam cries out and his hands fly to his face, bright red pouring between his fingers.

"Oh my god, I'm so sorry!" I say.

Sam shakes his head, his eyes wide and shocked. I can't even see his face for all the blood. It drips onto the boat's white floor and drenches Sam's shirt.

Quinn blinks at him, frozen. I think she's in shock. I run around the back of the boat, looking for a towel or rag or something, but can't find a single thing made of cloth.

"Where are the towels, Sam?" I ask. He tries to answer, but his words are clogged and total gobbledygook. I'm about to scream at the sky because this whole adventure went from amazing and exciting to a horror show in three seconds flat. Finally, I spot my bag on a seat. Surely there's something in there that will mop up the mess that is Sam's face.

I shove my hand in, feel something soft and cottony, and pull it out.

"Here!" I press it to Sam's nose and he grabs on to it, tears and snot mixing with the blood and making a total mess of the—

Oh. God.

"Is that a . . ." Quinn starts to ask, but she can't even say it. Because yes, Quinn, yes it is. That is Kate's black, lacy bra smooshed up against Sam Blanchard's broken nose.

CHAPTER

13

By the time we get back to Juniper Island, the afternoon sun is a blurry lemon drop in the blue sky and Sam's entire face is purple and green.

I guess it's safe to say that the first Kissing Quest attempt didn't go well. At all. On the ride back to the island, I can't even look at Quinn. I can't look at anyone, I'm so mortified. She keeps telling me it's okay, that, hey, everyone probably gives the first guy they try to kiss two black eyes and a broken nose and then a lacy bra to mop up the mess. I nod and smile, but really, I'm dying inside. Theoretically speaking, of course.

Marisol is pretty ticked, though. Not at me, she said. Sam's nose was an accident, but I guess she got some good shots and was hoping to go down again after a break. But when Nathan came out of the wheelhouse and saw his son gushing blood, he called it quits.

Now Sam's on his way to the hospital, Quinn's on her way back to Sandy Dunes with her fuming, blue-haired mom, and I'm walking home with a bloody bra in my bag.

New Life, as it turns out, is a little more complicated than I thought it would be. I mean, obviously, I know that I need to *want* to kiss someone for this whole thing to work, but how do I know I want to? One thing's for sure: I knew when I didn't want to, and I didn't want to kiss Sam Blanchard.

I'm thinking up all sort of ways to convince Kate to let me go over to Sandy Dunes and see Quinn and make sure she doesn't want to bail on the Quest—and on me—when I hear voices coming from my front porch.

"...just needs some time," Kate is saying.

"She won't even let me look at her right now."

I freeze. Hearing Lena's voice is like sprinting into a brick wall. I squint through the bright sun and, sure enough, I see Kate and Lena sitting on the porch stairs. The same truck from last night is parked in the driveway. It's mint green and looks super-old, like it's from the middle of the last century or something. I duck behind the big oak in our front yard, its shadow tucking me away.

"Like I said, it might take some time," Kate says. "How long are you staying in Port Hope?"

Lena picks at a loose thread on her jeans. "Indefinitely. I've lined up some voice lessons while I'm here."

"Wow. Okay," Kate says.

"Is that all right?" Lena asks.

Kate sighs. "You can do what you want."

"But are you okay with it? I need to know."

Kate doesn't answer at first. My heart is going wild in my chest, a hummingbird buzzing around a feeder. I can't figure out what I want Kate to say.

"I don't know," Kate finally says, so quiet I almost don't hear her. It's the perfect answer, because I don't know either.

"That's fair," Lena says.

"You . . . you still go to meetings, right?" Kate asks.

"We talked about this last night."

"Talk about it again."

"Yes," Lena says. "Every week. Sometimes more."

"And you've found one in Port Hope?"

"I have," Lena says. "They meet in the Methodist church basement, right near the house I'm renting. Don't worry about me, Katie."

"It's hard not to. I've worried for eight years. Actually, even longer than that."

"I know. I'm sorry."

"Are you?"

Lena sighs and rubs her forehead with both hands. "Yes. I told you, I'm good now. That's why I'm here. I would never try to put myself back into her life if I wasn't positive I was ready."

"And you haven't been ready for the past eight years?"

A beat. I hold my breath. "I know it sounds terrible, but no. I wasn't. I'd be okay for a while, only to start drinking again. But I'm ready now, I promise."

"Well, maybe Sunny's not," Kate says.

"I get that. I just want a chance."

"I'm trying, Lena, but Sunny has a mind of her own."

Lena smiles and I kind of want to run over there and slap it off. And I kind of want to watch her smile again. It's confusing.

"Of course she does," she says. Then the smile fades. "I never dreamed she'd get sick."

"What parent does?" Kate asks.

I tense up at that word—*parent*. It's not like it applies to Lena. At all.

Lena sighs and shakes her head. "I'm so sorry you went through everything alone. I'm sorry I didn't call for so long. It felt easier, at the time. Not only for me, but for you and Sunny. I didn't want to mess up your life and I was such a mess for so long. If I'd known—"

"I wasn't alone. I had Dave. And I had Sunny. She's really strong."

"I can tell. She's just like you."

Kate doesn't say anything to that, but a little knot gets all tangled up in my throat. I swallow it down. Inside the house, our kettle screeches from the kitchen and Kate stands up.

"Orange blossom tea still your favorite?" she asks, wiping under her eyes.

Lena looks up at her and smiles. "You remembered."

"I remember a lot of things." Then Kate disappears inside the house.

"Thank you," Lena whispers long after the screen door clicks shut. Her voice sounds super-sad, talking to no one.

I stand there and watch her for a couple of seconds. I wonder how long I'm going to have to wait out here until she leaves. I want to get inside and lock myself in my room and hide under the covers and stare at my picture of Lena until my eyes blur.

But I don't need to look at a picture. The real Lena is right here. Still, a picture is safe. A picture doesn't talk or give reasons or ask questions.

Lena stares at her lap and runs her fingers over one of the tattoos on her wrist. My heart gets all fast and jumpy, because she looks lonely.

Something tugs at me, like a knuckle knocking against my ribs. It nudges and nags until I'm walking toward the porch. Lena lifts her head, and her eyes widen when she sees me. My eyes probably widen too, because it's just plain weird that she's real. That she's sitting on my porch. That she sees me too.

I sit down next to her but scoot as far away as I can without falling off the step. I set my bag down and fiddle with the strap. I'm not sure what to do now. I kind of want to throw up. Or scream. Or ask a ton of questions. Or cry.

"Hi, Sunny," she says, her voice all whispery and soft.

I nod and don't look at her.

"I came by to talk to Kate," she says. "I didn't mean to surprise you."

Shrug. I guess I'm going for the silent treatment. The nice thing is, she lets me. She doesn't pile a whole bunch of questions in my lap. She gives me a second to get my breath back and figure out if I actually want to sit next to the lady who grew me in her body for nine months and then gave me away.

After five long minutes, I still don't have an answer. Maybe there isn't one. I wrap my arms around my legs and pull my knees to my chest. I sneak a glance at her. Both of her arms are completely covered in tattoos, swirling up from her wrists to her shoulders. There are a lot of suns on there. All sizes and shapes, some with elegant, curling rays and some with knifelike points and some with just a formless glow surrounding the ball of light.

133

"You didn't have all those tattoos in your picture," I say.

She tilts her head at me. "My picture?"

My face feels hot as I realize what I just admitted. I stay quiet. I don't want to tell her that I have a photo of her tucked in my nightstand that I stare at every night.

When I don't answer, she holds out her arms, inspecting them herself. "I got all these in the past few years."

"All of them?"

"Every single one."

"You like suns a lot."

She smiles, this time looking at me instead of her arms. "Why do you think your name is Sunshine?"

"I don't know. Because you're weird?"

She laughs. "Well, that's probably true. But I also like suns. I mean, I hope I do. These aren't coming off." She rubs at a sun on her upper arm that's half hidden behind a coil of thorns.

"Why?" I ask.

"Why the sun?"

I nod. "And why..." I tap my chest, hoping my question comes across. My middle name is Kate's name, but I've never asked where my first name came from. I've wondered about it, though. I know there are other people in the world with my name, but it's usually just Sunny.

Period. Not Sunshine, which is my legal first name. It's on my birth certificate and everything.

Sunshine Kathryn St. James.

"Well," Lena says, clearing her throat. "The sun is powerful. Life-giving."

"But it can hurt too," I say. "Like, if you have too much of it. And it gets covered up by clouds and hides at night."

Lena nods and touches a little sun on her wrist that's surrounded by a bunch of dark clouds, like a storm approaching. "All true. But I think that's why I love these images of the sun even more, you know? Anything good in life isn't all good, right? There are levels, layers. Everything that's beautiful can turn ugly and everything that's dark can be given some light. Nothing is only one thing. And the sun, it's the same every day, shining on and on, but every day is different too."

"And it's big," I say. "It always makes me feel supersmall when I see those diagrams of the solar system and how the sun is like this big old basketball next to a bunch of little golf balls and marbles."

Lena smiles and nods. "Yeah. Exactly."

We go silent again and I'm glad. My mind is going a mile a minute. Behind me, I hear one of the floorboards in our entryway squeak. When I turn, I see Kate holding a cup of tea. She smiles at me and kisses her finger before pressing it to the screen door. Then she drifts away and I can't decide if I want her to come back or not.

"Sunny, can I ask you something?" Lena says.

I turn back around. "Yeah, I guess."

"Well, I was wondering if you might let me ... see you a little."

I glance at Lena. She's not looking at me. She's knotting her fingers together and breathing sort of hard, but trying to act like she's not. She's super-nervous and I'd be lying if I said I wasn't a little glad.

I let the question sit there for a few seconds, because I'm not sure what my answer is yet. Still, I don't think I'll say no. I've got too many questions. At the same time, I'm scared to ask a whole bunch of them. My hands shake just thinking of all the answers she could give for leaving me, for showing up now and acting all sorry.

Then, the spark of an idea. There might be a way to get some inspiration for Step Three of my New Life plan and figure out some things about Lena all at the same time.

I could never ask Kate for help with this. Never in a million years. She'd totally freak out and say I was too young, but I'm twelve and a half. If that's not too young to have your heart ripped out and replaced, it's not too young for anything, in my opinion.

But Lena. Lena has tattoos. Lena wears stomping boots and torn jeans. She seems like she'd be cool with my quest. I don't know. Either way, I open my mouth and more words fall out.

"I have a question first," I finally say.

"Okay," Lena says, turning to face me. "Shoot."

I take a deep breath and take the plunge. I still have a New Life plan, after all, and I'm sticking to it, come long-lost mothers or Margot or bloody noses or whatever. "What do you know about kissing boys?"

CHAPTER

14

Lena looks at me with one eyebrow way up in her hair. I can do that too, but Kate can't. I guess now I know where I get it from.

"Kissing boys?" she says.

I nod. "I've never kissed anyone and I want to. Really bad."

Her mouth quirks up on one side and I can tell she's trying not to laugh.

"It's not a joke," I say.

"No, no, of course it's not." She clears her throat. "I was expecting a different question."

"Like what?"

"Like pretty much any other question."

"Well, I have those too, but let's start with this one."

She blows out a breath through both cheeks. "Okay. Well, um, I've kissed a boy or two."

"I figured. But how?"

"What exactly do you mean by how?"

"Just...how?"

"It's not something you can really plan, Sunny. It just happens if you want to and the other person wants to. You figure it out as you go."

"Okay, but that's the thing. How do I know when I want to?"

She tilts her head at me. "Sunny, do you have a boyfriend?"

"I don't need a boyfriend to kiss someone, do I?"

She rubs her eyes and takes another deep breath. I'm stressing her out, I can tell. "No. But as the adult here, I feel like I should tell you that it's a more enjoyable experience if you at least like the person a little."

It's not like I didn't pick up on this from all Kate's young adult novels and old movies. Romance, they call it. Swooning and feelings and flutters. That's the key to wanting to. It's why I want to kiss someone so bad in the first place. Because when you like someone and they like you back, even when they don't have to? That's kind of like magic, isn't it?

Only one problem.

"But I don't like any boys. I don't know any boys. At least not really. I've been sick, remember? I haven't really been hanging out with a lot of people lately."

"I know." Her eyes go all soft and I'm sure she wants to talk about me knocking on Death's door and her being gone and how sorry she is, but I'm not ready to go there. Not yet.

"So what do I do?" I ask.

She sighs and folds her feet under her legs. "I think you focus on yourself and your friends."

"I think that's a super-boring grown-up answer."

She laughs and I like the sound. It's kind of deep and gritty, like it's out of practice and just getting started up again.

"Fair enough," she says. "How about...think about the kind of person you want to share your first kiss with, and then keep an eye out for them."

"Okay, that's a little less boring, but I still need to figure out how to kiss the guy."

"Have you talked to Kate about this?"

"Are you kidding?" I say. "No way. She'd probably take me to the doctor or something."

"I doubt it. Kissing is very normal, as long as you want to do it."

"When was the last time you kissed someone? Did you make the first move or did he?"

"This is not how I expected our first conversation to go." She presses her hands to her cheeks and I let her stew a bit. Finally, a deep breath. "It's not something I can just tell you about. At least, I don't think. You have to live it. Experience it."

"Well, I just *experienced* a best friend who may or may not think my whole plan is stupid. Oh, and let's not forget the bloody nose."

"Bloody nose? What? Are you okay?"

"Not my bloody nose. The boy's."

Lena winces. "Really?"

"It was like a geyser." I mime a fountain spurting from my nose and Lena laughs. I tell her the whole story—including Quinn's and my argument and my wild elbow and Kate's bloody bra that I have to figure out how to sneak into the wash—and she laughs even more.

"Wow. That is an epic first-attempt story."

"Epically awful." I rest my chin in my hands, defeated.

She lets me brood for a few seconds and then comes out with a real zinger.

"Okay, fine. I'll tell you about my first kiss. Are you ready?"

I turn so I'm facing her, tucking my legs underneath me to mirror her. "Yes, I'm so ready."

She grins and takes a shaky breath. I take a shaky breath. I can't tell if it's because I'm finally getting a first-kiss story that doesn't involve Margot saying how amaaaaazing it was and making me feel like I'm about five years old or because it's Lena. Maybe a bit of both.

"It was your dad, actually," she finally says. She says it so super-quiet that I almost don't hear her. She looks down at her hands and picks at a callus on her forefinger. "I was around your age."

"You met my dad when you were twelve?" I ask.

"We were ten when we met. But we didn't kiss until we were almost thirteen. His family came to Mexico Beach every summer for vacation."

"You only saw him during the summer?"

She nods. "But we wrote to each other a lot during the year. We even talked on the phone some."

"Did Kate know him too?"

"She knew him more when we were older, but when we were kids, it was mostly just him and me. His family rented a house right next to mine and... well, it was pretty much love at first sight."

"At ten?"

She laughs and shrugs. "When you know, you know."

I chew on that for a second. I definitely knew something when Quinn suggested I kiss Sam, but it was that I one hundred percent didn't want to kiss him.

"So, how did you end up kissing?" I ask.

She doesn't answer right away. For a second, I think

she's going to change her mind about telling me. For a second, I think I want her to change her mind. My heart is beating like a wild horse, but then a tiny smile pulls at one side of Lena's mouth. She glances at me and grins a little wider.

"Come to think of it, I'm pretty sure he planned the whole thing."

"He did?"

She laughs and nods. "Like I said, we were almost thirteen and it was our third summer together. Our town had this really big bonfire on the Fourth of July and everyone camped right on the beach——"

"Hey, Juniper Island does that too."

"Yeah? It was pretty fun."

"I didn't get to go last year. Or the year before that."

She nods, her eyes instantly sad. "Maybe this year."

I shrug, but secretly, I think, *Yes, please, ugh, let me go.* "So what happened?"

She tells me about how she and Kate and some of their other friends met Ethan—that's my dad—on the beach and they roasted marshmallows for S'mores by a fire, and how Lena had started playing guitar the year before and she'd brought it to the bonfire because she wanted to show Ethan how cool she was.

"You wanted to impress him?" I ask.

"So much."

143

"Did you?"

She grins. "He asked me to show him some chords. I still remember my heart was beating so fast because I had to get kind of close to him to help move his fingers and I couldn't breathe."

I swallow hard, because my throat kind of aches. My mom. This is my mom telling me about my dad. My mom, who I've wondered, wondered, wondered so much about every night for so long.

"So what happened?" I ask, desperate for more.

"He asked me to go for a walk while the fireworks were going off."

"And?"

"And I did and during the big finale he asked if he could kiss me and I said yes."

"He asked you?"

She nods. "Never kiss a boy who doesn't ask, Sunny."

I file this away for later, because all I can think about right now is that my parents kissed for the very first time ever when they were thirteen while fireworks exploded in the sky.

Suddenly, my stomach hurts. Not in a bad way. In the kind of way it used to hurt when I would lie in bed, my ankles swollen and my breathing super-loud because my lungs were trying hard to make up for what my heart couldn't do, and I'd want, want, want a new heart so bad, everything ached. It's the same kind of ache I get when Dave sings his whiny kissing song and I read a kissing scene in one of Kate's young adult books under the covers. It's the ache of wanting your dreams to come true. I definitely didn't have that ache today when I saw Sam, but I know it's possible to have it with a real person.

Just like Lena did.

I glance over at her and she's smiling down at her hands, her eyes all hazy like she's remembering stuff.

Remembering my dad.

It hits me like a lightning bolt. Or, actually, like a firework, fast and bright, exploding with a *pop* and then spreading through my whole body like a sunburst.

My mom. She's my mom. And she's talking about how it all started. My family. Our family.

"Sunny?"

I flinch, Lena's face swimming in front of me.

"You okay?"

I nod.

"You sure? You look pale."

I press my hand to my chest, my heart jackhammering underneath. If you cracked me open right now, I'd bleed questions all over the place. But before I can ask any of them, Kate opens the screen door and pops her head out.

"How are things out here?" she asks.

"I'm not sure," Lena says. She tilts her head at me, a question in her eyes. But all I do is stare at her because I'm noticing this itty-bitty mole right under Lena's eye and how I have the same one. I'm noticing that our hair is the color of a midnight sky and both of our bottom lips have a little dip in the middle like a peach or a cherry. I'm noticing that she has flat, square fingernails just like me and she picks at her cuticles just like I do. I'm wondering if my dad's hair was really straight, just like mine and Lena's, and if he liked my name or thought Lena was a little bonkers for naming me after a giant ball of gas in the sky. My curiosity is on fire. It's always been there, a little spark every night while I ran my fingers over Lena's photo-face. But now it's an inferno. I want more stories about my parents, about Lena, about my dad.

"Sunny?" Lena asks, glancing at me.

I rub my temples, my head twirling like a baton.

"Let's come on in, all right, Sunshine?" Kate says, holding her hand out to me. I get up and grab her fingers.

"I'm okay," I say.

"I know, sweetie," Kate says, but she doesn't sound like she knows it at all. Still, I'm exhausted. Between the Sam debacle and Lena, my brain feels like a roller coaster.

"Yeah, I need to get going," Lena says as she stands, stuffing her hands into her pockets. "But before I go... Sunny, have you ever been surfing?"

146

"Surfing?" Kate says before I can answer. "No, she absolutely has not."

Lena keeps her eyes on me. "Would you like to?"

"Surfing?" I say. "Like with a surfboard on the ocean and stuff?"

Lena nods. "It's something I started doing the past few years."

"You can't be serious," Kate says.

"I wouldn't have her riding actual waves," Lena says. "Just paddling out, talking through the basics." She turns back to me. "You can invite a friend if you want to. I can't go tomorrow, but I'd love to take you out on Monday."

"Out of the question," Kate says.

"We'd go over to the east end of the island," Lena says. "I've heard it's good for beginners. But like I said, we won't do anything dangerous."

"Surfing *is* dangerous," Kate says.

"Katie, come on."

"Are you serious?"

I listen to them argue back and forth.

Surfing. Real surfing in the ocean. My heart nudges me again, a curious little knock against my ribs. Surfing would go right along with Step One of my *New Life* plan, in which I do awesome amazing things I've never done before. Plus, I could get more stories out of Lena. Maybe I'll get enough stories to understand why she left me.

Maybe I'll get enough to actually forgive her.

"I want to go," I say, loudly enough that Kate and Lena stop arguing.

"Sunny—" Kate starts, but I cut her off.

"It's my choice, Kate," I say. "You said you didn't want me to regret anything and that you'd support whatever I decided..." I trail off, not wanting to say *about Lena* right in front of Lena, but Kate knows what I'm talking about.

She stares at me and I stare back. Lena is still as a statue. Finally, Kate looks down and nods, her jaw tight. She waits for me while Lena and I exchange numbers, but the air around us is all fizzy, like a shaken-up soda can.

"Thank you, Katie," Lena says to Kate after she puts my number into her phone. "Thank you for this."

Kate doesn't answer. Instead, she laces her fingers through mine and leads me inside without another word.

☀

Later, after Kate stuffs me full of pills and broccoli and Ensure, she snuggles into bed with me. This is our thing, our tradition every night for as long as I can remember. We turn off all the lamps and leave on the little white lights around the canopy, and the whole room looks like we're floating under an ocean beneath a starlit sky.

But for the first time ever, I just want her to leave.

I need to think.

I need to think and think and think.

And I can't think and think and think with Kate whispering all these words against my hair every five seconds.

"You're sure you don't want to talk about Lena?"

Breathe in.

"If you change your mind about surfing, that's okay."

Breathe out.

"She should've asked me first. Then I could've talked to you about it. Prepared you a little. I called Dr. Ahmed and she said you should be fine as long as you take it easy, just like swimming."

In.

"Are you sure you don't want to talk?"

Out.

"Sunny, I know you. I know what it means when you get quiet."

"That I'm super-tired?" I finally say.

She slides her thumb down my cheek and sighs. Apparently the time for joking has passed. "That you're overwhelmed and you're worried and you think you can handle it all on your own."

I huff a breath. "Maybe it just means that I need to think about stuff a little before I talk about it."

"Okay, that's fair. But, honey, you just talked to Lena for the first time ever. I know you must be feeling—"

"You don't know how I'm feeling at all." My words

come out like a whip on a horse's back. Kate feels the sting and flinches. She's always saying this kind of stuff—*I know how you feel. I know this is hard. I know, I know, I know.* But she doesn't get it at all.

"Sunshine—"

I turn over and face the window, focusing on all the dark outside, all the hidden stuff. Kate lies there for a minute, but finally, she whispers a soft "Okay," and squeezes my shoulders once before she gets up and leaves.

I flop onto my back and glare at the ceiling for a good ten minutes, waiting to feel excited about surfing, about talking to Lena and that amazing story she told about her and my dad. And I am excited, but it's all mixed up with other stuff too. I feel mad and like I want to cry and maybe even scream a little. Everything aches, like I'm all bruised up. It's like before I got sick, when I would run really hard down the beach and my whole body would get all tingly and relaxed, but the next day my legs would be so sore I could barely walk. But the only thing that would make me feel better was to run again, harder, until all that pain was gone.

I roll over and grab my phone off my nightstand, along with the picture of Lena out of the drawer, and open up my music app. I type *Lena Marks* into the search bar. One album pops up. It's called *Shallows* and she made it before I was born. I don't listen to it all that often. It's too hard. Music is too full of feelings. Staring at a picture, I can think whatever I want about Lena, but listening to her voice, right in my ear, singing about love and stuff...well, that's harder.

My thumb hovers over the first song. I pop in my earbuds and press Play. I stare at Lena's photo-face while a soft, ghostly piano starts...then guitar...then a voice that sounds so sad, so pretty, so...

I start crying. Then I cry and cry some more, from one song to the next, until I taste salt on my lips and it almost feels like I'm back in the ocean, just a human girl floating around with a mermaid.

Now that I've seen you up close,
you look exactly like me.
Or maybe I look like you.
Sometimes I forget that I made it all up,
the mermaid in the sea
and me in the sand.

CHAPTER
15

On Sunday, I almost convince myself that the whole conversation with Lena was a dream. I don't talk about her at all. I guess Kate got the message that I've locked up all my Lena thoughts good and tight, because she doesn't ask any more questions. We just sit on the couch while I eat my weight in butterscotch pudding and watch bad movies all morning.

In the afternoon, Kate takes me to the bookstore for a couple of hours so she can get next week's schedule done. We barely talk on the way there or on the way back.

I do, however, stick a song I wrote into a book in the middle-grade section called *Hello, Universe*, which is just too perfect for words. The song is the one I wrote about Lena right after she showed up in my hospital room. I'm just sitting there in a cute little alcove in the kids' area, reading through my songs in my notebook, and before I know it, my eyes stick to this pretty blue cover and the most perfect title ever, and I grab the book off the shelf and stick the paper inside.

My heart pounds for so long afterward that Kate brings me home early and takes my blood pressure. I smile the whole time she pumps the cuff around my arm, thinking of my song hiding out between the pages of a book, waiting to be found, like a little treasure.

Kate and I have just finished up eating dinner—broccoli and chicken casserole with a side of Ensure—when the doorbell rings. I'm almost positive it's Dave, because it's always Dave, and I stay in my sluglike position on the couch, all set to watch my third rom-com of the day. So when Kate opens the door and I see Quinn's blue hair shining under the porch light, I sit up quick.

"Hey, Sunny," she says as Kate lets her inside.

"What are you doing here?" I blurt. She frowns and freezes. My stomach coils into a tight knot. I haven't talked to Quinn since the Sam debacle yesterday morning. Not a single text or anything. My face feels like I could cook a steak on it.

"I can go," Quinn says.

"No!" I shove the blanket off my legs and stand up. Dark gray fleece pools around my feet. "I mean, no, don't go. I'm glad you're here."

She smiles and exhales loudly. "Okay."

Kate shifts her eyes between us, a tiny smile on her lips. "You must be Quinn," she says. "I'm Kate."

"Hi, it's great to meet you," Quinn says. "I hope it's okay I came by."

"Of course. My closing manager just called in sick, so I actually need to head back to the bookstore for an hour or two. Your timing is perfect."

I grit my teeth. Translation: *You can make sure Sunny doesn't drop dead while I'm gone.*

"Sunny, you'll be all right?" Kate asks as she grabs her purse.

"Yup."

"I put your pills out on the counter."

I scowl.

"Just take them, okay?" She smacks a kiss to my forehead and waves at Quinn as she heads out the front door.

"Sorry," I say, untangling my feet from the blanket. "Want to go to my room?"

Quinn nods but doesn't move. She's wearing a snug navy tee with light blue whales all over it and dark skinny jeans. She's so freaking cute, I can't even take it. I look down at my boring gray tank top and plaid pajama pants, both of which I think are Kate's, now that I think about it. I roll my eyes at myself.

"Um . . . do you need to take those pills?" Quinn asks.

"Ugh, not you too."

"I'm just saying, I'd rather not have to dial 9-1-1 while I'm here, you know?"

"Not your idea of fun?"

"Not exactly."

"I take the pills at bedtime, so you can pipe down."

She lifts her hands in surrender and I lead the way to my room.

"Whoa...cool," she says as I open the door. The white lights are on and the lamps are off. Everything looks watery and calm.

"I like it," I say, plopping onto my bed.

"So, about yesterday," she says, sitting down next to me.

My stomach flutters. "We don't have to talk about it."

"I didn't mean to push you to kiss Sam. I thought that was what you wanted."

"I thought so too, I guess. It was just weird, you know? Once it was really real."

She nods. "I wanted to make sure you were okay."

"I think so. Just confused."

"About what?"

I swallow down a knot in my throat and shrug. "I talked to Lena last night."

"Lena? Wait...you mean..."

"My mermaid."

"Your mom mermaid?" she asks.

155

"Yeah," I say. "She's taking me out surfing tomorrow."

"Holy swearword."

"Major holy swearword."

"Are you okay?" Quinn asks. "What'd you talk about? Did she say why she left you?"

I sigh and fall back on the bed and stare up at my canopy. "I know, actually."

"Oh."

I roll the words—the why—around in my head for a few seconds before I actually say them. "She's an alcoholic. Do you know what that is?"

Quinn nods and lies back too, twisting onto her side and propping up on her elbow. She doesn't say anything. She just looks at me.

"She couldn't take care of me," I say, "so she left me with Kate. She was supposed to come back after she got better, but..."

"She never did."

"Not until now," I say.

"Wow."

"Yeah."

We sit there in the quiet for a few seconds, letting it all sink in.

"Did you ask her why she took so long?" she finally asks.

I shake my head. "I heard her tell Kate she just wasn't

ready and didn't want to mess us up, but I don't know. I'm not sure I want to hear whatever she might tell me. Once you know something, you can't ever unknow it. It's there, forever in your head, and..." *What girl wants to know forever that she wasn't enough for her mom to give up something that was bad for her anyway?* is what I want to keep saying, but I don't. I just think it. I think it over and over and over again.

"I'm a weirdo, I know," I say.

"No, you're not. I get it. At least, I think I do. Sometimes I get so mad at my mom because she makes me travel so much. I mean, it's fun, but sometimes, I just want a house that's mine, you know? I want a friend I've known for years and years. I want to go to the same school and wave at teachers I had the year before in the hall. I want to ask her to stop, even if it's just for a year or something. She could teach at a college. She could work at the aquarium in Port Hope. Or any aquarium. She has a PhD in oceanography and everything. But if I ask..."

"She might say no."

"Yeah."

I can tell Quinn doesn't want to leave at the end of the summer. I don't want her to leave either. I mean, yes, I know I've only known her for a few days, but she's my BFF. I can't even think about saying goodbye to her. I can't even fathom walking into middle school—with Margot and all her friends there, laughing at me behind their locker doors—without Quinn.

"The aquarium in Port Hope is really awesome," I say. "I haven't been in a long time, but Kate took me when I was seven and then I went there on a field trip in fourth grade."

"I can't wait to go," Quinn says. "My mom has a big presentation there with another oceanographer in a couple of weeks about the dwindling population of sea mammals on the East Coast."

"That's good, right?"

Quinn shrugs. "I guess. She's always doing these presentations, though. Doesn't mean she'll take a job."

"Oh."

Quinn sighs big and loud. "Port Hope's aquarium is amazing, though. It has the biggest whale shark on the Eastern Seaboard. They named her Juliette."

"That's a funny name for a shark."

"I think it's perfect. It's all graceful, but powerful, just like whale sharks."

I grin at her. "You really like all this ocean, science-y stuff, huh?"

"Yeah, I guess." Then she smiles and shakes her head. "No, I do. I actually really love it. I just wish . . ."

"What?"

"That I could love it and stay in one place at the same time."

I watch her face, and she just looks so sad that I scoot closer to her, my forehead almost touching hers. Almost, but not quite.

"That stinks," I say.

"Sometimes, yeah."

We lie there for a few seconds, the silence like a nice fleece blanket around us. I like this kind of quiet, the BFF kind where you're not alone but can think and you know your best friend is thinking too and it's all okay because you know that all the things you're thinking are safe.

"You know what's weird?" she asks.

"What?"

"I don't really remember stuff."

"What do you mean?"

"Like, I remember things, but sometimes, specific memories from when I was a little kid are super-fuzzy. I thought about it a lot and so I Googled it and you know what? A lot of our memories are connected to places like our house and school and, I don't know, a park we go play at every weekend. I don't have any of those familiar places where I can put all my memories. Isn't that weird?"

I can't tell in this light, but it almost looks like she's

got some tears in her eyes. "I don't think it's weird. I think it's sad."

"Yeah? Me too, I guess."

"I'm sorry."

She shrugs. "Hey, it's nothing compared to what you've been through."

"Don't say that."

She smiles. Her free hand is spread out on the quilt between us and I reach out and loop my pinkie around hers. She smiles even wider and curls her finger tight.

"Lena and I talked about kissing," I say.

Her eyes go big and round. "You what?"

"I asked her what she knew about kissing."

"What'd she say?"

"She said kissing was a lot better with someone you actually liked."

Quinn nods. "That's what I was thinking. And neither of us really liked Sam. I mean, not like that."

I don't say anything for a second. I'm thinking about liking and how you know when you like someone and how you know when that liking means you want to kiss them. Then Quinn clears her throat and I realize I've been staring right at her mouth.

But I wasn't. I was just thinking, right? Because this new heart doesn't *wonder* about certain stuff anymore.

Stuff that gets me laughed at behind closed doors by my best friend.

"You don't like Sam, do you?" she asks.

"Huh?" I swallow and it feels like there's sandpaper in my throat. "No way. I mean, he's cute. But . . . no."

Her mouth—which is kind of shiny because she must have on some lip gloss or something, not that I noticed—twitches into a tiny smile. "I didn't think so. With Sadie, I—" But she cuts herself off and her shoulders curl around her neck.

"Sadie?" I ask. "Your friend from Alaska? What about her?"

"Nothing, she just . . . I think she'd say the same thing. About liking people before you kiss them."

I want to know more about this Sadie girl, but I can't figure out a way to ask that doesn't sound like I'm being super-nosy. "Kissing is heavy-duty personal," I say instead.

"Yeah," she says. "It's like, faces really close and mouths touching and maybe even"—she leans forward like she's telling a secret—"tongues."

I giggle and feel my face warm. "I can't even imagine that."

"Me neither. It's . . ."

"A lot."

"So much."

She stares at me and I stare at her and something feels weird in my stomach. Thinking about being that close to someone—really, really close, knowing they want to be that close to you too—is scarier than I thought it would be. Quinn's kind of close to me right now and my body feels all buzzy with nerves or something. And she's just my friend. I might literally pass out when it's a boy I'm going to kiss. Quinn is so pretty and funny and smart, she won't have any problem finding a boy who'll want to be with her. I bet she'll be super-cool throughout the whole kiss. I want to be like that.

"So...how are we going to find someone we like?" she whispers.

"I don't know," I whisper back. Then we just keep staring at each other and my stomach keeps on doing weird things and I feel like I'm about to light up like a sparkler on the Fourth of July. I keep opening my mouth to say something, but nothing comes out. My mind is all jumbled up, like a jigsaw puzzle with too many missing pieces. Quinn watches me and I watch her and my breathing is so loud, I just know it's giving away how weird I'm feeling right now.

"Let's Google Lena," I blurt, because I need to stop feeling weird and because I've been wanting to Google her all day but I don't want to do it alone and I sure don't want to Google her with Kate.

"Yes," Quinn says, sitting up and clapping her hands together. "Let's do it."

I grab the laptop Kate got me for Christmas last year off my nightstand and settle against the headboard. Quinn squishes up next to me and I open the browser before I type *Lena St. James* into the search bar.

There are a bunch of hits, but nothing that looks like my Lena. No Twitter or Instagram or Snapchat.

"Wow, does she even exist?" Quinn asks, squinting at the screen. "I thought everyone our parents' age at least had a Facebook page. My mom's on hers constantly."

I shrug and then type in a new name: *Lena Marks*.

Her face pops up immediately. She's just there...thirteen years younger and bare-armed.

"Is that her?" Quinn asks.

I nod, my eyes devouring the screen.

"She's...gorgeous."

"Yeah."

"You look just like her."

"Do I?" I glance at Quinn and she's looking right at me. She nods and I feel my cheeks go red. But Quinn's right—I look just like Lena. Especially like this, younger and flat-bellied and without any tattoos or those dark circles I noticed under her eyes last night.

There are more than photos too. There's the link to

the iTunes page where you can stream *Shallows*, as well as all these sites with a ton of information on them.

All about Lena.

I click on the first site, a Wikipedia entry, then I go quiet as I read.

Lena grew up in Mexico Beach, Florida, just like Kate and Dave, and when she was eighteen, she moved to Nashville. Kate moved there too, although the bio doesn't say that, of course. It doesn't mention Kate at all, but I can't help sticking her in the stories, piecing together all the bits of information Kate has offered over the years. Like how she and Dave went to college in Nashville, some school called Belmont. But Lena didn't. Lena moved there to be famous.

At least, that's what I think, because none of the Internet sites say anything about college. But they do say a whole lot about how Lena was only in Nashville for about a year before she caught the eye of some agent, and a year after that she made *Shallows*, which got really popular, really fast. Then, for about a year after that, she toured all over the country singing her songs, and about a year after that, the year I was born, she dropped off the face of the earth.

Like, there's no more information about her. I even find some music blogs that wonder if she died and her family is covering it up, but obviously that's not true.

164

There's nothing about her being an alcoholic. There's not even anything about my dad. I know Lena had me when she was twenty-two, so it's not hard to connect the dots.

Lena gave up her dream because of me.

CHAPTER

16

Kate doesn't say anything as she coats my whole body in SPF 40,000,000. I sit in the kitchen chair, not saying anything either. When we hear Lena's truck rumble up the driveway, Kate smears one last handful of white goo onto my back and caps the bottle with a loud *snap*. I stand up, my legs wobbly with nerves, and stuff my towel into my beach bag, which Kate has loaded down with about eleven bottles of Ensure, extra sunscreen, crackers, and carrot sticks.

We still don't say anything, though, as we head out to the porch. Lena gets out of her truck and waves at me. I wave back, but my stomach feels like there's a thunderstorm happening in there, all lightning flashes and rumbles. Lena doesn't come up to the porch and I'm glad. I need a second to get a grip.

"Okay," Kate says, taking a deep breath. She tucks a loose strand of hair behind my ear. "Be safe, all right?"

I glance up at her. Her eyes look a little red, a little wet. "I will."

"I mean, really safe."

I manage a tiny smile. "The safest."

She nods and looks away, but then she pulls me into a hug and kisses the top of my head. I want to roll my eyes at her, but I don't. I hug her back.

Kate walks me down to Lena's truck and I get in before anyone—me included—changes their mind about this whole adventure. Kate and Lena talk for a second, but soon, Lena's sitting next to me and we're ready to go, two surfboards piled up in the bed of her truck. I relax into the white leather seat.

It's barely six o'clock in the morning, the sun pinking up the sky, but Lena says early-morning surfing is the best. Kate watches from the porch as Lena turns the truck around, watches us roll down the driveway, and she probably keeps on watching long after we're out of sight and heading toward the east end of the island. I feel a twinge of guilt, but I swallow it down. I'm going surfing, after all. I'm living.

Once we're through downtown and on the island's main road surrounded by thick pines and oak trees— cleverly named Juniper Island Road—Lena rolls the windows down and sticks her arm out, riding the air with her palm. I keep stealing a bunch of glances at her, glad that the wind is too loud for us to talk. I just need a minute like this, some time to watch this weird lady with tattoos who's the whole reason I'm alive.

Well, not the whole reason, I guess. I pat my chest and take a deep breath, feeling the thrum-thrum under my fingers. I wonder if my donor ever got to surf. I sure never thought I would.

East Beach on Juniper Island has the clearest water and the biggest waves. It's also free of all the rocks that dot the west end, so it's a perfect spot for surfing. At least, that's what Lena told me.

After we park in the gravel lot, Lena goes around to the truck's bed and starts unloading the boards. One is bright pink and a lot smaller than the other neon-green one, so it's clearly a kid's board. My chest warms, thinking how Lena must have gone out yesterday and rented a board just for me.

I grab my bag and we head toward the beach. My heart flutters and flits, nerves tingling my fingertips.

But all my nerves disappear when my feet hit the sand. The ocean is there, just like it always is, my constant friend. It's never let me down, not once. The sun is rising over the water, spilling pink and orange and purple over all the blue. It's just about the most amazing thing ever. I've never seen the sunrise like this. Before I was sick, there was no way I was ever going to get up early enough to drive over to the east side of the island to see the sun come up. And, after I got sick, there was no way Kate was ever going to let me get up that early. So, this... this is...

This is New Life.

Tears pile up in my eyes and I go ahead and let them fall.

"Sunny?" Lena's ahead of me a little, but she drops the boards in the sand and doubles back. "You okay?"

I nod and wave my hand at the sky.

She turns to look at it and takes a deep breath. "I know. It's one reason I wanted to come to the east side. There's nothing like it, huh?"

I shake my head. I can't remember the last time Kate just... stopped. Even when we sit on the porch and listen to the ocean hit the rocks, she's always worrying her fingers into knots and tossing me glances to make sure I'm still there.

Lena's not doing any of that. She's watching the earth wake up, just like I am. I kind of want to take her hand. I can't get any words out, but I want to do something, something big to mark this moment, and holding Lena's hand seems pretty big to me. Before I can take the leap, though, she squeezes my shoulder and asks if I'm ready to ride some waves.

And you know what? I so am.

※

"Lie on your stomach and paddle," Lena says, so I lie on my stomach and paddle.

It's not as easy as it sounds. The salty waves roll around me. They keep swelling up and smacking me in the face, and even though mine is a kid's board, it feels about as big as a car. And the water is cold. The sun is still creeping up on the earth, so it's not super-warm yet, and Lena didn't have a Sunny-sized rash guard for me to borrow. Still, I'm on a surfboard. I'm going to surf.

We go out pretty deep, even deeper than I went out on the day I met Quinn. The sea is calmer out here and Lena says we don't need the waves yet. She sits up on her board, one leg over each side.

I do the same. Except instead of sitting tall like I'm riding a horse, I promptly lose my balance and plop into the water. Good thing there's a leash around my ankle.

"Whoa, there!" Lena says, and I spit and sputter salt water from my mouth. She holds on to my board as I climb back on, careful not to make a total fool out of myself this time.

"I meant to do that," I say.

"Of course you did."

I grin at her and find my balance.

"I just want you to feel the sea right now," she says. "Feel the board under your body, feel how it interacts with the water. We'll get to the waves later."

I nod and take a deep breath. The sun is still rising, turning the sky from orange to lavender-gray, the first signs of blue peeking through. But I'm not really looking at that anymore. I'm looking at Lena watching the sky. She has on a long-sleeved black rash guard over her black bikini—one thing I do know about her is that she likes black—and she has this tiny smile on her face. Her eyes are soft. She looks...happy.

"Why did you start surfing?" I ask.

She glances at me, her eyes still all gentle, the exact same amber-brown as mine. "You know about me, right? That I'm an alcoholic?"

I nod.

"Well, I haven't had a drink in a long time. Three years, four months, and eighteen days. Today will be nineteen, actually."

The number bounces around in my brain. It's higher than I thought it would be. "You've...you've been okay for three whole years?"

She sighs and looks out at the water. "That's a complicated question, Sunny. Okay isn't a word I usually use to talk about my recovery. It's ongoing and it's not easy. Every day I have to fight for it."

"Why? Why couldn't you just stop drinking if it was bad for you?"

"I wish I had an easy answer for that. For a long time, I told myself I could. I could stop anytime—and I tried." She sighs and looks even harder at me, her eyes all hungry. "I tried, Sunny. I tried to stop and I tried to keep you. I did."

I frown and look away from her. It's the first time she's mentioned me in all of this and I'm not sure I want to go there. In fact, I'm pretty sure I don't. Because I don't get it. I don't get why she couldn't keep me, if she really wanted me.

I guess she feels me closing up, because she clears her throat and moves on. "Anyway, after the first year of being sober, my sponsor, Danielle—that's the person who helps me when I'm really struggling—suggested getting a hobby. I was still songwriting, and that helped a lot, but I needed something physical so I could stay healthy. Something that was good for my mind too."

"And surfing is good for your mind?"

"What do you think?"

She waves her hand at the sky and sea as we bob on the boards. The sun is warming up on my shoulders, pulling freckles out of my skin. The air is salty and full.

"This isn't surfing, though," I say.

"It's part of it. You have to learn how to read the sea, the swells. You have to learn how to be patient and daring at the same time."

"Why did you need to learn patience and daring?"

"Everyone does, don't you think?"

I drag my fingers through the water while I think about that. The sea is cool and clear, and below I see tiny fish swimming in circles. I feel them nipping at my toes.

"I think I had to have a lot of patience when I was sick," I finally say. "Because there was nothing I could do about it, you know?"

Lena's soft eyes go totally gooey. "Yeah, I can see that."

"And then, when we found out I got a heart, I needed some daring. The surgery was scary. But maybe I had daring the whole time I was sick too. Because sometimes, before we knew I'd be okay, I just wanted to go to sleep and not wake up. I mean, I didn't want to die, but I was so tired. But then I would wake up and I'd get out of bed and I'd keep hoping and trying. Maybe that was kind of daring."

I've never said any of this to Kate or Margot or Dave. I've only ever thought it in my bed at night when it hurt to breathe and my oxygen tank puffed air up my nose and all I could do was cry after Kate fell asleep next to me.

"Sunny," Lena says, "I think you're the most daring person I know."

I shrug. "You don't know me very well."

She doesn't say anything to that, but her gooey eyes go sad. I didn't say it to be mean. I said it because it's true and she knows it.

"I know one thing," she says after a few seconds. "You're daring enough to go on an epic kissing quest, even after giving a guy a bloody nose."

A laugh busts out of my mouth. Somehow, of all the things she could've said, that was the perfect thing.

"I don't know," I say. "Quinn and I decided you're right. We need to like the person first. It'll just be less... weird, I think."

"Agreed. So what's your next strategy?"

"Um... meet a boy I like?"

She laughs. "Solid plan."

That's my exact plan, actually. I even changed my New Life plan to fit it and everything.

Step Three: Find a boy I like and kiss him.

"You met... Ethan on the beach, right?" I ask.

Lena nods. "I was trying to do a cartwheel and failing pretty hard."

"Right in front of him?"

"Right in front of him. He laughed and helped me stand up and then he showed me how to do it right."

"He knew how to do a cartwheel?"

"He did and it was perfect. He could do a roundoff too. He was always full of surprises."

She goes quiet for a second and her eyes are way, way far away. I feel a knot tangling up in my throat. I gulp it down.

"So I need to . . . be really bad at gymnastics on the beach?" I ask.

She cracks up at that. "Worked for me. But I've met more people than just your dad, you know. Friends and people I've liked." She winks at me when she says that. "I've met people at the mall, at the skating rink, at fairs, in line buying guitar strings, at the doctor's office when I had the flu, at concerts. People you might connect with are everywhere, Sunny."

I think about how I met Quinn, how she just appeared right next to me in the ocean like a magical mermaid. It's pretty much the best meeting story ever, if you ask me.

"Wait . . . so . . . you've kissed other people? Other than my dad?" I ask.

"Well, yeah. We were only thirteen, you know, and he lived in Michigan. Way far away for two teenagers. I dated people. So did he. After tenth grade, I didn't even talk to him anymore. His family stopped coming to Mexico Beach and we grew apart."

"So . . . how did you . . ." I wave at myself, hoping she gets what I'm asking.

She smiles at me. "Funny story, that."

"Yeah?"

She leans over, resting her elbows on her board. I do the same and if we weren't floating in the middle of the ocean, I'd almost feel like we were at a slumber party, sharing secrets.

"So, I was nineteen and I'd just signed with my manager in Nashville," Lena says. "I was all set to record my first album, but you have to get studio musicians. You know, those people to fill in the instruments you don't play, make it sound rich and full."

I nod, entranced.

"The second day of recording, I was in the booth about to lay down a vocal track and in walks this guy in a leather jacket with floppy brown hair and green eyes."

"Oh my god. Was it—"

"You bet it was. He was my drummer, hired by my producer, and his name was Ethan St. James."

"No way."

"Right? He couldn't believe it either. A week later, we were dating and never looked back."

"Wow."

She nods, a little smile on her face.

"Did you love him a lot?" I ask.

She sits back up and blinks at the sky for a couple of

seconds before looking back at me. "So much. You have his nose, I think."

Instinctively, I press my finger against the tip of my nose.

"When we found out we were having you, we were..." She sighs and runs her hand through her wet hair. "Well, we were surprised."

"Um. Gross."

She grins and pushes my board a little, but then pulls me back. "But we were excited. We got married and rented an apartment about the size of a walk-in closet and we were so happy."

"You were? Even though you quit music because of me?"

Her eyes go wide and her mouth drops open. "Sunny. Sweetie, that was...I didn't..."

"But you did, didn't you?"

She presses her mouth super-flat, but finally, she nods. "But I wanted to. I loved making music, but the music scene wasn't good for me. There were parties and touring and unpredictable schedules and, well, just a lot of things that were bad for me that I had a hard time saying no to."

I frown, about to ask her what kind of things, but then, I know. "Like drinking alcohol?"

"Yeah. Exactly. So when I got pregnant with you, it

made sense to quit. Or at least take a break. Your dad agreed and, Sunny, like I said. We were happy."

Her eyes are shining when she says all this and my chest feels warm and melty. But then everything hardens up quick. Because if she was so happy to have me, to give up her whole big famous music career for me, how did she give me away only four years later? And even more than that, how did she stay away for so long?

"Where've you been all this time?" I ask, and immediately wish I could swallow my own tongue.

She pushes her palms into her board and looks at me. "At first? Nashville. I stayed there after your dad died and...well, after everything fell apart. Then, about four years ago, I knew I needed to get out of Nashville if I was really going to get serious about getting sober. I'd had some good long spells without drinking, went to these meetings called Alcoholics Anonymous that helped, but I'd always fall back into it. It'd just take one call from an old friend, one show at a venue I used to play at. So I moved to this coastal town on Long Island in New York called Montauk. It's small and quiet. That's where I started surfing. I taught private voice lessons there."

New York. She lives in New York. She was in New York when I got sick. She was in New York when Margot spit all over our friendship. It's so weird, thinking about Lena all the way up there in those colder ocean waters.

What did she do all that time? Who did she talk to? Does she have friends? A roommate? Does she go on dates? My mind spins with thousands of questions. Before Lena showed up, all my questions were about the past, wondering about her and my dad and why she left and never came back. But now, with that one little word—Montauk—I can't stop thinking about this whole life she's had without me. I want to know more, more, more. But I don't. I don't want to know any of it.

I stare out at the water for a while, trying to calm down my brain. I wish Quinn was here. She could talk to Lena about regular stuff and I could listen and think and keep all my questions behind my teeth. And Quinn would love surfing. I wonder if she's ever surfed before. Probably, she's done everything before. Except have her first kiss, I guess.

My heart flips and flops as I think about kissing. I sit up straight on my board. "I think I've felt the ocean enough."

Lena clears her throat. "Right. Let's do this."

"I'm ready."

"Okay, all you're going to do for now is stand."

I pull a face at her. "*Stand.* That's it?"

"Talk to me again after you've tried it."

I would roll my eyes, but, hey, I'm the one who fell off the board just trying to sit on it.

"All right," she says, "lie on your stomach with your head up. Put your hands on the board beside your shoulders, like you're going to do a push-up."

"I haven't done a push-up in two years."

She frowns. "Are you okay to do this?"

I wave a hand as I pitch forward to lie down. "Actually, I've never done a push-up."

"Sunny."

"I'm fine. Carry on, O Surfer Queen."

She smiles and I smoosh my palms against the board. The water is almost eye level, the sun a hazy golden ball right in front of me. The world looks amazing from here—small and big all at the same time.

"When you're ready, push your upper body up and sweep your feet under you, planting them on the stringer."

"The what?"

"That line in the middle of your board."

"Then just say *that line in the middle of your board.*"

She sighs. "Watch me do it first. You have to turn your body as you do it so your feet are facing the side of the board."

I turn my head and watch her lie down and then gracefully pop up on the board, her body crouched like she's ready for a fight, hands out just above her waist. It's a thing of beauty, let me tell you, and I want to be the master of it.

"Okay, watch me go," I say.

She sits back down on her board and flourishes her hand at me. I press my hands into the board and push up, bringing my feet under me at the same time. I plant them on the line in the middle of the board—pardon me, the *stringer*—and keep my legs bent. I'm about to shoot Lena a triumphant grin when the board tilts to the side. Then it tilts more and more. I try to even out my weight, but I might as well be grape jelly wiggling around in a bowl. The board flips all the way over and I splash into the ocean.

For the second time today, I come up sputtering. I climb back on the board while Lena cracks up.

"Easy as pie, right?" she says.

I glare at her, but a smile tugs at my mouth. I haven't moved my body around this much in a long, long time. Kate would probably be freaking out right now, but I feel totally awesome. I feel like this is what it was all for, all that patience and daring.

I lie down on the board and do the whole thing over again.

And topple into the sea again.

Then I do it again.

And so it goes—*push, jump, splash . . . push, jump, splash*— for at least fifteen minutes. I'm breathing hard, my heart slamming against my ribs, but I keep going. I keep going and going because I want to do this. I need to do it, to know I can, to let this new heart and whoever gave it to me stand on a surfboard surrounded by the sea and know it's alive.

"Sunny."

Push, jump, *splash.*

"Sunny, stop."

Push, jump, *splash.*

"Sunny!"

Push, jump—

Arms wrap around my waist and pull me gently into the sea. I'm breathing way too fast and I swallow some water. I choke and spit, my head spinning.

"Breathe, baby, just breathe," Lena says, one arm tight around me. She's holding on to my board with the other, her face pressed against my head. "Breathe, baby."

Baby.

Something about the word makes me want to scream at her. Or cry. As my breath slows and the ache I didn't even notice was going on in my chest starts to dull, my body picks crying.

Tears well up and spill down my cheeks, mixing with the sea. Lena holds me tighter, and I can feel her body shaking against mine while I cry harder and harder. In fact, I'm all-out sobbing now. I want to hold on to Lena, but I don't want to. So I let my arms drift in the water, my body limp as a dead fish.

182

"We've got time, Sunshine," Lena says, her face still smooshed against my wet hair. "We've got all the time in the world."

On the way back to my house, I'm so exhausted, Lena insists that I lie down in the backseat on the soft white leather. There's hardly enough room in this old truck to fit all my limbs, and the seat belt is all twisted around my stomach, but I don't even care. I use my turquoise and navy-striped beach towel as a pillow and watch the pale morning light skip around in the window above me.

"Don't tell Kate," I say.

"What?" Lena asks. She turns down the song playing from her phone, some moody music Dave would probably love.

"Kate," I say. "Don't tell her what happened in the ocean."

She shakes her head. "Sunny. I have to. This is your health we're talking about."

"But I'm fine. I just overdid it. I won't next time, I promise."

She glances back at me, a smile pulling at her mouth. "Next time?"

"Well... yeah. I mean, if you want."

"I want. I very much want."

I tuck my arm under my head, relieved. I didn't even surf today, but I know I'm totally hooked. Floating in the middle of the ocean, figuring out how my body works with it, works against it. I want that. I want it so bad.

Lena turns the music back up and we ride like that for a couple of miles. I'm smiling to myself just thinking about being out there on the water again when I spy a plastic baggie of Cheerios peeking out of Lena's bag on the floorboard. My stomach growls—I was way too nervous to eat all that much this morning, much to Kate's dismay—and I reach down to grab the dry cereal. The baggie is caught on something, so I give it a good yank and a bunch of other stuff tumbles out.

There are a few tubes of lipstick in funky colors, like blue and purple and sea-glass green, and a bottle of moon-gray nail polish. There's a package of wet wipes, a bald baby smiling out at me on the front. And there's this weird salmon-pink owl with a heart-shaped hole in the middle about the size of my palm. It's soft and squishy, and I can't figure out if it's supposed to be a giant keychain or some kind of stress-reliever toy or what.

But what really hooks all my attention is a black notebook. It's small, maybe a little bigger than a deck of cards, and when I flip through the pages super-fast, it's packed full of tiny, slanted handwriting in blue or black ink.

I shove all the other stuff back into Lena's bag. Then I

turn onto my stomach and split the journal open with my thumb, right to the middle where the latest entry is. It's dated yesterday.

> So relieved that Sunny has agreed to see me. I can't imagine what I would've done if she'd refused. All of this for nothing. Not that I would've blamed her. But there's so much at stake now. J says I need to—

I let the notebook fall shut before my eyeballs see another word.

"You all right?" Lena asks from the front, turning down the music again.

"Mm-hm," I say, because I don't trust my voice at all.

"Almost there."

I sit up just as we're turning into my driveway. Our little house looms up ahead, all soft gray paint and dark red roof, the red-and-white striped lighthouse tall and pretty behind it.

The truck bumps along the gravel and there's Kate sitting on the porch swing with Dave, waiting to make sure I didn't drown in the ocean or whatever.

"Hey, did everything go all right?" Kate calls, jogging toward the truck. Dave stays put, but he sticks his tongue out at me.

Lena rolls her window down and hangs an arm outside. I hold my breath.

"Yeah, great," she says.

I breathe.

"I think Sunny might be a natural," Lena says.

"Well, let's take it slow," Kate says.

"We are, Katie."

"All right, I'm just saying."

They go back and forth like this for a few seconds, but all I hear is a bunch of blah, blah, blah, because I've still got Lena's journal in my lap, hidden under my towel.

"Are we still on?" Lena asks, turning to look at me in the backseat. Kate rounds the truck and opens the passenger door for me to get out. "For surfing in a couple of days?"

"Yeah. Yeah, that sounds awesome," I say, grabbing my bag from beside me. I push the front seat forward and before I know it, I'm out of the truck and walking toward my house with Kate's arm around my shoulders, the corner of Lena's journal digging into my ribs as I hug my towel to my chest.

CHAPTER

17

Surfing wore me out, but I can't sleep. I'm thinking about my heart a lot, how it let me go out in the ocean today, and listening to it thump-thump-thump in my chest. And I'm thinking about my dad while I listen to Lena's album over and over again, paying super-close attention to the drums. Then, while I do that, I'm thinking about Lena and her life in Montauk and how she's friends with someone she calls J.

My brain feels like a cup overflowing with water, thoughts spilling everywhere. I lie in bed with the little black notebook I pretty much stole right out of Lena's bag resting on my chest. I watch it move up and down, up and down with my breathing.

I haven't read any of it yet. At least, not past that one

little snippet in the car, but I feel like those words were enough to chew on for a few years.

She was relieved I let her see me.

But...all of what would've been for nothing?

But...who in the holy heck is J?

I pick up the notebook and flip through it. The pages are crinkly from the all the writing and there are a few round light brown stains from a tea or coffee mug.

It's wrong. It's super-wrong. I know this, but I can't stop myself from opening to the first page and running my fingers down the writing. The entry is dated a few months ago, way back in February.

Which would've been about a month before she called Kate for the first time.

> Tonight's meeting was hard. I can't lie, I wanted a drink, which is why I went to a meeting in the first place. Danielle met with me after at Café Marzoli and we drank coffee and talked. So much coffee. I used to hate coffee, but now it seems like the only thing that will calm me down.
>
> "You're ready," she tells me, but I don't know.
>
> J says the same thing. Says I'll never forgive myself if I don't try. Says S will be fine, that she'll

adjust. That when she's older, she'll understand and never know any different and she'll be so grateful to know her whole family.

Danielle agrees, but that's the thing. It's not S I'm worried about all that much. I mean, I am, but I know she'll be all right.

It's me.

It's always me. I'm scared I'll fail. I'm scared Sunny will reject me. I'm scared Kate won't even consider it. I'm scared, scared, scared. And so I sit with Danielle and drink a gallon of coffee until I feel a little less scared.

Breathing is hard, but I reread it again. And then again. A meeting . . . that must be the ones she goes to for being an alcoholic, because I know Danielle helps her with all that. There's J again, and now there's an S.

S . . . S . . .

S has to be me, right? That I'll be all right. That I'll be grateful to know my whole family.

I tear through some more pages—flip, flip, flip—and finally find the entry at the very end of March that I'm looking for.

I did it. I called K. She didn't answer, but I did it and I didn't drink and I didn't pass out and

189

I'm still breathing. I left her a message and now I just have to wait and hope. J took me out for a nice dinner to celebrate, but I could barely eat a thing. I'm so nervous. I just want to hold S and never let go. I'm never letting her go. Never.

A drop of salty water plops onto the page, smearing the blue ink. Lena's writing blurs and I can't wipe my face fast enough. My nose burns and runs and my throat aches something awful.

I'm never letting her go. Never.

I grab my phone and find Lena's name, my thumbs trembling over my screen as I try to think of something amazing to say. But I don't want to talk to Lena right now. I want to talk *about* Lena.

I switch over to another name and type Hi into the text box. As soon as I hit Send, though, I realize how late it is. There's no way Quinn's up. There's no way she's—

Three little dots bounce onto my screen, followed by
Hey. You're awake?

I breathe out a big huge breath.

I guess I am, I text back. So are you.

I like staying up late. Shh, don't tell my mom.

Secrets are safe with BFFs.

Always, she says.

I squeeze the phone tighter, relief opening up my chest.

So how was surfing? Quinn texts.

It was great. I mean, I didn't really surf. Just learned how to stand.

Stand? That's it?

Hey, it's hard! I text. Still fun, though.

That's amazing, Quinn says. How was it with Lena? Weird?

My thumbs hover, wanting to talk, talk, talk, but now I'm not sure how to answer Quinn's questions. My mind is like mush. Plus, it's nearly midnight and it feels like someone's yanking on my eyelashes and I've been crying. I'm all wrung out, like a wet rag squeezed of all its water.

I don't know, I finally text. The truth.

She doesn't text back and then my phone rings, belting out a Truth Lies Low song—the kissing song, of course—so loudly, I drop it in my covers. I grab it, scrambling to silence it and slide my finger over the screen.

"Hello?" I whisper, like I don't know who it is.

"Hey," Quinn says.

"Hey."

"Is it okay that I called?"

"Yeah, but you didn't have to."

"I know," she says. "But it's a big deal, right? Hanging out with Lena for the first time?"

"Yeah. I guess it is." My voice is all trembly. I swallow

a bunch of times until it smooths out. I want to tell Quinn all about Lena's journal, but that feels wrong. I already stole the thing, I don't want to spill Lena's deepest thoughts to the whole world too. My eyes ache, though, a bunch of feelings still hiding behind them just waiting for me to let them out.

"Do you think you can love someone and hate them at the same time?" I finally ask.

"Yeah, totally," Quinn says. She doesn't even miss a beat.

"Really?"

"I feel like that toward my mom sometimes. Like, I love her, right? She's my best friend, pretty much, and the only thing that never changes about my life. But it's her fault that she's the only thing that never changes, and sometimes? Yeah, I hate her for it."

I burrow deeper into my covers. "That makes sense. I just . . . I feel everything when it comes to Lena, you know? I'm excited she's here. And I want to know everything about her. And I'm so stinking mad at her, I can barely see straight sometimes. And I'm nervous too. Because what if she doesn't like me?"

"Impossible."

"She left me once, though."

"Sunny. You're . . . you're amazing, okay? And she's your mom."

"She left me, Quinn."

She doesn't say anything for a second. I wish we weren't on the phone. I wish she was here or I was at her house so I could see her face. Because what if Quinn's wondering why Lena left me too? What if she's wondering why she's my only friend even though I've lived on the island most of my life?

A tear slips down my cheek and I brush it away fast. I'm so tired of feeling like this.

"She's back," Quinn says softly. "Right?"

"Until when, though?"

Quinn sighs into the phone. "I wish I could hug you right now."

That makes me smile. It makes me smile really big, right through the tears. "Me too."

"Well, I'll just have to hug you super-tight tomorrow."

"What's happening tomorrow?"

"Kissing Quest, full force."

I sit up in my bed, my smile going even wider. "Really? You still want to?"

"Totally. We just need to find someone we could totally fall head over heels in love with. Easy peasy."

I laugh. "Hey, we should go to the pool by the pier. There are always a ton of boys our age hanging around there."

"Boys," Quinn says. "Right."

There's a beat of silence before she clears her throat and says, "Let's do it. Meet you there around nine?"

"Perfect."

"Awesome. Now...why is it so hard to stand on a surfboard?"

I smile and lie back down in my bed, telling Quinn every detail about surfing, which, it turns out, she's never done. Then we start talking about all the other stuff we've never done and want to do, like parasailing and riding a horse on the beach. We talk about small stuff too, though. Like eating lunch at the same table, in the same seat, with the same people every day for a whole school year. Like holding hands with someone at the movie theater. Like picking out a dress for our first school dance. We talk about everything and nothing and it's amazing.

Next thing I know, I'm blinking awake in the morning light, my phone is still smooshed against my cheek, and Quinn is deep-sleep breathing on the other end.

I woke up smiling
because I fell asleep
with your voice in my ear.
I forgot what it was like to have
someone on my side,
someone to laugh with,

someone to wonder with,
someone to trust.

But then,
the morning light
was really bright
and I remembered.
Then I wondered.
Then I worried.

Will
    you
        break
            my
                heart
                    too?

CHAPTER 18

Later that morning, I walk to the pier. It's this area down by the ocean with a bunch of shops and cafés and a huge community pool with a slide and waterfalls and even one of those lazy rivers with an actual current curling around the whole thing. It's pretty amazing, all clear blue and natural stone, like a miniature water park by the sea.

I remember Margot and me freaking out when they were building it, we were so excited. We were in fifth grade, before my epic collapse in recess and *dilated cardiomyopathy*. But by the time they were done, I was sick, and of course, Kate wouldn't let me go. Slides were too pulse-pounding. Waterfalls were too...waterfall-y? Who knows what Kate's reasons were. The point is, I never got to swim here. Not until today.

The day is cloudless and hot, the sky a brilliant turquoise. The pool has just opened and I don't see Quinn anywhere, so I find a couple of bright white lounge chairs near the deep end and dig into my bag. I take out the song I wrote this morning after I woke up and go back outside the pool gate onto the sidewalk, looking for the perfect spot for my words.

It takes a couple of minutes, because it can't be too obvious or so hidden that no one will ever see it, but finally, I find it.

Right between the new playground and the pool area, there's this big sculpture of a humpback whale with her calf on her back that's been there forever. I'm talking big. I used to climb on it when I was really little. Actually, I used to climb on it when I was ten. Oh, who am I kidding? I'm going to climb on it right now.

I step onto the big whale's back, the little baby right next to me. I climb up, up, up, right onto the mama's head. I stand tall and look out over the sparkling sapphire ocean on the other side of the sidewalk and rocks; it's so close at high tide, I can almost touch it. I breathe in the delicious salty air. Then I bend down and stick the song right into the mama whale's mouth.

After I jump down, I pat the whale's head while I make sure the piece of paper is nice and secure, but still visible.

I want someone to read it, after all. My stomach flips and flops just thinking about it, part terror and part excitement. But I always feel that when I put a song out into the world, so I'm hoping that's normal.

"Sunny, hey!"

I whirl around to see Quinn waving at me from inside the pool area. She found my bag by the deep end and has already taken off her cover-up. I yank my hands out of the whale's mouth and wave back.

"Hey!"

"What are you doing?" she asks.

"Nothing. Just...you know...looking at the whale."

"Isn't she pretty? Stay there, I want to see her too." She starts toward the gate and my palms get all damp.

"No!" I yelp.

She freezes, frowning at me. "Why not?"

"Um...I'm just...ready to swim."

I don't wait for her to answer, just hightail it back through the gate and over to the deep end.

"Sorry I'm late," Quinn says, and then she pulls me into a tight hug. All the air goes out of me and my arms dangle at my sides for a second. Finally, I get my brain on right and wrap my arms around her back. She smells like coconuts and the tang of sunscreen.

"What was that for?" I ask when we pull away.

She tucks a blue-black strand of hair behind her ear. "I told you I'd hug you the next time I saw you, remember?"

I do. I do remember.

"Thanks," I say.

"BFFs," she says.

My breath feels shaky, but I try to hide it by smiling extra big at her. She's got on a different bikini today—this one is black with little yellow suns all over it.

"I like your suit," I say.

She glances down at it and grins. "I wore it for you."

"You...you did?"

"Hello, there are sunshines on it. Really bright and pretty ones, don't you think?"

"Um...yeah." They are pretty. They're super-bright yellow and the rays are curled like they're waving in the breeze.

Quinn smiles at me and I smile back, or I think I do, but my chest feels all warm and my belly feels all fluttery and it's distracting. I'm about to say something really funny and clever, something like *Well, I'll need to find a suit with some Quinns all over it,* but she starts pulling a third chair over to ours and then I'm all confused.

"What are you doing?" I ask.

"Margot came over to our cottage this morning with her dad to check the refrigerator—it's making this really weird noise, like a dying bird or something—so I invited her to come."

I blink at her. Then I blink some more, hoping she said Pargot or Hargot or pretty much any name other than the one I think I heard.

But no such luck. While Quinn lines up three chairs and then lays out her fluorescent pink towel, I see Former Best Friend flouncing toward us in a super-chic black-and-white polka-dotted tankini like she's the queen of... of... of something really cool.

I rub my forehead and tell my thoughts and my heart—not to mention my gag reflex—to chill.

"Hey," Margot says when she reaches us.

"Hey, you made it," Quinn says.

I glower.

"Yeah, thanks for inviting me," Margot says.

I glower some more.

"Sunny, you okay?" Quinn asks.

I snap my spine straight and nod, focusing on laying out my towel.

"I heard you gave Sam Blanchard a black eye," Margot says as she sits down on the chair next to me and takes out a tube of SPF 15.

"What?" I say, but I heard her. My cheeks catch on fire and my mouth starts watering like I'm about to puke. Of all the people I never, ever, ever wanted to get wind of the Sam Blanchard Debacle—as I shall now always think of it—Margot is at the top of the list. "Where'd you hear that?"

"From Sam," she says. "I saw him on the beach yesterday. His face is about five different colors. He said you gave him a bra to wipe his nose?"

I don't say anything. If I do, I'll start crying. Or spew fire. Neither is a great option. Instead I take off my cover-up and make sure the SPF 4,000,000,000 that Kate put on me this morning is all rubbed in. I'm still in my boring one-piece, but I'd rather have a boring one-piece than deal with people staring at my scar. Then I plop down onto my chair and take out this comic book called *Lumberjanes* that Dave brought me the other day and bury my face in the inky pages.

"That must have been embarrassing," Margot says, and I glare at her. She's looking at me all wide-eyed and concerned, though. Her face reminds me of when Jack McCoy dared me to pull out my barely loose tooth in second grade. Not one to back down from a dare, eight-year-old me yanked that tooth right out. It bled so much on the playground, blood all over my light blue tunic dress, that I started bawling right then and there. Margot held my hand the whole way to the nurse, telling me how no one would remember anything by the next day.

"Why do you care?" I ask now.

Margot frowns at me, a glob of creamy sunscreen in her palm. "Why wouldn't I?"

I shrug and flip a page in my comic, waiting for my throat to stop aching. "I don't know. Don't you have cooler friends to worry about?"

She huffs a big breath. "I can have more than one friend, you know."

"I know."

"No, you don't." She smacks her palms together, spitting sunblock all over her towel. She rubs the cream into her legs. "You hated it when I started hanging out with Eliza and all of them."

I open my mouth to tell her that's totally not true— that she's the one who didn't want me around her new friends—but I can't. Because it is kind of true. It had been Margot and me for so long, maybe I didn't know how to share her. Especially after I was already sick. Well, I sure can share her now. Her swim team friends can have her.

"Who's Eliza?" Quinn asks quietly.

"Margot's best friend," I say before Margot can answer. "She tells them all her secrets. Even mine."

Margot's mouth drops open. She blinks at me and I look away. I can't tell if she understands that I know that she told them all about my wonderings, but I don't really want to know. I just want her to go away.

"Um...okay..." Quinn says, and I feel bad. I'm making this awkward and Quinn doesn't deserve that. "So, what's your comic about, Sunny?"

I lower *Lumberjanes* and look at the cover. Margot is still staring at me. I can feel her eyes trying to bore right through my forehead and into my brain. I don't look at her. "It's about these five girls at a camp, and they—"

"I thought you only liked reading kissing books," Margot says.

My eyes snap to hers. Her jaw is all tight and her green eyes look cold and hard, like emeralds.

"What?" I ask.

"Kissing books," she says slowly. "You love them. That's all you used to read, remember?"

Breathe, Sunny. Breathe.

"Did you?" Quinn asks, smiling at me.

"I—"

"She totally loves all of Kate's YA books," Margot says. "Especially the ones with kissing in them. Remember that one you read with the two girls making out?"

This time, my mouth drops open. A weird silence wiggles in among all three of us, and my heart is about to bust out of my chest. I glance at Margot, expecting her to be grinning in triumph, but she looks away and her cheeks are all red. I stare at the pool, the blue water blurring as I try to think about what to say. Of course I remember that book. It was a great book. It was cute and sweet and was about these two girls who were the only two drama counselors at the summer camp for little kids. They really hated each other at the beginning, but then they started liking each other. Like, liking each other like that. I remember crying when I finished it, but I don't know why. The story just made me feel…well…I don't know.

Normal, maybe.

But then I had to open my mouth and tell Margot all about it. Then Margot had to go and make promises she never, ever meant to keep. Then everything changed that night in my room two weeks before her terrible, awful slumber party.

"It was a good book, right?" Margot asks softly when I just sit there and gulp the air as quietly as possible. I'm not sure what she's trying to do. Her voice sounds all comforting and encouraging, but she knows me and she has to know I don't want to talk about this. She has to know I'm about to scream.

I sit there, fists clenched, trying not to think about that book. Trying not to care that Margot's totally embarrassing me right now. I've got a brand-new heart and this one doesn't wonder about kissing girls anymore. I bet I could read that book about the girls falling in love and just think it's a nice story now. I bet I wouldn't cry at all. I bet

I'd just be happy for them and then fall asleep dreaming about having a boyfriend.

"Yeah, it was good," I say, keeping my eyes on *Lumberjanes* and my voice nice and even. I'm breathing hard, but I can get it under control. I can.

"What was the title?" Margot asks.

I flick my eyes to Quinn, who's staring at me. I can't figure out what kind of stare it is, but I'm not taking any chances that it's the kind that'll get me laughed at.

"I don't remember," I say, even though I do.

"It's cool if you like that book," Margot says. "Any of those books."

She's staring at me now, her face all soft and hopeful, and it makes me so mad. It makes me feel like I'm made of fire.

"You didn't think it was cool at your slumber party," I say, my voice low and mean.

Her eyes go wide, just like I knew they would. We stare at each other for a few seconds and I know that she knows that I know. Quinn stares at her lap and bites on her lower lip.

"Sunny," Margot says, her voice all trembly. "I didn't...I—"

"I'm burning up," I say, standing, which isn't a lie. I'm sweating bullets.

"Hang on," Margot says, her face falling into her serious-talk look. A look I've had enough of, to be honest. "Do you think you and I could—"

"I'm going in," I say, ignoring her. Then I bolt toward the pool before she can say anything else. Because I may be done wondering about all that stuff that made her betray me, but I'm not done being mad at her for it.

I dive into the deep end and keep going until my fingers hit the bottom and my ears pop. The water is cold and delicious and I wish I could stay under here forever. As fast as I can, I swim toward the nearest waterfall, trying to get under it before I have to come up so Quinn and Margot can't see me. I kick like a frog and my lungs are about to burst, but I make it. I break the surface and hang my hand on the rocky wall right next to one of the slides to keep my head above water.

I turn and look out through the waterfall. The pool is getting more crowded and everyone is all blurry, wavy lines and colors. Every now and then, someone whoops as they zip down the slide. I want to whoop and zip, but my body feels all frozen. I press my hand to my heart, feeling the thrum-thrum-thrum going fast from all the swimming I can do now, and wonder if my donor ever dealt with an evil best friend. If they ever had someone who was supposed to love them no matter what, who had always acted like they did, and then turned on them like a flipped pancake.

Then, for some reason, all these *supposed to love you* thoughts make me think about Lena and how I can tell she's super-happy to spend time with me and talk to me, but how she's been gone for so long, so she can't love me all that much, and now there's water in my eyes that's not from the pool. I squish closer to the white and gray and brown rocks and let a few tears fall, sniffling and snuffling like a baby.

"There you are."

I gasp at Quinn's voice and, wouldn't you know it, my mouth is right where it needs to be to suck in a whole lungful of water. I cough and splutter, gripping the rock wall so I won't slip under.

"Sorry!" Quinn says as she swims toward me and grabs on to the wall with one hand too, patting me on the back with the other.

I wave her off and hack a little bit more. "It's fine."

"You okay?"

I roll my eyes, so unbelievably tired of that question, a motion Quinn doesn't miss.

"Sorry," she says again.

"Stop apologizing," I snap.

I don't look at her to see if she flinches, but the silence

that follows is enough to tell me she probably did. She doesn't say anything else. Just holds on to the rock wall next to me, her legs swirling underwater as she watches me.

"I'm sorry," I say, because I know I'm acting like a jerk. "Margot just...she bugs me."

"Why? She seems nice enough."

I snort.

"Did you two have a fight?" Quinn asks. "She said..." She trails off, a frown wrinkling up her forehead.

"She said what?" I ask. My heart is a giant gong in my chest.

"She said you were best friends. For a long, long time. And then you just stopped talking to her a few months ago. Did her new friends—Eliza and all of them—did you not like them?"

I swallow hard, that memory of me spilling all my secret wonderings into Margot's treacherous lap wiggling its way into my brain again.

I take a minute to breathe, my face to the rocky wall. I'm trying to figure out what to tell Quinn without telling her everything that happened with Margot at that slumber party, when she swims really close to me and lays her head on my shoulder. It calms my heart right down.

"Margot did something," I say quietly. "She...she told her new friends some stuff. Stuff about me."

Quinn lifts her head and looks at me. "Like what?"

I open my mouth to just say it—*I used to wonder what it would be like to kiss a girl*—but I can't get the words out. I can't do it. What if Quinn wrinkles her nose at me the moment I say it? What if she laughs? What if she swims away and never comes back? So I shake my head and lie. "Just... stuff about when I was sick."

She stares at me for a second and I can feel my face go all red with the lie. I don't like lying to Quinn, but the truth is worse.

Isn't it?

"I'm sorry," she says. "That had to be hard, on top of being sick."

"It's okay. I'm over it."

Another lie.

She puts her head back on my shoulder. I breathe out and lean my head against hers. She really is the best. We stay like that for a few seconds. Our feet keep brushing underwater and my knee rams into hers once, but she just laughs and keeps her head right on my shoulder. It's nice. It's really nice.

"I read a book about girls liking each other once," she says quietly.

I snap my head up and stare at her. "You did?"

"Actually, I've read a whole bunch."

"You have?"

"Yup. And it's got me thinking."

"You're... you're thinking about girls kissing?"

Her face goes crimson and she looks away. "Just kissing in general."

I nod, waiting for her to go on, but then her eyes are back on me and we just stare and stare and stare at each other and I'm not sure what it all means but my stomach is doing that weird thing that it did in my room the other night when we were lying on my bed and I can't decide if I'm about to cry or laugh or what.

"Anyway, I've been thinking about when we find someone we like," she says. "What do we do then?"

"Um...I have no idea."

"It's always so easy in the books. Like, not easy, but there's this perfect moment, you know?"

"Like at a party where they both feel lonely until they find each other."

"Or while they're studying in a corner at the library and one of them finally decides to confess their feelings."

"Or on the beach on the Fourth of July and fireworks are going off over the ocean."

She grins at that one. "Yeah. Or hidden under a waterfall at a pool."

My stomach lurches and I look around. We're tucked under the waterfall, yeah, but this area is also partly under the slide, so it's kind of darker, like we're in some magical cave, and all the pool water gives it this gauzy blue glow.

"This really would be a great kissing spot," I say.

"It would."

"What's the first thing the two people who are about to kiss might do?" I ask.

"Once they know they want to kiss?"

"Yeah."

She swallows really hard. "Well. One of them would probably touch the other person's face. Have you ever noticed that? There's always lots of face-touching in the books."

I nod. "Like this." Then I don't even know what I'm doing. But I reach out and glide my thumb over Quinn's cheek. Her skin is soft and so is her smile and it makes my breath all shaky.

"Exactly like that," she says. "Let me try." Then she slides her thumb over my cheek too and a super-nervous laugh falls out of my mouth. She drops her arm and laughs right along with me. There's lots of laughing. Good thing, because I might puke if there wasn't.

"They'd probably hold hands too," I say.

"Most definitely."

Then we press our palms together and lace our fingers together and our breathing is loud and mixing together and everything is together, together, together. I don't know what's happening. We're just walking through a plan, right? We're just...thinking.

211

From the other side of the pool, a bunch of high school girls bust out laughing. I yank my hand from Quinn's and look around, but no one can see us under the waterfall like this. I can only hear those girls. That's enough, though. My stomach coils into a tight knot.

"Okay," I say, "so that's what we might do when we find a boy we like."

Quinn doesn't say anything, and for a second, I think she can tell how hard my heart is pounding and how my body is shaking all over. My hand tingles from holding hers and I shove it through my wet hair.

"Yeah," she finally says. "That's what we'll do."

I nod and keep my eyes on the blue water. "I'm cold. I'm going to go sit in the sun for a while. I'll be on the lookout for some cute boys. Because, you know, we need a boy to like."

"Sunny—"

But I'm already diving under the water. The world goes crystal blue and quiet as I leave her behind.

☀

I don't sit in the sun. I don't sit anywhere. When I get back to the lounge chairs, Margot's still there, but now, someone else is there too.

Eliza.

Swim team captain.

The girl who said she thought I had a crush on Margot. The girl Margot laughed with and gave all my secrets to. She's sitting in Quinn's chair wearing a plum-colored bikini, her dark hair all long and loose around her tan shoulders.

"Hey there, Sunny," she says.

I ignore her. I grab my towel and stuff it into my bag. Then I shove my feet into my flip-flops and don't even bother putting on my cover-up. I just toss it over my shoulder.

"Sunny, what's wrong?" Margot asks, sitting up.

I ignore her too. I ignore Quinn, who I can see climbing out of the pool a few feet away. I ignore the way my heart feels like it's caught in my throat and my eyes are blurring with tears. I ignore the whole world and walk away until there's no one left to ignore.

What does it mean to wonder
what it would feel like...
What it would be like...
What she would say...
What they would think...
if they knew
I held your hand like that?

I think you know how it feels,
but if I ask you if it's true,
will you laugh too?
Because maybe it's all in my head.
Maybe it's all in my old heart,
stuck like a memory that I can't forget.

But if I have a new heart,
shouldn't that mean that
I don't wonder
what it would
feel like?

CHAPTER

19

I write the song in the public bathroom by the pier. Not the most inspiring place, sitting on a toilet lid in a little stall that smells like pee while scribbling out your totally-freaking-out thoughts, but it had to be done. I wouldn't have made it to my house. I would've exploded or imploded or deploded or something.

On my way home, I stick the song into the hollow of an oak tree about half a block away from the pool, next to Kingston's Pharmacy. I barely slow down enough to make sure it's secure. I'm terrified Quinn will come after me. Or worse, Margot.

When I get home, I thank the stars above that Kate's at the bookstore, because all I want to do is call Lena. I'm shaking, tears finally pouring down my cheeks. I don't even change out of my wet swimsuit before I tuck myself into my room and dig my phone out of my bag. My hands tremble as I tap on Lena's name.

But it just rings and rings and then goes to her voice mail.

I end the call. Quick.

I'm breathing hard and toss my phone onto my bed so I don't call her back. Because what in the holy heck would I say anyway?

Um, hey, Lena, what does it mean to practice holding hands with a girl and feel all—

Nope.

Um, hey, Lena, you know when you're with a girl and your stomach gets all fluttery and—

Uh-uh.

I groan and face-plant on my bed. Then I roll over to my side and see the auger shell Quinn gave me on the first day we met just sitting there on my nightstand, all la-di-da. I grab it and run my fingers over the swirls while I think, think, think.

Holding hands with Quinn like that under the waterfall, it was just practice. It didn't mean anything. Even Quinn said that was what we could do if we ever found a boy to like. This new heart doesn't wonder about girls like that. It doesn't even matter what Margot told Eliza and the whole swim team. I like boys. Only boys. As in Step Three. I've got to stay focused.

A fresh wave of tears blooms in my eyes. I wipe them away fast. I don't even know why I'm crying. Nothing happened. *Old Sunny* is gone. I'm *New Sunny*.

But I don't feel like *New Sunny*. I don't feel like *Old Sunny* either. I feel all mixed up, a thousand different Sunnys swirling together like a kaleidoscope.

I put the shell back and shove my hand under my pillow, taking out Lena's journal. My chest gets all tight just looking at it. I know I should give it back, but it feels like a little peek into Lena's brain. It feels like . . . maybe it's not so wrong to read it, because I missed out on eight years of having a real mom, so in a way, her journal is just helping me catch up.

I take a deep breath and flip through the inked-up pages, searching for that first day Lena showed up in my hospital room back at the beginning of May. Surely, she wrote about that. It was pretty epic. Epically awful and awkward.

Finally, I find it. It's scribbly, the handwriting way worse than the other entries. As soon as I start reading, I find out why.

I saw her today. I actually saw her. My Sunshine. She was so beautiful. She was pale and thin, but she was the most beautiful thing I've ever seen. She wouldn't talk to me. It broke

*my heart right in half, but I'm trying to stay
positive. She just had a heart transplant, for
crying out loud. J says I've got to give her time.
D said the same, when she called to see how it
went and make sure I wasn't feeling tempted
to drink. I'm not tempted. Not even close. If
anything makes me never want to take another
sip of alcohol again, it's my girls.*

I can barely read the last part, it's so messy. I can tell
Lena's upset. I squint at the last word, figuring she must
have accidentally added an *s* to girl. She was feeling a lot, just
like I am. My heart beats faster and faster with every word.
I touch my finger to the scar on my chest and keep reading.

*But then I start thinking... why couldn't I
stop drinking when Sunny was a little girl?*

*D says that's a useless way to think, but I
can't stop thinking it.*

*"You were a different person," D says. "You
didn't have the support system you do now. You
were drowning in grief. Everything is different
now."*

*And she's right. I know she is. But, my god,
Sunny had a heart transplant. She's been sick, my
baby, and her whole heart got replaced. I can't*

218

believe I missed it all. I can't believe I let her go
through all that without me. I can't believe I
stayed away so long, that I didn't know she was
dying.

I don't know if I'll ever fully forgive myself.

I don't know if Sunny will either.

But I'm going to try. For S. For me. I'm going
to put my family back together.

Tears flow down my face. They're hot and mix with
all the other tears I've already cried today, making my face
feel tight with the salt. I hug the journal to my chest and
try to get a grip, but I can't stop picturing Lena in some
rented house in Port Hope, scribbling all this down while
she cried too. I want to hug her.

Or yell at her.

Because I can't believe she missed it all either.

Next to me, my phone buzzes. I pick it up and my
heart leaps up into my throat.

It's a text from Quinn.

Hey. Are you all right?

I stare at my phone. No way I want to deal with this
right now. My heart hurts so bad and I just want to dive
back into Lena's journal and figure her out. Figure us out.

Yeah, I text back, because if I ignore her, then that
clearly means I'm not all right at all.

Okay, she texts. I wait for her to say more, but she doesn't. Probably because we held hands in a weird way and now things are weird.

I shake my head, hoping the thoughts fall right out of my ears or something, and then my phone buzzes again, this time with a call.

I yank it up, terrified I'm going to have to talk to Quinn because I can't really ignore her when she knows I was just by my phone.

But it's not her. It's Lena.

I slide my finger over the screen super-fast.

"Hi," I say.

"Hey, you," she says. "I saw you called but you didn't leave a message. You okay?"

In the background, I hear a bunch of noise. Some dishes clinking and a baby babbling, like she's in some busy restaurant. But still, she called me. She saw that I needed her and she stopped whatever she was doing for me.

I get under my covers and sink down into my bed, breathing a whole lungful of air for the first time since leaving the pool. "Yeah. I'm fine."

"Fine, huh? You know, whenever I tell my therapist I'm fine, she makes this really annoying sound in her throat, like a buzzer going off for a wrong answer, and tells me to try again."

"Wow. She sounds horrible."

Lena laughs. "She's not. So, Sunny, try again."

"You go to therapy?"

"Yes, I do," she says. "I have for about three years."

"Does it help?"

"It really does."

I swallow, wondering what it would be like to spill all my wonderings into a stranger's lap. Which, if I'm being honest, is sort of what I'm doing right now.

"Do you think I'm weird?" I ask.

"What do you mean?"

"I just, well, you didn't know me before, you know? When I was sick. Or even before that."

There's a pause, but then she sighs and says, "I know, Sunny."

"But you wanted to, right?"

She sighs and when she speaks, her voice is all shaky-sounding. "So much, you don't even know."

I smile a little, even though she can't see it. I could tell she wanted to know me in her journal. But it's a whole different ball of wax, hearing her say it.

"Okay," I say, "but now I have another person's heart in my chest."

"Sunny, you're still you."

"But am I? Like, the one I was born with is totally gone. I like butterscotch pudding now. Isn't that weird?"

"Butterscotch pudding is disgusting."

221

"Exactly. Except it's the nectar of the gods!"

She laughs.

"I feel different," I say. "I mean, of course I do, because I can breathe okay now and do stuff and my doctor says I'm doing really good. But also, I feel the same sometimes too. Like, the old me is all mixed up with this new me and it just feels like I'll always be weird and wondering weird things no matter what. Am I still me? Or am I just a different me?"

She's quiet. So quiet that I say "Hello?" just to make sure she didn't hang up on me.

"I'm here," she says, and clears her throat. I'm freaking her out again. After all, she left me when I was only four, and four is a really cute age. I was totally adorable when I was four. But there must have been something, right? Something in me that made her choose drinking over me. Now I'm even worse because my heart isn't even mine; it's not the one she gave me.

My throat starts to ache. "We don't have to—"

"No, Sunny, it's okay. I'm just thinking through my answer."

"Oh."

"It must be hard," she says. "All these feelings, all these thoughts."

"Yeah. Sometimes. But I've had hard feelings and thoughts before."

"Everyone does."

"Not like me," I say.

"What do you mean?"

I shake my head, even though she can't see me. Margot—not to mention every girl at that slumber party—made it super-clear that not everyone has the kinds of thoughts and wonderings I do. Or did.

"Nothing," I say. "It's just a lot sometimes."

"I can't imagine what it feels like to be you. But I do know what it feels like to start over. And, yeah, it can be a little weird. But that's not a bad thing. It just means..."

She trails off and I'm holding my breath, but before I can beg her to finish, there's a knock on my bedroom door.

"Sunny?" Kate calls.

I shove the phone under my pillow and pretend to be napping.

The door opens.

"Sunny, are you on the phone?" Kate asks. "I heard you talking."

I don't budge. I'm really, really good at looking like I'm asleep, thanks to all those times when I was sick and I was supposed to be resting but couldn't turn my brain off and didn't want Kate to worry that I couldn't sleep on top of everything else. The key is to keep your eyes closed, nice and loose, without squeezing them. Also, relax your mouth and breathe deeply.

Kate walks over to my bed and pats the sheets a little, probably looking for my phone, but she doesn't go searching under my pillow. For a split second, I think about opening my eyes and telling her everything I'm thinking about, but I'm afraid I'll sound all ungrateful for my new heart and I'm not. I'm just... trying to make it fit in my head like it fits in my body.

Finally, she sweeps her hand over my hair and leaves. When I hear the door click shut, I yank my phone out from under my pillow.

"Are you still there?" I whisper, sure that Lena's long gone.

A beat. Then, "I'm still here."

"So... what does it mean?" I ask.

"What?"

"Starting over. What does it mean that it's weird?"

Lena sighs. "It means that you get to do something that not everyone gets to do. That's what weird means, doesn't it? Doing something or being someone out of the ordinary. Not following the pattern everyone expects you to follow. That's all."

I think about that and Margot's stupid party comes back to me. How all those girls laughed at me and made me feel like the worst girl in the history of girls, all because I wondered about something they didn't. I think about Quinn holding my hand under the waterfall and how...how...I didn't really feel weird at all.

I felt scared.

"You know what helps me sometimes when I start thinking about stuff like this?" she says.

"What?"

"I write it down."

I grip her journal in my hands and swallow hard. "You do?"

"Yeah. Journal entries, songs. It helps to get it all out."

"Actually, I sort of do that too." And then for some reason, I tell her all about my songs and how I've started sticking them around town. It makes me feel even weirder as I'm explaining it, but I guess it is kind of weird. When I'm done talking, Lena doesn't say anything for a second, which also makes me feel weird.

"I think that's amazing, Sunny," she finally says, and I breathe out a big breath.

"Yeah?"

"Brave."

"Well, not as brave as trying to surf."

"Braver, I'd say."

"I'm not sure if they're even songs. A melody never comes into my head when I'm writing them and they don't rhyme. Like, at all. I guess they're really bad songs."

225

"They sound like poems to me."

I blink at my ceiling, my mouth dropping open, because of course they're poems.

"Free verse poems," I say.

"Exactly."

"Like Emily Dickinson."

"And Sylvia Plath and Pablo Neruda."

"Who?"

She laughs. "Look them up. It sounds to me like they're your people."

I smile, tucking the names away for later. "Can we go surfing again soon?"

"Of course. I told you we would."

"Tomorrow?"

"Absolutely. But we'll have to do it in the afternoon. Is that okay?"

Again, I wonder what in the world Lena does when she's not with me. I know she's renting a house somewhere near the Methodist church in Port Hope and that she's giving some private voice lessons, but that's it. How long is she really staying here? Does she miss Montauk? Does she talk to J or D on the phone? Do they visit her here? Thinking about Lena's whole other life without me, all the people who might have replaced me, makes my stomach hurt. I can't bring myself to ask any of my questions.

I turn onto my side, Lena's journal hugged close to my chest. "Yeah, okay," I finally say.

"I'll pick you up around noon," Lena says. "See you tomorrow, weirdo."

I can hear the smile in her voice and my heart feels all warm and steady. It feels good. It feels . . . normal.

"See you tomorrow, weirdo," I say back.

I lost my heart but kept on breathing.
Now all the mirrors show the same face,
but I don't know the girl inside.
Does anyone know her?
A thousand years ago, she was lost in the
    ocean
but now she walks on the land.
Is she me?
Or am I her?
Or is she a new girl
who looks like
someone I used to be?

CHAPTER 20

Over the next few days, I write about ten more poems and stash them all over the island. I tuck them away in that little blue birdhouse in the park and in the tip jar at the coffee shop where Kate buys her sachets of lavender green tea.

They're all about...stuff.

Wondering kind of stuff.

Handholding, kissing kind of stuff.

I try not to write about it—I'm done wondering, after all—but it's like my hand or my brain or maybe even my heart takes over. Every time I lie on my bed or sit on the front porch with a piece of paper and a pen, I mean to write about, I don't know, the mind-blowing double chocolate cake doughnut from Yeast Juniper Island Bakery that Kate has finally started letting me eat, but that's not the stuff I end up thinking about.

But think, I do. And I write and write and write until my head feels nice and empty, until my heart feels slicked clean like all the gunk got washed out. Then I start thinking about Quinn again and I have to start the whole process over.

Let's just say I've written a lot of poems.

Today, it's rainy out, the sky a puffy gray. I'm sitting on the front porch and waiting for Lena to pick me up to take me clothes shopping when my phone buzzes in my bag. I choke down a sip of Ensure and set the can down next to me, then dig out my phone.

Hey, Quinn texts. **Want to go to the beach today?**

My Ensure threatens to come right back up. I haven't seen Quinn in a week. Not since the pool. She's texted a bunch, always asking me to hang out, and I take forever to answer her. I want to say yes. Every time, I want to say yes, but then I remember holding hands with her under the waterfall and the way my stomach felt all funny. Then I remember that all the wondering about kissing and hand-holding I've been doing lately isn't about boys. It's not even about girls, really.

All my wondering is about Quinn.

I shake my head, trying to knock all those wonderings right out. They're too scary, too risky.

229

I can't, I text back. I'm going shopping with Lena.

Not a lie.

Okay, she says. Text me later?

For sure.

Maybe a lie.

I mean, I want to text her. I want to *see* her. She's my BFF and I don't want to mess that up, but what if I feel...and what if she doesn't feel...and what does all that mean...

I groan and rest my forehead on my knees.

"You okay, sweetie?" Kate says, coming out the front door.

I snap my head back up and grab my Ensure, sipping dutifully. "Yeah, fine. I just...don't want to finish this gross drink."

Kate sits down and nudges me with her shoulder. "I wish I could go shopping with you," she says. She's dressed in her raincoat with a ratty Nirvana T-shirt and tattered jeans, because today is inventory day at Cherry Picked Books. She and Dave and the staff go through every single book in the whole store and make sure they're all in the computer and figure out which books aren't selling and need to be sent back to the publisher. It takes all day and a lot of the night and sounds so boring, I almost fall asleep every time Kate tells me about it.

"Yeah, me too," I say, and then, because I'm thinking about the kind of clothes I want to get, Quinn pops back

230

into my head. I pretty much love everything Quinn wears. I want the same kind of cute and snug printed tees. Also a bikini, preferably bright blue with suns all over it. And a pair of black shorts. Also some dark skinny jeans. All mine are too loose.

"Just don't get any tattoos while you're out," Kate says.

"I don't know. I kind of want a big old sun on my bicep."

She laughs and puts her arm around my shoulders, running her hand down my hair. I lean into her and smell her familiar smell—books and clean wax from the candles she loves to burn at night.

"You like her," she says.

My heart jumps into my throat. "Who?"

"Lena."

I relax a little but pull away so I can frown at her. "Am I not supposed to?"

"No, sweetie, of course you are. It's just..."

But she trails off, her eyes all distant and glazy-looking as she holds me tighter.

Lena and I have been surfing three times this past week. I can stand now and everything. But whenever Lena comes to the house to pick me up, Kate gets all weird. She always lets me go, but she grills Lena for at least ten minutes, asking a bunch of questions about how deep in the ocean we go and how far Lena lets me get from her and when we take breaks and how much water I'm drinking. I'm amazed she doesn't ask Lena to write down every time I take a deep breath.

Now, I can see all the wheels turning in Kate's brain, all the worries. Before I can beg her to chill out, Lena's truck bounces up the driveway, the horn honking happily.

"Hey, you two!" Lena says as she slides out of the driver's seat. "Ready for some serious shopping?"

Kate's arm drops from my side as I leap to my feet. "So ready." And I so am. I'm so, so tired of all the drab stuff in my closet. *Old Life* Sunny stuff.

"First, I have a surprise for you," Lena says, grinning.

"What is it?"

She waves me to the back of her truck and I bound off the porch.

"Sunny, it's raining," Kate calls behind me.

"I won't melt!" I singsong, and keep running. Kate makes an annoyed noise, but she follows me, and we meet Lena at the truck bed just as she's pulling down the tailgate. The rain is barely anything, the kind of drizzle that Dave likes to call spit-rain.

"Ta-da!" Lena sings, flourishing her hands.

And, um, yes, *ta-da* indeed. Because there, lying on the worn bed of her truck, is a gorgeous, shiny, sparkling, bright blue surfboard.

With a gorgeous, shiny, sparkling, bright yellow sun right in the middle.

My mouth drops open. "Is . . . is that for me?"

"Wait, there's more," Lena says. She disappears for a second and opens the back passenger door. I hear the rustle of a bag and when she reappears, she's holding a short-sleeved black rash guard, just like hers. Except this one has a yellow sun on the chest. It matches the one on the surfboard.

"I love it," I whisper, reaching out to touch the smooth fabric, rain already beading up on the surface. "Is all this really mine?"

"Completely and totally yours."

Kate clears her throat. She's got her arms folded and she's staring at the board like she expects it to sprout wings and fly away.

"I mean, if it's okay with Kate," Lena says.

Kate doesn't say anything. She reaches out a finger and runs it over the edge of the shiny board. "What was wrong with the board she was using?"

Lena's mouth opens and closes a few times. "Well, it wasn't hers. I rented it and Sunny seemed to like surfing so much. A surfer needs a board all her own."

Kate nods, real quick and tight and over and over again, just like she did when Dr. Ahmed first told us I was sick. *Nod-nod-nod-nod-nod-nod.*

"I can keep it, right?" I ask Kate, because wow, this board is so pretty. Kate seems upset, but I have no idea why. It's just a surfboard and I want it so, so bad. I can already feel the waxy surface under my bare feet, see the ocean water moving over that bright sun as I rise up to ride my first wave.

"Kate?" Lena asks when Kate just keeps staring at the board. Kate startles and smiles at me.

"Of course you can keep it, honey," she says. Nod-nod-nod-nod-nod-nod.

I squeal and throw my arms around Lena's neck. "Thank you, thank you, thank you!"

Lena laughs and squeezes me tight. "You're so welcome."

"When can I try it out? Right now? Please say right now. I'm ready to catch a real wave, you know I am."

Last time we were out, we were in the shallows, where the waves are running toward the shore, and Lena started showing me how to catch smaller waves. I had to stay on my stomach until I got the hang of it, but I still had to get the board positioned and learn to read when a wave was starting to break.

Lena starts to answer, but Kate cuts her off. "No way. It's wet and stormy."

"It's wet, not stormy," I say. "And the ocean is already wet."

"The water is choppy. You can see it from here." Kate waves her hand toward the gray sea to our left. There are some definite whitecaps out there, ribbons of water turned inside out by the wind, but so what?

"Surfers need to learn to surf in all conditions," Lena says. "It's a safety issue. Weather can change quickly on the sea."

"Safety?" Kate says. "Safe would be not going out at all."

"You can't swaddle her in bubble wrap forever, Katie."

Kate's jaw clenches. "Lena."

"She'll be fine. She'll be with me and I've been doing this a long time."

"Surfers die all the time."

"Yes. Inexperienced surfers."

"That's not true. Professionals get hurt just the same."

"What, did you Google it?" Lena asks.

"Maybe I did. I'm Sunny's guardian. I'm legally responsible for her."

Lena stares at her and Kate stares back and my chest starts to hurt.

"I'm sorry," Lena finally says, real soft and low. "I don't mean to overstep, I just—"

"You promised Sunny shopping. We can talk about this later," Kate says. Then she pulls me into a hug, her T-shirt good and damp now, and presses a kiss to my forehead. "Bye, sweetie. Be sure to get some winter shirts today, okay?"

"Um. Yeah. Okay," I squeeze out through a tight throat.

Kate doesn't say bye to Lena. Lena doesn't say bye to her either, but watches Kate flip the hood of her raincoat up and get on her sunshine-yellow beach bike, the one she always rides into town, and pedal away. Even after Kate's long gone, Lena just keeps staring off down the road, her fists balling up and releasing, balling up and releasing.

"Lena?"

She doesn't answer at first, but finally she nods once, takes a deep breath, and looks at me. "Ready to try out your new board, Sunshine?"

CHAPTER
21

After Lena and I duck into the house to change into our bathing suits—and my new rash guard—we head straight to East Beach. We don't talk much on the way there. The rain sprinkles the windshield, but barely, and I can't decide if the knot in my stomach is excitement or terror. Probably a little bit of both. This will be the second time I've lied to Kate about where I was—the first being the boat that resulted in the Sam Blanchard Debacle—but I didn't get hurt and Sam's fine. So it all ended up okay.

"Kate always was a worrier," Lena says, like she can read my mind. Or, more likely, we're both stewing over the same thing.

"Yeah, tell me about it. She wouldn't even let me go swimming at the pool when I was sick. In fifth grade, right after I got diagnosed but was still going to school, she wouldn't let me go on this field trip to a farm in Calder Heights."

"Those baby goats can be really dangerous."

I snort-laugh. "She thinks so."

"She's just looking out for you. I know that."

"Yeah, but how about letting a girl go play miniature golf every now and then?"

"She wouldn't let you play miniature golf?"

I shake my head. "Last year, Margot invited me to go with her and her mom. Kate said nope." I don't mention that I had passed out four times that same week. I also don't say that Kate had called Dr. Ahmed to ask about miniature golf and Dr. Ahmed was the one who said no. Details shmeetails.

"I guess tiny windmills and bright orange golf balls are pretty risky," Lena says.

"Ha ha."

She grins at me and then her face goes all serious. "I get where she's coming from. I do. But I meant what I said before. Surfing in this kind of weather is important. Not only to understand what the ocean is like, but to understand what you're capable of. You need to have confidence to surf, or you really will get hurt. I wouldn't take you out if I didn't think I could keep you safe. This'll be good for you, trust me."

I look at her, her eyes focused on the road. The same eyes as mine. "I do trust you."

She reaches over the middle console and slips her hand under my palm, squeezing tight. I look down at our hands and it feels like there's a hummingbird fluttering around in my chest. A really, really happy hummingbird.

I'm holding my mom's hand. First time ever. Or, at least, the first time I remember. The rain plinks even harder on the windows and I'm holding hands with my mom, like it's any other day, like we do this all the time. I smile and peer closer at our fingers. We both have freckles here and there, tiny dots like constellations making shapes on our skin.

Eventually, Lena pulls her hand free—but not before she squeezes mine one more time—and turns into East Beach's totally empty gravel lot.

"Are you ready?" she asks, shutting off the truck and stuffing the keys into her bag.

"I was born ready," I say. "Or actually, reborn ready."

She lifts a brow at me.

"Sorry, heart transplant joke," I say, which only makes her frown. "I'm fine. I'm ready." Then I throw open the door before she can start to doubt her decision to take me surfing.

She must not have a whole lot of doubts anyway, because she meets me at the back of the truck, and soon we're running toward the sea with our boards tucked under our arms. Mine's smaller than hers, but it's heavy, which helps keep beginners from getting tossed around in the waves like a rag doll. I'm pretty winded when we reach the water.

"I've already waxed up your board, so we're all set," she says. She has to yell a little over the wind, and I finally take a good look at the ocean.

It looks mad.

Like, really mad.

It's churning and spitting and there are whitecaps all over the place. A little deeper out, there are some pretty big swells, which means good surfing.

It also means my stomach is churning and spitting just like the sea.

"You okay?" Lena asks, stepping closer to me.

I nod. At least I think I do. I'm too busy staring at the water, which looks like it kind of wants to eat me, to know what I'm really doing.

"Hey," Lena says. She takes my chin in her hand, which forces me to look at her. "You don't have to do this. We can go change in the truck and go shopping instead. You say the word."

I nod again and for a second, I think I'm going to turn tail and run. I don't want to die, after all, and Kate spent a ton of money on all my medical bills making sure I didn't. Someone gave me their heart so I wouldn't.

But.

I still can't run more than half a mile without wheezing. I can't hang out with Lena without making Kate all worried. I can't forget about what Margot did. I can't find a boy I like. Even if I did, I probably couldn't kiss him without causing him some kind of bodily harm. And I really can't figure out what to say to Quinn next time I see her.

But I can do this, right?

I can dive into the ocean and find the perfect wave, a wave meant just for me, and I can stand up on my very own surfboard and ride that wave until I hit the shore.

I can do it.

"I can do it," I say, this time out loud.

Lena tucks a piece of already-wet hair behind my ears. "You can do it."

I plunge into the water. It's dark gray and the rain is still falling—not too hard, but hard enough that I have to wipe my eyes—and start paddling out to the deeps.

Lena lets me go. She doesn't call me back. But she's right behind me, I know that, and that makes me even more determined to do this. I only want Lena to know this Sunny, the brave one with a strong heart and steady feet.

We go deep, but not so deep that the waves have evened out. It's wild out here and the swells bop me all over the place. It's like a roller coaster—not that Kate's ever let me on one, but this is what I imagine it might be like—and I fall off my board a couple of times.

"That's part of it," Lena says when I climb back on and straddle my board. "Just watch for that bit of white at the top of the wave. You'll know when you see the right one."

I nod but don't say anything. My heart is pounding. I think I'm shaking, but I can't tell if I'm cold or nervous or having some sort of heart episode, or what. I keep my eyes on the waves, though. The way they're breaking, the roll of the water as it pushes toward me.

Then I see it.

Hi, I whisper to the water, and I know it hears me. The wave is perfect—not too big, but big enough to scare the pants off me if I was wearing any.

I shift my weight back and use my arms and legs to angle my board toward the beach.

"Okay, you've got this," Lena says.

I'm too busy trying not to scream to answer.

I grip the sides of the board and slide my legs back so that I'm lying down on my board. Then I start paddling. I paddle, paddle, paddle, waiting for that perfect wave to pick me up.

Then I feel it behind me. A gentle lift. I paddle harder,

angling down the wave instead of heading straight toward shore, just like Lena taught me. I look over my shoulder, hoping the wave hasn't broken yet. There's a sharp edge at its top, like it's just about to topple.

"Now, now!" Lena yells.

I stop paddling and jump up, sliding my feet onto the stringer and doing a push-up. I wobble big-time, but I stay crouched and by some miracle I don't fall off. The rain splatters in my face and the wave feels huge. Like I'm on top of a skyscraper, the world nothing but tiny ants below.

I laugh and I think I might be crying, because oh my god, I'm surfing. I stay low, my body like a comma, and try to control the board with my leg muscles, moving it through the wave. It doesn't move all that much. I'm about as strong as a baby mouse. Still, I'm on my feet. I'm teetering like a slowly spinning top, but I'm on my feet.

It's amazing. I'm a surfer. I surf.

The wind combs salty fingers through my hair and the sea splashes over my legs, on my arms and face. I careen toward the shore. My balance lurches and I duck a little lower, evening out my weight. I never want to get off this board. I want to bend down and run my fingers through the water like I've seen super-cool surfers do on videos. I want all the people on the beach—well, the people who would be on the beach on a clear day—to watch me and *oooh* and *aaah* because I'm amazing.

Sunny St. James—the heart transplantee turned professional surfer.

I can't believe I get to do this.

I tap my hand to my heart, giving it a little high five. I sway on the board even more when I do it, but it's worth it. Because finally, finally, my heart is doing something right.

The shore looms ahead through a gauzy gray curtain of rain. I'm almost there, almost there—

The world flips upside down as my board flies out from under me. My back hits the sea with a stinging *smack*. I flail my arms and legs to get my head above the water, but I can't find the surface. It's like I'm a tennis ball and the ocean is the racket, volleying me back and forth, back and forth.

My board is still tied to my ankle and I yank it toward me. I reach out and finally feel an edge, but it's too thick and slippery to grab on to. I kick my feet as hard as I can, trying to go up. Something sharp scrapes down my forearm. It hurts like fire, but I keep kicking. The sky has to be there somewhere. I'm not going down like this.

Finally, I see some light. It's gray and blurry, but it's there, right below me. Which means I'm upside down. I flip myself around and kick and just when heaving a lungful of salt water starts to sound like heaven, my head breaks the surface.

I gulp at the air. Gulp and gasp and chew and lick and anything I can possibly do to get oxygen in my body faster.

"Sunny!"

Lena's voice isn't far. She's swimming frantically through the water. I put my feet down, my toes barely scraping the sandy bottom.

"Are you okay?" Lena yells.

I nod, feasting on air, and look around for my board. It's floating about ten feet behind me, innocent as can be, still leashed to my ankle.

Lena reaches me, her own board trailing behind her like a puppy, and scoops me up. Literally, she picks me up under my armpits and devours my face with her eyes.

"Did you hit your head?" she asks. "Did you?"

I open my mouth to answer, but I guess I'm not fast enough because she barks the question again.

"Sunny, did you hit your head or not?"

"No. No, I'm fine. I just got turned around under-water."

She nods, but she's still holding me, breathing heavy. I'm breathing heavy. The whole world is breathing heavy.

Then I smile.

"What are you grinning at?" she asks, but her mouth twitches too.

"I surfed."

She lets out a long breath. "Yes, and almost drowned."

"Yeah, but I didn't. I'm okay. I made it on my own. Isn't that why you brought me out here today?"

She tilts her head at me and her eyes go gentle. "Yeah. Yeah, it is, Sunshine. You did good."

I laugh, but it feels thick in my throat, like it might turn into a big old cry any minute. My whole body hurts, but at the same time, it feels amazing. Alive. I'm alive.

Lena's still holding me, but I press my hand to my heart, a reflex. It's pounding under there, happy and steady.

"Oh god. Sunny, you're bleeding."

"Huh?"

"Your arm."

I bend so I can see my forearm and yes, yes, I am bleeding. A big red gash stripes my skin from my elbow to my wrist, which explains why that area feels like the fire of a thousand suns.

"You must've cut it on a rock or something. Come on." Lena sets me down and we swim toward the shore. "I've got a first aid kit in the truck."

We drag our boards onto the sand and then carry them to the parking lot. It's still raining and the beach houses that dot the shore are covered in drizzly fog.

After loading up our stuff, we get into the truck and

Lena cleans my arm with hydrogen peroxide and Neosporin before she covers it with a large white bandage. Her brows are all furrowed and wrinkly while she does it, but I can't stop smiling.

When we're heading toward home, I'm still grinning so hard, my cheeks start to ache.

"I wish Quinn could've seen me," I say. It pops out before I can stop it. I didn't mean to say that. I don't want to think about her at all, but what I said is true. I really do wish she could've been here as my BFF.

"You can invite her to surf with us sometime," Lena says. Then she winks at me. "I'd love to meet your Kissing Quest partner in crime."

"Um...yeah..." I feel my face go atomic red.

"How's that going?"

I gulp, thinking about Quinn's hand pressed against mine. I can't think about being under that waterfall without my stomach going all butterscotch pudding-ish on me.

"It's...we're...sort of taking a break," I say, even though Quinn and I never said that.

"Oh, no, why?"

I don't answer right away. I have questions about kissing and feelings and holding hands bubbling up, questions I'm not sure I want to ask because they're all about Quinn. And I'm looking for a boy to kiss. Only boys.

"Sunny?" Lena asks when I sit there like a zombie.

"I don't know," I finally say, shoving the questions down until they're practically in my toes. "Just because."

"Ah, yes. An excellent reason."

I roll my eyes at her, but she just grins. "You know, it's okay to put this whole kissing thing off for a bit. Until you're ready."

"How do I know when I'm ready?" I ask quietly.

She gets this soft look on her face. "Oh, you'll know. You won't be able to stop thinking about it, about the person you like, and every time you see them, all you want to do is hold their hand or kiss them or just listen to them talk for hours and hours."

My pudding-stomach wiggles all over the place. "Is that how it was with my dad?"

Her smile fades a bit. "Yeah."

"Have you...have you ever had that with someone else? Someone you...maybe shouldn't like like that?"

She frowns at me, just like I knew she would, because here I am being weird again. Laugh-worthy weird. Margot-whispering-behind-my-back weird.

"Never mind," I say before she can answer.

"No, sweetie, what do you mean 'shouldn't like like that'?"

But I just shake my head. We're home anyway, bouncing

up my gravel driveway, the top of the lighthouse completely covered in clouds.

Except when Lena circles the car toward the front porch, there's someone sitting there, right on the steps. Someone who's not Kate. Someone who's not Dave either. Someone who is most definitely Quinn Ríos Rivera.

CHAPTER

22

Quinn stands up and looks at me. I look back at her. She waves at me with one hand. A black-and-purple-plaid backpack is hooked on her elbow. She doesn't smile, though. Or, actually, she does, but it's tiny and barely there. Nervous. God, why is she nervous? There's no reason to be nervous, right?

She doesn't move closer to the truck. I don't get out of the truck. I just sit there, totally not nervous, and breathe so loud and heavy I fog up the window.

"Sunny?" Lena says as she cuts the engine. "Is that Quinn?"

I nod.

"Do . . . you want to get out and go say hello?"

I nod, but I don't move.

"Okay, what's going on?" she asks.

"Nothing," I say too fast.

Stay cool, Sunny, I tell myself, but it's way too late for that. I'm the opposite of cool. My heart is flopping around in my chest like a fish out of water and I'm sweating, my skin prickling.

"Well, whatever this *nothing* is, you can handle it," Lena says. "You just surfed, remember?" She nudges me with her elbow and opens her door. Then she jogs toward the porch and starts chatting up my BFF while I stare at them from inside the truck.

I take a deep breath—or maybe a billion—and then I open the door.

When I reach the porch, Lena and Quinn are both smiling and Lena's asking Quinn all about her amazing blue hair.

"I love the different shades of blue," Lena's saying when I walk up. "Sunny, isn't her hair amazing?"

I nod, because it is amazing. So is her smile and her dark, dark eyes and the black T-shirt she has on right now with little unicorns all over it. They have rainbow-colored tails and horns and are somersaulting all over the place. Those unicorns are amazing too.

I'm suddenly super-aware that I'm in nothing but my bathing suit and a sand-covered rash guard. I fold my arms and clear my throat, wishing I'd thought to drape myself in a towel.

"I'm going to grab your board, Sunny," Lena says, squeezing my shoulder. "It was lovely to meet you, Quinn."

"You too," Quinn says.

Then Lena jogs off toward the truck and Quinn and I stand there in silence. Closer up, I notice that her eyes are all puffy and red, like she's been crying or something.

"So that's Lena," she finally says.

"Yeah, that's Lena."

"Did you go surfing?" Quinn asks, which gets a little smile out of me.

"Yeah. I actually rode a wave," I say. "Like a real one."

"That's awesome!"

"And I have a battle scar to prove it." I hold up my arm, super-proud of the tiny dots of blood seeping through the bandage. I might need to get that changed.

"Oh, wow, are you okay?" Quinn touches my arm gently. So gently, I barely feel her fingertips near the bandage, but I still get all goose bump-y.

I pull my arm back.

Quinn clears her throat and looks away. "Anyway. I came by because I thought, maybe..." She sets her backpack on the porch and unzips it. She digs around a towel and a pair of flip-flops and her grass-green bikini and finally pulls out two black bottles with the words *Arctic Fox* over the top.

"This one's called Girls' Night," she says, holding up

one of the bottles with an image of a lavender fox on the front. Then she hands me the other. "And this one's Aquamarine." The fox on that bottle is, well, aquamarine, and then I remember that first day we met on the beach.

"You want to dye our hair?" I ask.

She smiles—that tiny, nervous smile again. "Well, I was ready to redo mine anyway, and you said I should do lavender, right?"

"And you said I should do aquamarine."

"Yeah, exactly. I have the bleach and everything in my bag. It's okay if you don't want to. I know it's a lot, to dye your hair, especially when your hair is dark like ours, and I can just go if you want me to, but..."

She trails off, waiting for me to say something. And I'm trying. Oh, I am trying. It has to be the perfect thing so she knows I don't want to kiss her at all, even though I'm the one who touched her face first under the waterfall. Even though I'm the one who said we should hold hands. Even though I'm the one who's acted all weird ever since, when, if we were really just *practicing*, it shouldn't feel weird at all.

So, yeah, the next words I say have to be perfect.

Which is probably why I keep blinking at her, my mouth opening and closing like a catfish's. When I stand there, not saying the perfect thing for what feels like a millennium, Quinn's face droops and she slips Girls' Night back in her bag.

"Okay," she says. "It's okay. I'll see you—"

"Let's do it," I blurt out. Not exactly the most perfect words, but they're the right ones. I *want* to dye my hair. I want to do something that *Old Life Sunny* would never do, never even think about. Never wonder about. Never mention to Former Best Friend in the cone of silence. Before Quinn came along, I never thought about dyeing my hair.

And I miss Quinn. There, I said it. I miss her bad. Just as my friend, though. Only my friend. My friend who I think is cool and who has amazing clothes and who I sort of want to be like. But there were tons of times I sort of wanted to be like Margot too. Like, how easy it was for Margot to talk to boys and how she always had her nails painted all pretty. Whenever I painted my nails, they looked like I was bleeding pink or periwinkle or whatever all over the place.

This thing with Quinn, it's simple envy, that's all. Though my stomach never got all tingly-feeling like this with Margot, but it's probably because I'm hungry and I just surfed and almost drowned and I'm about to dye my hair for the first time ever. All that kind of stuff can really mess up a girl's guts.

Quinn's hand freezes on her bag and she pulls the bottle back out. "Yeah? You sure?"

I nod.

She exhales loudly. "Good. That's good." Then she bites her lip and I just know she's about to say something I don't want to hear. Call it heart disease intuition, that sixth sense when my whole body can tell when someone needs to talk about something serious.

"Look, Sunny, about the other day—"

"What are you girls going to do for the rest of the afternoon?" Lena asks as she comes up the steps with my sand-covered surfboard. She sets it against the house, right next to the front door. I've never been so happy to be interrupted by a grown-up in all my life.

"We're going to dye our hair," I say.

Lena flinches. "I'm sorry, what?"

I hand her the bottle of Aquamarine. "Won't this look amazing on me? You'll help us, right, Lena? Maybe we can do streaks, kind of like Quinn's. She's changing to this really pretty lavender."

Lena blinks at me, then rubs her forehead. She stands there for what feels like a long time, staring at the bottle of hair dye, reading the label, sighing. Quinn and I make eyes at each other. Not *those* kind of eyes. The kind that say, *What the heck is happening?*

"You really want to dye your hair?" Lena asks.

"Um... yeah."

"Why?"

I glance at Quinn, who shrugs.

"Because...it'll look cool?" I say, but it comes out like a question.

"Is that all?" Lena asks. "Really?"

I frown at her and scratch my bandaged arm. Grown-ups are so weird sometimes, but as I stand there with sand in my swimsuit, I look at my beautiful, perfect surfboard, the sun right in the middle, and I know it's more than looking cool. It's more than just doing something new and fresh.

"I guess I want to feel like me," I finally say.

Lena smiles but doesn't say anything. She just hands me the bottle and jogs to her truck. She opens the driver's-side door and takes out her backpack, then runs back through the rain, which is really coming down now.

"You ready to rock some blue hair, Sunshine?" she asks.

I glance at Quinn, who smiles at me, her blue hair curling into her eyes. She's so pretty and my stomach gnarls and snarls, but only because I want to be that pretty too.

That's the only reason.

I gulp a big breath and dig my house keys out of my bag. "I'm so ready."

☀

My bathroom is pretty much destroyed. There are blue and purple smears all over the white countertop and on two of

256

Kate's fluffy white towels, which are now scattered over the clean white tile. Also, my scalp stings something fierce from the bleach, which smelled so terrible and made me so dizzy, Lena had to crack open the bathroom window.

But.

I have blue hair.

Not just blue hair. Aquamarine, from my roots to the very ends. I decided against the streaks. I didn't want subtle. I wanted a full head of beautiful blue hair. Quinn did the same and she looks amazing with the lavender. I was right, that day on the beach over a week ago. The color goes perfectly with her skin and eyes. She looks so pretty, now I'm thinking I should've gone lavender too.

But then I look at myself in the mirror, a plain black tank top on now after my shower to wash off all the dye and sand, and I think I look pretty darn good.

I look like me. My hair has always been pretty straight, but Lena put some kind of serum in it to make it super-shiny. It looks like the ocean under a summer sun.

"You look like a rock star," Quinn says. She's not looking at me, though. She's pawing through Lena's makeup bag, which has so much cool stuff in it, it's overwhelming. Lena said we could pick out some things we wanted to try while she took a shower in Kate's bathroom. She was a mess after helping us, hair dye all over her arms and even a little on her face.

"I do?" I ask.

Quinn nods and takes out a tube of blue lipstick. It matches my hair perfectly. "You should try this color."

"I didn't even know they made blue lipstick."

"They make all kinds of lipstick."

"Green?"

Quinn smiles and rummages around in the bag some more before pulling out another tube. She uncaps it and rolls up the bottom, revealing a dull apple-green color.

"Wow," I say. "That looks like...puke."

Quinn cracks up and tosses it back in the bag. Then she hands me the blue. "Come on, you try this and I'll try"—she digs through the sea of eye shadows and liners before pulling up another lipstick—"this one."

It's bright lavender, the exact shade of her hair. She turns toward the mirror, sliding the color onto her mouth perfectly. I've never seen her in makeup before, so I have no idea how she knows how to do that. I've never put lipstick on in my whole life, but how hard can it be?

I uncap it and roll it over my mouth, just like I would with ChapStick. Which...turns out to be a mistake. It's everywhere. It looks like my mouth is just a giant circle of blue instead of anything, you know, mouth-shaped.

"Oh...wow," Quinn says, laughing.

"Shut up." I grab a hunk of tissues from the box on

the back of the toilet and start wiping. What's worse, my cheeks are fluorescent red.

"Have you never put on lipstick before?" Quinn asks.

"Obviously not," I snap, tossing the used tissue into the garbage.

"It's okay," she says quietly. "I can help you if you want."

I take a deep breath and try to relax. I don't know why I'm suddenly so annoyed. It's just lipstick. It's just Quinn.

"I'm sorry I laughed," she says.

I shrug.

"You looked cute," she says. "I wasn't laughing at you. I only know how to do all this stuff because my mom lets me wear it when I'm at home. Just for fun. She won't let me out of the house with it on. It's okay that you've never worn it."

I glance at her and she's looking at me with these big wide eyes that look really sorry. I hand her the lipstick and sit on the bathroom counter. "Okay, show me how it's done."

She smiles and then gets really close.

Like, really, really close. Her stomach bumps against my knees and her face is right in my face. Then her cheeks look a little flushed, but maybe it's just the heat in the bathroom. It's still steamy from showers and hair dryers. Plus, the window is open, letting in all that salty, balmy air.

I wonder if my cheeks are red too. They probably are, because they feel like they've been set on fire. I smoosh my hands against the counter and feel the cool granite on my palms.

"Can I?" Quinn asks, her fingers hovering near my chin.

Oh god. I can't do this. She's going to touch my face. Again. But I don't really want to say no either. Maybe if she does it again, and I don't freak out, I'll get over... whatever this feeling is that I feel when I'm close to Quinn Ríos Rivera. Because, if I'm being honest, this roller-coaster sensation in my belly has been there from the first time I ever saw her floating like a mermaid under the ocean. But who the heck wouldn't have a sloshy-stomach feeling when meeting a girl underwater? Especially a blue-haired girl in a cool bikini who's traveled the world.

Right?

"Yeah, that's fine," I manage to say. Quinn's fingers touch my chin. She angles my face here and there, peering into my eyes, then looking at my lips, then looking in my eyes again.

Then she smiles, showing her white teeth and her pretty purple lips, and my mouth is all dry and I can't breathe. We had PB&Js before we dyed our hair, so I tell myself it's because I don't want to expel my peanut-buttery breath in her face. I tell myself a lot of stuff.

"You're really going to look like a rock star with this on," she says, then touches the blue color to my lips.

"We should get a picture," I say, but moving my mouth makes her hand slip and smear some lipstick down my chin.

"Oops." Then she wipes it off with her thumb, and my stomach is not calming down. At all. It's supposed to be chill by now.

She glides the lipstick over my mouth a couple more times and grins at me. "Perfection."

"Really?"

She nods and finally, finally, her hand drops away from my face. I slide off the counter and turn to look in the mirror. I look . . . different.

But somehow, totally like me.

My belly, however, is still jumping all over the place like a jackhammer. So is my heart. My face tingles where Quinn touched me and I keep thinking about the way Quinn's fingers felt when I held her hand under the water-fall and how, maybe, that felt like me too.

I squeeze my eyes shut and shake my head. No. No way. That wasn't me. That was . . . that was . . . Old Life Sunny. That was a girl who gets betrayed and laughed at during slumber parties. She slipped through for a second, just a second, but New Life Sunny is back and she's bright

261

blue and is putting on makeup and is going to find a boy she likes. She is.

"We should do eyeshadow," I say, rummaging through Lena's makeup bag again.

"Oh, yeah, totally," Quinn says. "I like—"

"And mascara. And eyeliner. Do you know how to put on eyeliner?"

"Um, not really, but I bet Lena does."

"We'll ask her when she gets out of the shower," I say. "And have her do some blush. Oh, and I wonder if she has some perfume. Boys like perfume, right? I hope they like blue hair. I bet they like purple. We should go out later and find some boys." I pause my word vomit for a split second to glance out the window. "Yeah, it's stopped raining, which means boys are on the beach. Boys are always on the beach. We can find some and—"

"Sunny."

"We just need to find two. That's all. Just two boys. I don't even care about liking them anymore, do you? Let's just kiss them, right? Let's just get it over with. And then—"

"Sunny," Quinn says again. "Stop."

I chug a breath and bite down on my blue lips and blink a whole lot, trying to stop the stinging in my eyes. I stare down at Lena's makeup bag. It's bright orange and covered in little gray skulls. They look cute, exactly like something Quinn would have.

"Sunny, I don't think..." Quinn trails off and takes her own big breath. I glance at her and she's not looking at me. She's biting her lip too. She's blinking a whole lot too.

"You don't want to do the Kissing Quest anymore, do you?" I ask.

She shakes her head and honestly, I'm for-real relieved. I can figure the kissing thing out on my own. It's too confusing with Quinn. Too...I don't know. Just too much.

"Okay," I say. "It's okay. I get it. We don't—"

"No, Sunny, you don't get it."

I blink at her.

"I do want to do the Kissing Quest," she says.

"You...you do?"

She nods. Bites her lip. Blinks her eyes. "I just don't want to kiss a boy." She still doesn't look at me when she says it, but I sure am looking at her. I can't do anything but stare, stare, stare.

"Wh-wh-what?" I stammer, even though I heard her. I heard her loud and clear.

She shakes her head and wipes at her face. Her hand smears a little bit of purple lipstick onto her cheek. "I never wanted to kiss a boy. I just...I just said that because you did and I liked you and..." She blows out a big breath through puffed cheeks. "When you told me about the Kissing Quest, I wanted to be part of it with you and I thought maybe I could find a boy I liked, just like you. But I don't think I want that. I never really have."

"Never?"

She shakes her head. "Not yet, at least."

"Oh."

I want to say something else, something amazing, but I'm concentrating too hard on breathing to get any words out.

"Remember that girl Sadie I told you about?" Quinn asks. "Back in Alaska?"

I nod. I think I nod. It might be that my head has popped off my body and is rolling around on the bathroom floor. I'm not sure.

"I liked her. Like, I *liked* her liked her. And I thought she liked me. She even told me she did, but then her best friend found out and Sadie kind of freaked out and then..."

I'm holding my breath. My heart has stopped beating. "And then?"

"And then we moved here. My mom...she wasn't actually done with her work in Alaska, but things were bad. Like, school was really, really bad. They called me a lot of names and laughed at me in the halls. Wrote gross notes and stuck them on my locker about being gay and having crushes on certain teachers, which I've never had. They made fun of me because of my name, because I'm brown."

"What? You're... brown?"

She gives me this *Oh come on* look, but I'm lost.

"Because I'm Latina, Sunny. I was pretty much the only brown girl in the whole town." She sighs and waves a hand over her body. "Just... all of me. They hated all of me."

My heart breaks right in half. "Oh, Quinn. They're idiots. For real, they're so, so wrong. You're... you're..."

Smart.

Funny.

Beautiful.

Totally and unbelievably cooler than I will ever be.

It's all there, all these great words that are all true about Quinn, but I can't get them out. She shrugs and wipes her face again, because she's crying.

I don't even think about it. I grab her and pull her into my arms. I do it so fast and so hard, my elbow hits Lena's makeup bag and it clatters to the floor. Every single thing inside scatters all over the place, but I don't care. I need to hug Quinn. So I do and she hugs me back, her arms around my waist and her chin on my shoulder. Her hair is still damp and smells like the minty organic shampoo that Kate keeps in my shower.

I want to tell Quinn stuff. All about my wonderings and Margot's betrayal and how my stomach feels like butterscotch pudding when I'm around her, but maybe all

265

these thoughts about girls don't mean for me what they mean for Quinn.

Maybe I just...maybe I feel...maybe I'm only...

She pulls away and wipes at her eyes. "Sorry."

"Don't be sorry." I hand her a tissue, but I really want to hug her again. Or hold her hand. Or...well...anything to make sure she knows she doesn't have to worry about me turning on her or something.

She nods and then blows her nose and actually makes a honking sound. It's like a baby duck and it's hilarious and it makes us both crack up.

"Girls, you want some cookies?" Lena calls from the kitchen. I hear cabinets slamming open and closed and she must have found Dave's stash of soft-baked chocolate chip cookies that he hides in the back of our pantry and brings out when Kate's not around.

"Yeah!" I call back while Quinn furiously wipes at her face a bit more.

"You've got some..." I grab another tissue and then wipe the purple lipstick off her cheek. It's sticky, so I have to press kind of hard, Quinn staring into my eyes the whole time. Her throat bobs around and my stomach... well...it's doing what it always does around Quinn Ríos Rivera.

"Thanks," she says, taking the tissue and finishing the job for me. Then she motions toward the makeup-covered floor. "We should clean up this mess and then go eat about a billion cookies."

I laugh. "Deal."

We both bend down and start tossing makeup into the bag. All sorts of stuff I still want to try out someday. Glittery green eyeshadow and something called bronzer, lip gloss the color of a tangerine and carbon-black eyeliner with a tip so thick, it looks like it would take over my whole eyelid.

We're just about done when the bathroom door flies open. I turn to see Kate in the doorway, Lena right behind her. My heart starts running—no, galloping—like it's trying to escape my body. Kate takes in my hair, the mess of color all over the bathroom, the bandage on my arm. Her chest heaves up and down and a muscle ticks in her jaw.

Quinn slips her hand into mine and squeezes. I squeeze back.

CHAPTER

23

"Kate-" Lena starts, but Kate whirls around and jabs a finger right in her face, cutting her off.

"Don't," Kate says, her teeth gritted together. "Don't. You. Dare."

"It's okay," Lena says. "We just—"

"You don't get to tell me what's okay right now, Lena," Kate says. She turns back to me, her jaw clenched, her nostrils flaring with too-fast breaths. I've never seen her so mad. She's coiled like a snake about to strike. "Sunny, go to your room. Quinn, I need you to head home, okay?"

Quinn nods, but I hold on to her hand. "Kate, don't—"

"Sunny, you need to do what I ask. I am barely holding it together right now and, frankly, this is none of Quinn's business."

Her voice is sharp and kind of rude and I feel my cheeks flame up from embarrassment.

"It's okay," Quinn whispers, squeezing my hand again. "Text me later."

"She won't be texting you tonight," Kate says, her voice even more razor-y.

"What?" I say. "Kate—"

"Go to your room!"

Her yell echoes off the bathroom walls. Behind Kate, Lena watches, her face pale.

"I'm sorry," Quinn says, letting go of my hand and trying to edge past Atomic Kate, who's not budging.

"Quinn, wait—"

"It's okay," Quinn whispers. "It's okay, I'm sorry."

No, it's not okay and she shouldn't be sorry. Kate's acting like it's Quinn's fault I dyed my hair and I don't want Quinn to think anything is her fault ever again. But she's already down the hall and I hear the front door slam.

"Sunny. Your room. Now," Kate says.

"No."

She glares at me, but her eyes are shiny and her chin is trembling. I know her about-to-cry look and this is it. "Excuse me?"

"I didn't do anything wrong," I say.

"You didn't do anything wrong?" she echoes. "So,

going surfing when I expressly told you not to wasn't wrong?"

"We didn't—"

"You did. There's a salty, sand-covered surfboard leaning against my house right now. That rash guard is wet and on the floor in the hallway. And I don't even know what to say about the cut on your arm."

I glare right back at her, but my chin is bouncing around too.

"Kate, that was me," Lena says. "I took her surfing. I thought it was important and her arm is fine, I promise. Just a scrape. But you should've seen her. She was amazing and it made her feel confident out there. So don't be mad at Sunny. Blame me."

Kate turns around. "I do. I do blame you. This is not okay, Lena. This is not what I wanted to happen, at all."

"You're the one who told me she'd come around," Lena says. "You told me it was important that Sunny know I'd wait, as long as it took, for her to give me a chance. Well, she's giving me a chance."

"I wanted you to get to know your daughter and for her to know you. For her to know she was worth knowing. Don't you get that? I did not mean for you to go behind my back and take her into the ocean and dye her hair blue."

"I wanted it blue," I say, but Kate doesn't hear me.

"You have no idea," she says to Lena, her voice more shaky now than razor-y. "She may be your daughter, but she's my kid. I kept her fed and clothed. I watched her cry when she lost her best friend and wouldn't tell me why. I read to her every night. I felt my world falling apart when she got sick. I paid all the bills that insurance didn't cover. I wished, night after night after night, that she'd get a heart. I watched her grow into this beautiful, amazing person who I would do anything for, anything to protect. I did that, which you would know if you'd called or written, even once, in the past eight years."

"Katie—"

"No." Kate shakes her head, tears careening down her face. "No, we're done. You don't get to swoop in and undo our entire lives. She could've been hurt today. She could've *died*."

"But she didn't."

"Yeah. Today. But you lied to me. To my face. And she's not like every other kid, Lena. She's fragile."

Lena sighs and rubs her forehead. I don't know what to say. I knew Kate would be mad if she found out we went surfing, but this is more than mad. This is . . . destroyed.

"Please go," Kate says, looking right at Lena.

"Wait, what?" I ask. Lena just stares at her.

"You need to leave, Lena. Right now."

"Katie, that's not fair," Lena says.

"No, it's not," Kate says, "but I don't know what else to do here."

"She's fine," Lena says. "Sunny is fine. She proved to herself she could do it and she's—"

"You put her in danger," Kate says.

"Kate," I say. "She didn't. I just surfed, that's all."

"We need some time," Kate says. "We all need some time."

"Some time?" I say. Panic curls my hands into tight fists. "What? What are you saying?"

"Sunny, for the last time, go to your room!"

"No!" I turn to Lena. I want to grab her hands, but her arms are folded tight across her chest. "Lena, don't go, please."

Lena doesn't answer me, though. She stares at Kate and Kate stares back. Finally, Lena lets out a big breath and looks at me. "Sunny—"

"No," I say. "Please don't."

"Sweetie," Lena says, reaching out and tucking a piece of hair behind my ear. "Maybe Kate's right."

"She's not right! How could you say that?"

Lena takes a step closer to me. "She's right about taking a breather right now. This has been a lot, for all of us, and I want what's best for you."

I shake my head. "So best means leaving? Again? You're just going to leave me?"

Kate sucks in a breath and reaches for my hand. I yank my arm back.

"I'm not going anywhere," Lena says softly. "I promise. You have no reason to believe me, I know, but I won't leave. We're just going to take a few days so Kate and I can figure things out."

Kate doesn't say anything, but she's stiff as a board as she stares at the ground.

"But I want to go surfing again tomorrow," I say. "And you still need to take me shopping and I need to talk to you about... about..."

Liking.

Kissing.

Quinn.

The words bubble up and die before I can say them, but I know I want to say them all to Lena. She'd understand. She'd get it, all this confusion, all this starting over, all these big huge feelings in my stomach that I can't get rid of. I want to wade out to the deepest part of the ocean and bob on our boards while we watch the sun tick across the sky and tell her everything.

"You're not doing any of those things, Sunny," Kate says. "Not anytime soon, anyway."

My mouth drops open and tears leap into my eyes. I wait for Lena to protest, to tell Kate she's wrong, but she just stands there with her tattooed arms folded over her chest.

"Lena," I finally say.

She looks at me then, her eyes all big and sad. "I'll see you soon, Sunshine. I promise."

No, no, no. That sounds way too much like goodbye. It sounds like the end. It sounds like eight years without anything but mermaid dreams and a picture of a lady who has the same eyes as me.

I want to wrap my arms around her waist and never let go. I want her to fight for me. Because what if she doesn't come back? What if this is just like when I was four years old and she figured out I'm not worth all of this?

What if?

But she doesn't fight. She doesn't do anything but give me one more sad-eyed look and then turn around and leave.

Kate and I don't really talk about what happened.

Of course, she cleans my arm again, slathering it with a billion layers of Neosporin before covering it up with a hospital-grade Band-Aid. Then she takes my blood pressure. Then she calls Dr. Ahmed and yammers on and on to her about my surfing and the itty-bitty cut on my arm and hair dye. Like hair dye is going to make me suddenly sprint into cardiac arrest or something.

After she's pretty sure that I'm probably going to live,

at least for the next few hours, she tells me to go to my room. Again.

"That's it?" I ask, standing in the doorway to the kitchen, watching her fill up the kettle with water.

She nods, her jaw tight.

"Can I call Lena later?"

She flips off the water and slams the kettle down on the stove. "Sunny. Not now."

"Can I?"

"No."

"Well, when?"

"In a few days, all right? I need to think this through, figure out the best way for her to be in your life. I might need to talk to a lawyer."

"A lawyer? What for?"

"Honey, it's complicated. There are financial issues and...just a lot of things to think about, okay? I thought I was ready. I thought we were all ready, but—"

"This is stupid," I say, and my throat gets all tight. "You wanted me to talk to her. You kept saying I'd regret it if I didn't."

"I know that. I do want you to get to know her, but she can't do this, Sunny. She can't go against what I say and put your health and safety at risk."

"She didn't—"

"I'm your guardian. Legally. *She gave you up.*"

The last four words hurt and Kate knows it. She closes her eyes and shakes her head, but she doesn't take the words back. She doesn't even try to explain why Lena did what she did. Kate has always tried to explain. She's always wanted to help me understand that Lena loves me, that she gave me up for my own good, that there were good reasons for it all.

But today's different, I guess.

"Lena's just trying to help me," I say.

"Help you do what, exactly? Get hurt? Act like you're eighteen years old when you're twelve?"

"No."

"Then what?"

"Feel like I'm not about to drop dead all the time, that's what!"

Kate's face goes totally white. Tears spill fast down her cheeks. The kettle whistles, yelling like a banshee, and Kate still hasn't said anything.

It's still screaming when I stomp to my room, slamming my door so hard it rattles the whole house.

I wish I was a mermaid.
If I lived in the sea, I'd never get out,
never let my feet touch the sand.
Because if I was a mermaid,
I could swim the ocean wide with you,

the cold waters melting into warm.
If I lived in the sea, we wouldn't be here
and I wouldn't feel like this
because you never would have left me
alone.
If I was a mermaid, I'd fit with you like I
    should.
If I lived in the sea, I'd fit with me like I
    should.
If I was a mermaid, I'd sleep in the deep
and play in the shallows,
flipping my tail for the humans on shore.
They'd see a flash of color and shout.
They'd tell stories about me at night.
But I'd never let them get close enough
to hear my heart beat.
Mermaid girl.
Mermaid or girl?
Girl—real or not?

CHAPTER

24

Kate took my phone away. She says I need quiet time to think and get some rest. Well, I say she's turned into some kind of demon from the deep, complete with red-rimmed eyes and horns. And now Dave's here and he and Kate are talking, talking, talking out in the living room, probably about all the ways they can make my life miserable.

I lie on my bed and write. I write so much my hand cramps and I have to take a bunch of breaks. Then I scour Lena's journal, looking for anything to get rid of this knot in the middle of my chest, like my heart's arteries and veins and vessels are all tangled up.

She gave you up.

I shake my head and flip through the journal, landing on a black-inked entry toward the beginning of the book.

> *Sometimes I look at J and can't believe I've gotten this chance. I get to love again. I get to be loved again. Two years ago, I never thought this would happen. I had some chances, maybe, but I pushed them all away. Getting sober was so hard—it's still so hard—I wasn't going to risk a broken heart again. But now everything's different. And he wasn't the one who made me feel like I could do it. It was me. It was me working the program, me going to meetings, me calling D in the middle of the night if I had to. It was me believing that I had something to give someone else, finally, instead of just taking, taking, taking.*

I frown down at the page, my heart thumping all over the place. Because... because it sounds like this J person is her boyfriend or something. Maybe he's just a best friend, but it sounds super-romantic. I tuck this question away and keep on reading.

> *And now there's S. For the past few weeks, I cry myself to sleep almost every night, thinking about her. Thinking about how she's my life and I'm hers. Thinking about how I can't mess this up. I can't. Sometimes I look at S's face and*

I can't breathe, I love her so much. It's the scariest, best kind of pain, right in the middle of my chest.

I reread that part a couple of times, then I check the date on the entry. Lena wrote it in February. Way before she came to Port Hope for me. Way before she even called Kate.

So, if S is me, then...

I read it again. She must have had a picture of me. Maybe Kate sent her some over the past eight years, school photos and stuff like that. But...Kate said she could never get in touch with Lena, whenever she tried. The last number she'd had was disconnected. It had been years since Kate and Lena had talked. That's what she told me, that day in my hospital room.

But surely Lena had baby pictures of me. That's one thing I've been thinking about, actually. Kate doesn't have any of my baby stuff because our life together started when I was four. So Lena has to have something. She wouldn't throw it away, would she?

I sit up and run my hand over the crinkly journal page, imagining Lena looking at a baby picture of me and getting up the courage to call Kate, to come see me, to get her second chance. I try to settle the image in my heart and it almost fits, but it keeps popping out, like a puzzle piece that's just a hair too big for the only gap left in the whole puzzle.

I close the journal and stick it under my pillow. I feel itchy and bouncy and there's no way I can sleep after reading all that. They were supposed to calm me down, Lena's words, but all they did was stir me all up and stick all these questions in my brain.

I slide off my bed and tiptoe down the hallway, peering around the corner and into the living room. Dave's here and he and Kate are on the couch, their heads superclose. He has his arm around her shoulders, and his hand is playing with her hair.

I stand there for a few seconds, wondering if I should try to talk to Kate about Lena again. Maybe she knows who J is. Maybe she knows...something. I don't know, anything. But just as I'm about to step all the way into the living room, I realize Dave and Kate aren't talking.

They're...kissing.

Finally, they're kissing.

I wait to feel super-happy, because I'm always teasing them and I know that Dave loves Kate more than anything in the whole wide world. They think I don't know that he quit music to come be with her, to help her with the bookstore and me, but there's no other possible reason. His is the kind of love I read about in books and sing along with in songs. Especially his super-whiny songs. That kind of love is the whole reason I want to kiss someone so bad.

But I don't feel happy. I don't know what I feel, exactly, but it's not happy. My chest feels hollow, like I'm missing some super-important part of myself and I don't know where to find it. Everyone's got their life, their love stories that make them feel happy and grateful and all soft inside, and here I am with someone else's heart in my chest while Kate makes all the decisions and then goes and has all this fun smooching Dave.

I sneak back to my room and get into bed. I pull the covers over my head and squeeze my eyes shut so tight, colors explode under my eyelids. It's all bubbling up, too many thoughts all bumping into each other in my head. My heart pounds like it's about to bust right out of my chest, and I think it might. I think it really might.

I'm just about to cry or scream or pull out my blue hair, which I really do like a whole lot, when I hear a tiny *tap* on my window.

I peek out of my quilt and glance toward the glass. It's covered with sheer white curtains, so I can't see much. Plus, it's totally dark outside, almost eleven o'clock. But then I hear it again.

Tap.

Tap-tap.

I throw off my covers and run to the window, shoving

the curtains out of the way. I start to kneel on the cushioned bench under the glass, but I guess I'm a little too excited—or scared or nervous that it's an axe murderer tapping on my window or something—because my foot gets tangled in the bottom of the thin curtain fabric. I pull and tug, but it's like there's a tentacle wrapped around my ankle. I bend down to unwrap it, lose my balance, and go down hard. Even better, I bring the whole curtain rod and curtains down with me.

"Sunny, are you okay?"

I yank the curtains off my head and look around my room for the voice. It sounded like...Quinn. But a faraway Quinn.

"Sunny?"

Tap-tap-tap.

I peer at the window and see a hand pressed against the glass, fingernail tapping away. Her face appears a second later, purple curls everywhere, and I swear, I almost cry. I really, really do. But before I can get up and open the window, my bedroom door flies open.

CHAPTER
25

"Sunny?" Kate says, anger and panic mixing around in her voice.

I whip my head back to the window, but it's completely dark.

"Yeah," I grunt.

Kate hurries to where I'm sprawled on the floor, draped in drapes with a sore butt.

"What did you do?" she asks.

"What did I do? It's not like I tripped on the curtains on purpose."

She sighs and helps me to my feet and gathers the curtains into a ball before dumping them back onto the floor near my bed. Very un-Kate-like.

"You all right, Sunshine?" Dave asks from the doorway.

"She's fine," Kate snaps before I can even answer for myself.

Dave peers at me, eyes narrowed. Then he wiggles his fingers down his head and shoots me a thumbs-up. He likes my hair. I ignore him and he frowns, but I don't care.

"Go to bed," Kate says, heading for the door. "You should've been asleep hours ago."

"Yes, *Mother*," I say. But I don't really say it. I spit it, all venom, a name I've never been allowed to call her. It feels like a weapon now and I'm going to use it. It must be sharp too, because Kate stops in her tracks, her shoulders heaving up and down. She doesn't turn around to face me, though.

"Sunny," Dave sighs out.

"Well, she won't let me have my actual mom, will she?" I say. "A girl needs her mom, you know. Her real one."

Dave glances at Kate, who still hasn't moved. If my words really were a sword, they would've cut Kate in half. For real, she'd be in two pieces, blood all over the floor, her heart slowing, slowing, slowing until it finally stopped. I wait to feel some kind of triumph, but I don't. Instead my throat closes up and my eyes not only sting, but water. Like, a full bloom of tears right in my eyeballs.

I try to hold it together, but Dave can tell I'm about to lose it. Maybe Kate is too. She still hasn't budged. He comes into the room and takes her hand, so gently and sweetly, it makes all the tears start a sprint down my cheeks. Then they're gone and my door is closed.

I don't even wait to make sure they're out of earshot. Tears blur my vision, and I almost trip over the curtains Kate plopped right in my way, but I shake the devils off and make it to the window. It's locked up tight, but I get it unlatched and throw it open.

"Quinn," I whisper-yell into the dark. I don't see her anywhere. Not that I can see much, but more tears escape out of my eyes.

"Quinn!"

The word doesn't even sound like her name, my throat squeezing it until it's all broken up. I'm really bawling now, though I'm trying to be quiet about it. The last thing I need is Kate back in here, all mad but fussing over me just the same.

Trying to be quiet when there's a hurricane happening in your face is not an easy thing, let me tell you. I'm probably the color of a beet, blotchy and snotty on top of that. I'm not sure I even want Quinn to see me like this, except that I do. I do want her to see me like this because... because...

"I'm here," a voice says to my left. "I'm sorry, I dove into the bushes when I saw Kate come in your room and I got a branch stuck in my hair and—"

But she cuts herself off because I'm crying even harder now.

"Hey," she says, real soft and sweet.

"Hey," I say back, real hiccup-y and gross-sounding. I need a tissue.

"I texted, but you didn't answer," she said. "Then I called and it went straight to voice mail."

"Kate took my phone."

"Oh. I just...I wanted to make sure you were okay. That was intense. Earlier. With Kate and your...with Lena."

A fresh batch of tears spills over, but I manage a soggy laugh. "Intense. Yeah. Aren't you going to get into trouble for being out so late?"

She shrugs. "My mom sleeps hard and I have my phone if she wakes up. Even if she caught me, it'd be worth it."

I look at her and she looks back at me. "It would?"

"Totally."

"Why?"

She blinks a whole lot and I think her face goes a little red. But it's dark, so maybe not. "BFFs, right?" she finally says.

"Right." Hiccup. Sniff. BFFs are great. The greatest. In my opinion, they're the number one most important thing in a gal's life, in anyone's life, which is why finding a new best friend was a top priority in my *New Life* plan. But for some reason, I feel sort of let down by Quinn's answer.

Like I kind of, sort of, maybe wanted her to say something else.

Which is silly. And weird. And New Life Sunny isn't either of those things.

I shake my head and take a breath and, all at the same time, rub my eyes, which are still leaking. Sheesh, I'm a mess.

"Hey," Quinn says again, still soft and sweet. Before I know it, she's climbing through the window and standing in my room.

Quinn is in my room. I mean, she's been in my room before, but never in the middle of the night and never when I'm a crying mess and never, ever after she's told me she likes girls and definitely never, ever, ever after I just wished she'd said she came over to check on me because of BFFs and because of something a little bit different than BFFs.

I feel like I'm on my surfboard again, the wild sea under my feet, and I'm trying to keep my balance.

But I can't.

I'm about to fall. I just know I am. Right into an ocean so big, I'll disappear and no one will ever find me again.

I feel dizzy. My heart is totally out of control. This was not the plan. This was not on my list of amazing things to do if I got to live. I tap two fingers to my chest, trying to get my heart to calm down, to behave, to chill out because it's only Quinn.

But this heart is not having it. It keeps pounding, and my breathing keeps huffing and puffing.

"Sunny—"

"I'm okay," I say, but I sit down on the window seat anyway. I turn and lean my back against the frame, pulling my legs to my chest. Quinn does the same and it's such a tiny little bench that our knees touch.

"Your hair matches your room," Quinn says, whispering.

I look around and smile, picking up a long chunk of my hair and holding it against the walls. "It totally does."

"I love it."

I let my eyes meet hers. "I love yours too."

She takes a shaky breath. "I'm sorry about what happened. I feel like it's my fault."

"What? No way."

"But I brought over the hair dye."

"Kate's not mad about my hair," I say. "I mean, she is, but it's more . . ."

"Lena?"

A knot balls up in my throat. "Yeah. Lena."

"What's it like?"

"What's what like?"

She shrugs. "Being you. All this stuff with your heart and now Lena. It's . . . wow, Sunny. It's a lot."

I swallow hard. No one's ever asked me that before. Not even Kate. Not even when I was sick. She'd ask how I was feeling. She'd ask if I wanted to talk about Lena. But she's never, ever asked what it was *like*.

I take a deep, slow breath and feel my heart pounding under my ribs. Then I tell Quinn what I've only ever told Lena. That it's weird, to be alive. That it's weird to have someone else's heart, someone who died, and that sometimes I'm not sure what parts are me and what parts . . . aren't.

As I talk, I watch Quinn play with her fingers. Her nails are painted a pretty rose-gold color. I reach out and grab her hand. I tell myself I just want to look at her nails a little closer, but I'm not really sure about that.

I keep on talking, though. Then, somehow, Quinn's hand gets under mine and I move my fingers so they're tangled with hers and we're holding hands. We're holding hands like we did under the waterfall, like I always dreamed of holding hands with a boy.

Like I always *wondered* about holding hands with a girl.

Except now it's not practice and it's real. I know it's real, because I'm saying really real stuff to her and when I open my eyes, she's looking right at me and I know she gets it.

"That sounds hard," she says when I finally shut up.

I shrug. "Sometimes. But I'm alive, you know? And I shouldn't be. If my donor hadn't died when they did, I might have died too."

Her eyes get shiny and she nods. "That's so sad. And weird, because...I'm so glad you're alive. And if I'm glad, does that mean I'm glad they died?"

I give her a tired smile. "Welcome to my brain."

She squeezes my hand and I squeeze back. We don't let go.

"So, what's it like being you?" I ask.

She huffs a laugh, but then she sees I'm serious, that I really want to know, and she's quiet for a while. Her thumb moves over my first finger, back and forth, back and forth, making me feel all warm and happy.

"Lonely," she finally says.

"How come?"

"You know I hate all the traveling, right?"

"Right."

"But it's more than that. Like, all that stuff I told you that happened with Sadie back in Alaska. I just...I never fit anywhere. For the past couple of years, I was pretty sure that I liked...that I...well, you know."

I swallow hard. I don't blink. I don't breathe. Luckily, she doesn't look at me and keeps on talking.

"So, even if I'm not the only brown girl in whatever

town we're in, I'm always nervous that I'll...that some-one will..." She sighs and shrugs. "I just can't find any real friends, you know? My mom calls it 'finding your people.' But what if you can't? What if people you thought were your people laugh at you and forget about you?"

I nod, still unblinking and unbreathing. I thought Margot was my people, but I was way wrong. Kate and Dave are my people, but they don't know about all my wonderings, wonderings that I hoped were long gone but that keep creeping back into my head and heart. Then there's Lena, but there's still so much I don't know about her. So many holes and gaps in the eight years she was just a mermaid under the ocean.

But here's Quinn. Quinn, who's holding my hand. Quinn, who maybe, just maybe, not only *wonders*, but *knows*.

"I can be your people," I say, really super-quiet. Because Quinn is amazing. Quinn is smart and beautiful and she got laughed at too. She got betrayed too, and she's still here, being herself. She's still sitting in my room, holding my hand, like maybe, when I asked why she was here a few minutes ago, she wishes she'd given me a different reason than BFFs too.

"You can?" she asks, just as quiet.

"I mean...I'm not brown, and it seems like that can be hard."

She grins. "No. You're very, very white."

I grin back, but it fades quick. My heart is going buck-wild. My stomach too. "But I'm…I mean…I think I might…"

God, I can't say it. I can't do it. So I just squeeze her hand really, really hard. I scoot closer to her and hold out my other hand. She slips her fingers between mine and now both of our hands are all tangled up between us. She doesn't say anything. She does stare at me, though, not blinking, barely breathing, but that's okay. This is pretty much the most nonblinking, nonbreathing moment I can think of ever.

It's actually the perfect first-kiss moment. The little white lights in my room are super-soft and make everything look like we're underwater. We're sitting in a window seat. The rain from earlier is gone and the moon dips in and out of the leftover clouds. All I can hear is the sound of our breathing, nice and shallow like we can't catch our breath.

It's perfect.

It really, really is.

If I just had a boy I liked…

If I just had a boy…

I squeeze my eyes shut and imagine I'm sitting on my surfboard, waiting for the perfect wave. I wait… and wait…and then I feel the swell lift me up and I turn around and start paddling.

Patience and daring, just like Lena said.

When I open my eyes, I see Quinn and her purple curls and her dark eyes and how she's been the best best friend I've ever had and I know.

I just know.

I don't want to kiss a boy. At least, not right now. Because I don't like a boy right now.

I like a girl.

New Life Sunny likes a girl.

I lean forward a little, because if I know, maybe she knows too. I lean forward even more and she leans toward me and soon our foreheads are touching. She's breathing kind of hard, but so am I and I really, really hope that I don't puke in her lap before I have a chance to kiss her.

I have no idea how to do this, but if it's just about the angle, I need to tilt my chin up a little.

So I do.

My nose bumps into hers and I kind of want to laugh, but she's really quiet and still. I can't even hear her breathing anymore. My heart is speeding around my body like a supersonic plane. I turn my face a little and her bottom lip touches mine.

And then...

And then...

She's gone.

My hands are empty and her face isn't close to mine

anymore. In fact, it's way over on the other side of the window seat.

"Um, I'm sorry," she says, her arms hugging her body. "I just...I think I..."

She keeps swallowing, over and over. Then she stands up and my eyes follow her because this can't be happening, can it? I open my mouth a bunch of times to say something, say anything, say I was just kidding or...I don't know...practicing, but I can't get my voice to work.

"I need to go, Sunny," she says. "My mom...I'm sorry, I have to go."

Then she crawls out the window. I watch her jump on her bike and pedal away so fast, she's a blur in the dark. I rub my eyes over and over again, but when I open them, she's still gone. I even pinch my arm to see if maybe, just maybe, I'm dreaming, but pain shoots right up my elbow to my shoulder, good and real.

I thought Quinn...

I thought she...

I thought we...

I bury my head in my arm and try to cry, but I can't even do that. I'm shivering, my head so full of girls laughing and stories of girls kissing and hearts disappearing, I'm sure I'm about to shake to pieces.

I grab a pencil off my desk and the nearest piece of paper I can find, a bright blue flyer for the Fourth of July beach bonfire next week, and start writing on the back. I write and I write until a whole poem fills up the page.

Standing up, I stuff the poem—and all the other ones I wrote since Kate pretty much locked me in my room—in the front pocket of my backpack. I shove Lena's journal inside, along with a half-empty bottle of water that's been on my nightstand for at least a week.

Then I don't even think. I don't even care. Because right now, I need to talk to Lena. I need to see her and I need to tell her everything and I need her to tell me what to do and how to feel about all this. Because she knows what it's like to start over. She knows what it's like to be scared, to be patient and daring, and I'm betting she knows what it's like to be patient and daring and have everything fall apart. Kate doesn't know, because she won't even let me be patient and daring. She won't let me do anything.

No. I need Lena. I need my mom. I need her right now. So I pull on my black stomping boots, take a big breath, and toss my leg out the window.

I want to write a love song, but I'm not sure who
    it's for.
Maybe it's for you or maybe it's for me or
maybe it's for some boy with blue eyes and
    floppy hair
I have never met.

296

I feel something,
but is it just wonder or fear,
love or like?
Maybe I just want to be like you,
because you're smart and pretty
and your feet have been all over the world.

The girls I used to know,
the ones who sneer and shame,
they seem so sure
all the time.
Wouldn't that be easier?
Wouldn't that be safer?

On nights when I can't sleep,
my heart lights up and
I wonder, wonder, wonder.
I tuck it away.
Easier.
Safer.

But this heart is new and I think it
likes it when
you hold it in your hands,
gentle and sweet.
I thought you liked it too

and I thought I saw a flicker
of light in my heart.
A little brighter.
A little happier.
I thought it felt
a little more
like me.

But then you disappeared.
And when I touched my fingers to my chest
to make sure my heart was still there,
my hand went straight through
like it was never there at all.

CHAPTER

26

I land in the soft and sandy grass and freeze, waiting for an alarm to sound. For Kate's sixth Sunny sense to alert her to my daring escape.

But there's nothing.

My bike is stuck in the detached garage. Lifting that squeaky, rusty door would wake the dead, I'm sure of it. But when I creep around to the front of the house, I see that Kate's beach bike is leaning against the front porch, which will work just fine. Soft light fills the living room window, but I barely even glance at it as I grab the bike's handlebars. Now is the time for action, for doing awesome and amazing things I've never done before, and I'm not going to wait around for Kate to spot my shadow out on the front lawn.

I barely get my butt settled on the bike's seat and dump

my bag in the little metal basket in the front before my legs are pumping, pedaling away from my house.

At the end of the driveway, I slow down long enough to dig the poems out of my bag and hold them over my head. The papers, at least ten different pages, flap in the salty breeze for a few seconds before I let them all go.

I look back just long enough to see the wind pushing my words against the sky.

☀

Port Hope is a pretty big town, spreading inland for miles and miles, but the Methodist church is right off the bridge that connects to Juniper Island.

Which means, so is Lena. I remember her telling Kate she'd found a meeting at the church, which was near where she was staying. It shouldn't be that hard to find her. It's hard to miss that ancient mint-green truck.

I pedal over the Port Hope Bridge, which, if I'm being honest, is a terrifying journey. It's quiet and dark, not a car in sight, and the bike lane runs right along the edge so I can see the black water a billion miles below me.

I'm totally out of breath, my mouth dry and my heart pounding, but I keep going. I wheel off the bridge and bump up onto the sidewalk that runs along the main street. There are a few cars here and there as I ride toward the big steeple arching above the palm trees a few blocks ahead, but no one seems to notice me. No one slows down to ask what I'm doing or if I'm okay or if Kate knows where I am.

No one knows me here in Port Hope.

No one except Lena.

I ride faster and soon I spot the church. It's old, made of cream-colored stone and stained-glass windows that look like nothing more than spilled ink in the dark. Skidding to a stop in front of a sign inviting me to join the congregation for a barbecue this Sunday, I look around. Little streets veer off from here, all of them dotted with sleeping houses with wide front porches.

There's nothing else to do but pick one and go for it. I pedal down one street and then another, searching for Lena's truck. Then, on the third street, a wakeful dog spots me and starts barking, chasing me to the edge of its yard. I pump my legs so hard, they ache and my chest feels tight, but eventually the dog goes quiet again. My heart calms down.

Well, no, no, it doesn't. My heart is a wild beast, just like the dog. It's barking and gnashing its teeth, chasing the rest of my body, which feels like it's trying to leave my heart behind.

I'm just about to give up and collapse in a stranger's yard when I see it.

A mint-green truck in the driveway of a tiny bungalow with a stone porch in front of a bright yellow front door. In the dark, I can't tell if the house is green or blue, but that door is super-clear.

Sunshine yellow.

I pedal toward the truck and hop off my bike. It clatters to the ground and I run up the porch steps. Inside, it's all dark, but I don't even wait to get my breath back before I press the doorbell and listen to it echo through the house.

I wait, my breathing heavy, but I don't hear anything inside. No footsteps, nothing. I turn around and look back at the driveway. There's another car in front of Lena's. A gray four-door something or other. I stare at it, wondering if it belongs to whoever owns the house. Maybe Lena's just renting a room and the family is still here. Maybe Lena met some friends in Port Hope and it belongs to one of them. Maybe...

I swallow my last maybe as I squint through the dark to read the state on the car's license plate. It doesn't look like it says South Carolina. It looks like—

New York.

My stomach goes all tight. I step off the porch to get a better look, passing Lena's truck to peer through the windows of the gray car. It's a mess inside. Cheerios dot the floorboards in the back and there are a bunch of kid books on the seat. Board books. Like the kind they make for babies so they won't tear them up or get paper cuts or whatever. There's also a couple of diapers, a cloth that has little green stars all over it, and a baby's car seat.

There's a baby's car seat. As in, where a baby rides in a car.

I blink at it, at the sky-blue and gray fabric, at the pacifier that someone left in the seat. I blink and blink and blink, but all that baby stuff is still there.

My imagination gets going, thinking of all the reasons why Lena would be at a house where a baby lives.

Maybe a friend is visiting from New York.

Maybe whoever owns the car babysits a lot.

Maybe—

"Sunny? Is that you?"

I whirl around at the deep voice, almost choking on a scream.

"Whoa, it's okay," the voice says again. It belongs to a tall, skinny guy I've never seen before. He has brown skin and his dark hair goes in every direction all at once. He's just standing there in the yard, barefoot in a pair of plaid pajama pants and a purple T-shirt with NYU written across the chest in big white letters.

"Who...who are you?" I ask.

He looks at me for another second and then drags his hands through his hair. "It is you. Are you okay? How did you get here?"

"Um, how do you know who I am?"

He just stares at me and rubs his chin.

"Hello?" I ask. I think I'm being rude, but I don't know what else to say.

"Sorry. I'm Janesh," he finally says. "I'm ... I'm a friend of Lena's."

"Oh." I breathe out a world of relief. That explains the car, I guess. "Is she here?"

"Yeah, yeah, she's inside. I heard the doorbell, but she sleeps really hard and was up late last night with..." He frowns and shakes his head, hanging his hand on the back of his neck. This dude is weird.

"So can I see her?" I ask when he just stands there.

"I'm sorry," he says. "This isn't how I wanted to meet you."

I just blink at him, because huh? But then, as he keeps on standing there, not moving, it all clicks. Lena's journal, the way this guy seems to know all about me and how hard Lena sleeps.

"Your name," I say, "it starts with a J."

He nods, his eyes still wide on mine.

I stare back, not sure what else to say. This guy is more than Lena's friend. I know he is. He's the J in her journal. The one she's so glad she gets to love, the one who took her out to dinner after she called Kate for the first time in eight years.

"Let me go wake up Lena, all right?" he says, heading

toward the house. Clueless about what else to do, I follow him up the front steps. "Can you wait on the porch for me?"

"Why?" I ask.

"I just...I'd rather get Lena, okay?"

I huff a breath. "Fine."

He disappears through the yellow door and swings it closed, but it doesn't shut all the way. I press the toe of my boot against the bottom of the door and push it a little.

Then a little more.

It's about halfway open when I hear it.

A baby.

Crying.

CHAPTER

27

I freeze.

The baby keeps crying, but then I hear murmuring and the baby quiets down. A light clicks on, its glow spilling into the front hallway.

I push the door open all the way and stand there, waiting for Lena to come rushing out and explain all this. The baby squawks a little more and I walk into the house, following the sound and the voices.

"She *what?*" a voice calls out.

Lena's voice.

"She's outside on the porch," Janesh says. "It's the middle of the night, Leen. What's going on?"

"I don't know. I need to call Kate right now."

My feet glide through the house like I'm in a trance. There's baby stuff everywhere. A high chair at the end of a dark wood kitchen table. Cloth books and squishy toys all over the living room, soft blankets tossed over the dark leather couch.

The house is cute and simple, throw pillows and paintings on the walls. There's a lot of color—deep reds and oranges and dark purple. The air smells like orange blossom tea and milk. I keep expecting someone else to appear, like maybe someone who owns the house, but I only hear Janesh and Lena.

I tiptoe down a hallway off the kitchen and stop outside an open door. I don't look inside. I don't dare. I just listen.

"You need to go talk to Sunny," Janesh says. "She knows something's up. You should've told her right away."

"That was out of the question and you know it," Lena says. "I wasn't ready. *She* wasn't ready."

"You're stronger than you think you are. You don't give yourself enough credit for all you've done. How much you've overcome."

I hold my breath, waiting for Lena to say something.

"You don't know what this is like, okay?" she says quietly. "You've never left your own daughter. You would *never* leave Samaira."

Samaira.

"Leen, come on. Don't—"

"Just take her, all right? If Kate wakes up and finds out

307

Sunny's gone, she'll call the police. I'll never see Sunny again."

"All right. But, Leen, you need to tell her the truth."

"I know that. I will."

They go quiet and I hear a rustling sound, like maybe Janesh is hugging her. Then there's a soft cooing noise, kind of like a dove. The baby's in there. With Lena and Janesh. Only with them.

Knowing stuff is tricky business. Look at all that's happened. I knew Lena wasn't really a mermaid swimming free in the ocean, which meant she left me behind on purpose. Margot knew I wondered about kissing girls and it cost me my best friend. Then there's Quinn. As soon as I found out she liked girls—as soon as I knew—it all blew up in my face, losing me my second best friend in six months.

Knowing stuff is dangerous.

Knowing stuff hurts.

But I can't stop myself from stepping forward, closer, closer, until I'm standing in the doorway of a room with a big white crib in one corner. The room is lit by a single lamp with a blue whale for a base, and everything looks soft and warm. There's a cushioned rocking chair and paintings on the walls of watercolor starfish and dolphins and sand dollars. And the colors. The colors are perfect. Aquamarine and cerulean and sky.

Lena and Janesh are in front of the crib, holding a baby between them. Lena smooths her hand over the baby's head, which is covered in super-dark hair that looks just like Janesh's. Her skin is brown like his too, although it's a little lighter.

I breathe out as quietly as I can. The baby's his. Only his. This is Samaira and he brought her with him on his visit from New York. But then I notice a ring on Janesh's finger. A gold ring. Then I notice a ring on Lena's finger too. Silver-colored with a simple round diamond on top. I've never seen it before. She's never worn any rings the whole time she's been here.

And then I keep noticing more and more stuff. I keep knowing.

The baby squirms while she pulls on Lena's hair and I can see her whole face. I see freckles spilling over her nose and onto her cheeks. I see her eyes, which aren't dark like Janesh's at all.

They're amber.

Just like mine.

My mind hums and whirls. I think back to all those entries I read in Lena's journal, all the times she talked about S and my chest felt all warm and light, like I was loved, like I mattered.

But I don't think S is me. I don't think S is me at all.

"Mom?"

It's the first time I've ever called her Mom. The first time I've ever called *anyone* Mom. The word feels small when it falls out of my mouth, but it lands like a grenade and blows up everything in the room. Lena's head pops up and her eyes go wide. Janesh takes Samaira, who screeches and stretches her little arms toward Lena. Her onesie is bright blue. It has little yellow moons all over it.

"Sunny," Lena says, hurrying toward me. "Sweetie."

I feel her hands close around my arms. I think I even hear her saying stuff. Stuff like *It's okay* and *Let's go outside and talk* and *Are you all right?* But all I can see is Samaira.

S.

She's crying and Janesh is cuddling her, his cheek smooshed up against hers while he sways her back and forth. Lena pulls on me a little, trying to get me out of the room, but I can't budge. There's a baby in here. Lena's baby. Lena's *daughter*.

"Sunny," Lena says, "I need you to breathe."

I *am* breathing, I want to say, but I can't get my tongue to work. And maybe I'm not breathing, because my chest feels super-tight. Like, so tight, I may not be breathing at all. It's not the kind of ache I get when I swim or surf too hard. It's not even the kind of feeling I get around Quinn, all fluttery and nervous. This hurts, like a billion bricks just landed right on my sternum.

I back away from Lena, or I try to. I try to run. I try to disappear altogether, but my legs feel like they're full of wet sand. My whole body feels like that—fingers and toes, arms and chest.

"Lena," Janesh says.

"I know," Lena says. She kneels down and looks at my amber eyes with her amber eyes and Samaira's amber eyes.

I squeeze mine shut.

"Honey, take a deep breath, please."

"Lena, she doesn't look good," Janesh says. "Is it her heart? Should I call Kate?" He knows about my heart. Of course he does. He's Lena's . . . he and Lena are . . .

"Just give her a minute," Lena says.

I sink down to the floor and I grab at my chest, because that heart that everyone knows all about is pounding like a million hammers. It's going to break every one of my ribs and bust through my skin.

"Sunny!" Lena's hands tighten around my arms. Her face is super-close to mine and it's like looking in a mirror, except it's not.

"I'm calling 9-1-1," Janesh says.

Samaira cries and cries.

My chest bursts open, or at least it feels that way. It splits right down the middle. *Zip* goes the scalpel. Blood.

There should be blood everywhere. There should be blood covering the whole world when your heart gets ripped right out of your body, when your whole self spills right out onto the floor. But there's no red. No white walls and steel operating table. There are only blurry faces of a family I don't know right before everything goes dark.

CHAPTER 28

I must be dead again, because I dream about mermaids. This time, though, I'm the mermaid. My legs are gone, replaced with a graceful, sparkly aquamarine tail that matches my hair. I must've really kicked the bucket this time.

But unlike my other dead-dream, Lena's nowhere to be found. It's just me, floating in the blue water. The bright sun pierces through the waves, making my tail shimmer like sapphires.

Lena?

No one answers. I twist and twirl, looking for my mermaid, a flash of black hair and that iridescent tail, but all I see is blue, blue, everywhere. Deep blue that I can't see through. I can only see me and I'm all alone.

CHAPTER
29

Beep-beep-beep.

I open my eyes. The blue is gone, replaced with dingy white walls and a scratchy blanket over my very human legs, the familiar tug of a needle in my arm.

I'm in the hospital again.

Kate's right next to me, snuggled by my side in the bed just like she was right before I was wheeled down for my heart transplant over two months ago.

Beep-beep-beep.

I turn my head and watch my heart rate flashing on the monitor.

65 . . . 64 . . . 66 . . .

"Hi, sweetie," Kate says. She lifts up on her elbow and rubs her eyes, which means she's been lying here for a long time and probably fell asleep. Her arm is around my waist and she hugs me a little tighter. "How are you feeling?"

70 . . . 72 . . . 75 . . .

I keep waiting for the numbers to start falling, for alarms to blare and nurses to rush in to try to save me.

"Is my heart bad again?" I ask. I grip the blanket and pull it up to my chin.

"What?"

My body feels tired. And achy. And sick. Wait, do I feel sick? Or do I just feel tired? I definitely feel tired, like I just ran around the island a few times without stopping. I press my palms to my chest, both of them, and feel the thunk-thunk-thunk going on under there.

"Sunny, you're okay," Kate says.

"But I'm back. I'm in the hospital. Is my heart bad again? Did I ruin it?"

"No, sweetheart. Ruin what?"

"My heart. My new heart. I ruined it. I—"

"Sweetie, breathe."

"I . . . am . . . breathing."

Kate sits up and turns so she's facing me; then she takes my face in her hands and rubs my temples. "Look at me."

I try, but I think I'm starting to cry.

83 . . . 84 . . . 86 . . .

"Sunshine, look at me."

I finally get a big gulp of air and look at her.

315

My Kate.

Blond hair, blue eyes, the total opposite of me. She's always worried, always tired, always overreacting about my every little move, but she's mine. She's here and she's never left me and she's never laughed at me and she's never, ever lied to me.

I grab her wrists and she keeps massaging my temples, nice and slow, the way she knows will always eventually calm me down.

"You had a panic attack, sweetie," she says.

"A panic attack?"

She nods. "Trouble breathing, tight feeling in your chest?"

"Yeah. That's exactly what it felt like."

"Your heart is fine, I promise. Dr. Ahmed checked you out and your heart is doing exactly what it should."

"So why am I still here?"

"Well, you're a heart transplantee and you did pass out, so Dr. Ahmed wanted to keep you here for observation. Just for tonight. We'll be back home tomorrow, okay?"

75...77...76...

I relax into the bed, but only a little. Because now I'm thinking about my new heart pumping in my chest, but even though it's healthy and new and perfect, it's not enough. It'll never be enough. Not for Quinn and not for Lena. Never for Lena.

316

"Oh, honey, I'm so sorry," Kate says, reading my mind. She does that sometimes. When I get all quiet, she knows I'm thinking and usually about not great stuff. She lies back down and tucks her chin onto my shoulder, her thumb stroking my face.

"Did you know?" I ask.

"No. I didn't, I promise. But when Lena came to the hospital with the ambulance, she told me about it. Three years ago, she started giving private guitar and voice lessons in Montauk and Janesh wanted to learn guitar. That's how they met. And then—"

"Stop. I don't want to know any more."

"Honey, I know this is a shock, but—"

"You should be happy. Lena's gone, poof, out of my life."

"Sunny. That is not what I wanted. Nothing about this makes me happy."

I shake my head. "She has a baby. Like, a whole person. A girl."

"Yeah," Kate says, all quiet. "Lena told me about her too. Your sister."

The word echoes through the room like she yelled it.

A sister.

I have a sister.

I don't even know what to say about that. It doesn't feel real and whenever I think about it, it makes my chest ache with all sorts of anger and sadness and...something else that feels softer and lighter, but I don't want to feel soft and light right now.

For a while, Kate and I just lie in silence. I'm glad. I don't want to talk about it. No way, nohow, but I can't seem to stop thinking about it either. I can't stop thinking about how Lena's a mom. She's just not my mom. Not in any way that counts.

Kate's who counts. She always did and I was so stupid to think I needed anyone else. I snuggle in closer to her and I think Kate and I fall asleep, because when I hear a knock on the door, the room is dimmer, the light outside the window a silvery blue. Kate sits up and I open my gluey eyes to see Dave in the doorway. He and Kate glance at each other, their faces glow-y. I want to tell them that I saw them kissing, that it's okay with me, but then Dave's face gets real serious.

"Hey, Sunshine," he says. "You feeling better?"

I shrug. I'm not sure what I'm feeling, honestly.

"Um...Lena's outside," he says, dragging his hand down his face, all nervous. "She wants to—"

"No," I say. "No way."

Kate smooths her hand over my hair. "Sunny—"

"I said no."

Then I turn onto my side so I can't see the way they

look at me, the girl who'll never be good enough. Not for Margot, not for Quinn. Not even for her own mom.

Later, while Kate's getting some coffee with Dave and probably making out in a stairwell or something, I sit up in my bed and try to write a poem on a napkin left over from my rubbery-chicken dinner.

~~You left~~
~~You didn't want~~
~~You lied~~
~~Moms are supposed to~~
~~Why don't you love~~

But I can't even get a full sentence out. I ball up the napkin and throw it across the room. I'm done with this *New Life*. It's too hard and too messy. I'm going back to *Old Life* Sunny. *Old Life* Sunny who only likes boys and doesn't need a best friend and whose mom is a mermaid lost at sea.

CHAPTER

30

I'm on the couch reading a comic, which is where I've been and what I've been doing for the past week since getting home from the hospital. I've got a blanket tucked around my legs, a big old bowl full of buttery popcorn on the end table, and absolutely no pudding in sight. Even better, this comic isn't about kissing at all. It's not about romance or crushes or anything awful like that. It's about a bunch of kids on the run from their villainous parents.

Which means, it's basically the perfect story.

Kate keeps pacing around the house, shooting me all these worried looks. I don't know why, though. I've basically turned into a couch potato and I'm not asking her to do anything like surf the treacherous Atlantic or dye my hair some other wild color. In fact, I plan on asking Dave to take my surfboard to the dump and seeing if Kate will help me dye my hair back to black.

So, Kate should be happy. Kate should be ecstatic. I'm all safe and sound, tucked away in my little cocoon. True, I've barely said a word in the past week. Like, *yes* and *no* and that's about it. It's hard to talk when you're in a cocoon. But that's better than being in the big wide world that just wants to stomp all over me.

Still, Kate's constantly got that wrinkle between her eyes that means she wants to *talk* and probably talk about Lena.

Well, no thanks. Lena's called and texted about a billion times since I was at her house—her house, where she actually *lives* with Janesh and has for the past eight weeks—but I always ignore her.

She hasn't texted at all today. Maybe she's finally given up on me, which is fine by me. She has Samaira. She has Janesh. No wonder she took so long to come back and find me. She doesn't even need me anymore.

I rub my chest right where my scar splits me in two, which feels achy all the time lately.

"Sunny?" Kate says.

I keep my nose buried in the comic.

She lifts my feet and sits down on the end of the couch, setting my legs in her lap. I glance up long enough to confirm the telltale wrinkle and then look back down at my comic.

She sits there for a second, rubbing my feet. Behind us, the window is open, letting in the balmy air of a truly magnificent summer day. The air is warm but not stifling, and the sky is a perfect cloudless blue, the sun bright. I breathe in the salty air. I breathe it in real deep, because I also haven't been outside since getting home from the hospital. Not even onto the porch.

Apparently this, along with me not talking all that much and never asking to do anything fun ever, is doing the exact opposite of making Kate happy.

"Do you want to go have a picnic on the beach?" she asks.

"No thanks."

"How about a movie?" she asks. "We could drive into Port Hope and go to the theater. There's that new Pixar out. It's supposed to be amazing."

"No."

"Sunny. Sweetheart."

"I just want to read, okay?"

She sighs. "Sunny, I know this is hard—"

"Nothing is hard. Everything is fine."

"Sweetie, you love Lena. I know you do. I know it hurts that she didn't tell you the truth about her family. I wish she'd told you too, but you have to understand that her disease is complicated."

I sigh and let my book drop in my lap. A bunch of words crowd into my mouth and I let them loose. "I'm so tired of *complicated*. Grown-ups are always saying stuff like that, like kids can't handle anything, but really, you're the ones who can't handle it. You're the ones who are scared."

It's more than I've said in days and it leaves me all out of breath.

Kate sighs. "Yeah. You're probably right about that."

I stare at her and she stares at me.

"But we're all trying here," she says. "I worry that you—"

But whatever she was going to say is cut off by the doorbell. My whole body goes tense, just like it has every time my phone has buzzed in the past two days, because it's always Lena.

Kate gets up to answer the door and I throw the blanket off my legs, ready to bolt to my room and lock myself inside. I'm halfway to the hallway when I see a flash of purple.

Lavender, to be exact.

I freeze and look back toward the front entryway.

"Hi, Quinn, how are you?" Kate says.

"I'm okay, Kate, thanks." Quinn shifts from foot to

foot. She's got on a gray tank top with little rainbows all over it, and a cute navy blue bag with a big aquamarine whale on it hangs from her shoulder. "Is it okay that I'm here?"

"Of course, honey."

Quinn smiles and nods. "Is Sunny here?"

I mean to tiptoe all the way to my room and then pretend to be asleep, but my feet won't move. For real, they're glued to the hardwood.

"She is. She's just on the—"

Kate sees the empty couch and looks around. I'm not hard to spot, because, as I said, I'm cemented to the floor right near the hallway. Quinn sees me at the same time and does this awkward finger-wiggling wave thing.

"Hi," she says.

I blink at her.

Her shoulders slump.

Kate looks back and forth between the two of us and then clears her throat. "Well... I'll be in my room if you need me, okay?" She squeezes my shoulder and then kisses the top of my head before starting toward her bedroom.

I want to grab on to her and make her stay, but I don't. I just stand there, my heart pounding and my eyes already aching from tears building up. I didn't think it would feel like this to see Quinn again, but it's terrible. Awful. I'm mortified and I'm pretty sure my cheeks are bright red and I'm so, so tired of feeling like this.

Of feeling wrong and weird and like I'll never be good enough for anyone.

"What're you doing here?" I ask. It comes out sharper than I meant it to, but then again, maybe it comes out exactly the way it should.

Quinn takes a couple more steps into the living room. "I heard you were in the hospital. Are you okay?"

"I'm fine."

"I heard about Lena too. That she, well, you know..."

"Has a whole new family?"

Quinn winces and looks at me all sad. I hate it.

"How did you hear that?" I ask.

She shrugs. "Small town, I guess."

"Great. That's just great."

"That must've been hard. Finding out that she—"

"Look, I really don't want to talk about this." And I really, really don't want to talk about it with a girl I tried to kiss. My cheeks go all warm just thinking about it. I want to dive under my bedcovers and never come out.

Quinn frowns but nods. "I came by because I wanted to show you something. Is that okay?"

"I guess."

She walks over to the couch and sits down, setting her bag at her feet. I don't budge. Instead, I lean against the doorframe, still halfway in the hall. She watches me for a couple of seconds, but then I guess she figures out that I'm not moving.

"Okay, well..." she says, and opens up her bag. "I just...I wanted to show you..." She gulps some more air and stares into her bag. "Look, I'm really nervous. I'm worried you'll be mad and I know I already messed everything up."

Her voice is all trembly and soft and it makes me take a tiny step closer. Just a little one.

"Anyway," she says. "Okay, here goes." Then she digs into her bag and pulls out a clear soda bottle with a cork stuffed into the top.

It has a piece of rolled-up paper inside.

My heart just about pops out the top of my head. Before I can think, I'm across the room and on the couch, sitting right next to her. I take the bottle in my hands and turn it this way and that. I can see my handwriting peeking through a corner on the paper inside, written in dark purple ink.

It's my thank-you poem to my heart donor, the one I sent out into the ocean my first day back on the beach.

"What...where did you find this?" I ask.

"On the beach down by our cottage."

"When?"

"The day after we met."

326

"Did you... did you read it?"

She smiles a little and nods. "Yeah. I figured, it's a message in a bottle and it's supposed to be read, right? I've never found one and I thought it was amazing. So, yeah, I read it. I didn't know it was you, though. I promise, I didn't."

"How do you know it's me now?"

She swallows so hard I hear the gulp. "After I found out about your heart transplant, I wondered, because of what the poem talks about. But then... well, I found another one."

My eyes go wide. "You did?"

She dips back into her bag and pulls out a piece of paper. It has writing on it. Familiar writing. So familiar it makes my heart swell into my throat like a balloon. I take it from her and smooth it over my lap.

I woke up smiling
because I fell asleep
with your voice in my ear...

It's the poem I wrote about Quinn after we talked on the phone all night along. At the time, I was just writing about my new best friend, but now, after I tried to kiss her and know that I like like her, my words make my palms sweat.

"I found it that day we went to the pool," Quinn says. My stomach flip-flops, just thinking about being with her under that waterfall. "After you left," she goes on, "I walked around the pier and ended up by that humpback whale statue."

"And you just . . . took it?"

She winces. "I'm sorry. I was climbing up on the whale and I saw a piece of paper sticking out of its mouth. I remembered you'd been standing over there when I got to the pool, so it made me wonder, you know? So I took it out and read it. I figured, if you put it there, you must not mind if someone reads it, right?"

I don't say anything, because, yeah, that's exactly why I put it there. Except I never imagined *someone* would turn out to be Quinn.

"Anyway," she says. "When I got home, I compared it with the poem from the bottle and the handwriting looked the same."

I glue my eyes to the poem, speechless.

"I wanted you to know I found them," she goes on. "Because . . . because I wanted you to know that someone read them. And someone loved them. A lot."

I glance up at her and she's staring right at me. Her eyes are kind of shiny and I try not to feel about her the way I felt about her a few days ago, but I can't help it. It's all still there, swirling in my chest and my gut.

"Okay," I say, and look away from her. Then I scoot away from her a little too.

"There's a couple more," she says, as she pulls out a few more sheets of paper. I spy my handwriting again, scrawled over the ripped-out notebook paper, the poems I wrote after Kate said I couldn't see Lena for a while.

I wish I was a mermaid.
If I lived in the sea, I'd never get out...

"And...and this one," Quinn says, her voice so soft I barely hear her.

"Are you serious?"

She doesn't answer, but dips back into her bag and brings out—

Oh god.

—a bright blue flyer advertising the Fourth of July bonfire tomorrow night.

"I came by your house that morning after we dyed our hair," Quinn says. "I wanted to...I don't know... talk, I guess, but no one was here. Now I know you were in the hospital, but I waited on your porch for a while and I saw something blue stuck in a low branch of that big oak in your front yard. The other ones were in your bushes." She talks really quiet, like she's afraid I might explode.

And I just might.

I take the papers from her, but all I see is that bright blue flyer, my messy handwriting filling up the whole back. I remember writing it—panicked, scared, sad, mad—right after I tried to kiss Quinn and she left.

She left me sitting there all alone.

And then after that, everything else fell apart and now I'm still alone and scared and sad and mad.

"Just go," I manage to say. My fingers tighten on the paper and I'm trying not to lose it. I really am. That would just be the cherry on top, wouldn't it? To start bawling right there in front of the girl I tried to kiss and scared away who's now trying to tell me, all sweet and soft and stuff, that she doesn't like me like that. That she never did, that she never could.

It's too hard to love a broken heart. Lena proved that.

"Sunny," Quinn says. "Please, just let me—"

"Just go!" I yell it this time and silence settles between us. Quinn's breathing hard, but she doesn't move. I wait... wait... and sure enough, Kate pops her head out of her room.

"Everything okay?" she asks.

I take a deep breath to try to get a grip. Then I nod, even though, no, everything is not okay. Everything is falling apart. Everything keeps falling apart.

Kate doesn't say anything, but she doesn't go back in

her room either. Instead, she wanders into the kitchen and starts getting stuff out to make tea.

Quinn is frozen next to me. I steal a glance at her and her cheeks are wet. I look away.

"Okay, I'm sorry," she says quietly, and finally, finally stands up and pulls her bag over her shoulder. I sit there, staring at all the papers left on the couch. I can't look at her. I won't.

"I'm really sorry," she says again. Then she puts a new piece of paper I don't recognize on the coffee table in front of me. It's folded up into a neat square, just like that first note she gave to Dave inviting me to go on the boat with her and her mom. There's nothing but a little drawing of a bright yellow sun on the front.

After that, she leaves and I can finally cry and cry and cry.

CHAPTER 31

Of course. I can't start weeping on the couch without Kate noticing, but she doesn't rush over and yank me into her arms. Well, she does rush over, but then she just sits down next to me and rubs my back, pulling her gentle fingers through my still-blue hair while she waits for me to calm down.

Her eyes roam over the papers, but she doesn't touch them and she doesn't ask. I'm glad. I wouldn't know what to tell her anyway. I mean, I'm sure eventually, I would've told her that I think about girls sometimes, the way most girls only think about boys. But I was going to tell—

I was going to tell Lena first.

The thought brings on a fresh wave of tears. For the first time ever, I really feel like a motherless kid. Before Lena showed up, I hardly ever thought of myself like that because I had Kate. Because Lena was just some picture that I looked at every night. She wasn't real. But deep down, way deep down, I know that I missed her. I missed Lena, even though I barely remembered her, and I was so, so mad at her.

But now I can't go back to not remembering her. I can't go back to pretending everything is the way it was before I got my new heart.

It's not.

I'm different. I'm not motherless. I never was, because I've always had Kate. And now I've got Lena *and* Kate. And even though I love Kate a ton and would never, ever want to be without her, there's all this...this...Lena stuff in my heart now and I don't know what to do with it. Everything is messy and tangled up, and now there's a sister in there who I can't stop thinking about. I keep seeing her wild black hair and her eyes that look just like mine and I keep wondering what it would be like to hold her and read her a little board book and say things like *My sister is so funny. My sister is the cutest thing.* Even something like *My sister is so annoying* sounds amazing, because I never thought I'd ever get to say anything like that.

Sunshine and Samaira.

Samaira and Sunshine.

Kate keeps on rubbing my back, her hand making a soothing *shhh* sound over my tank top. I don't want to talk yet. I can't. So I let myself look over all my poems, all my words. I read over them and slowly, slowly, I get my breath back. Slowly, slowly, my eyes dry up a little.

But my heart keeps on beating.

I gather all the poems in a pile. It hurts to look at them. All of them. It hurts to think of all the other ones I wrote that are still stashed around the island or with some person who'll never know I wrote them. They all make my chest ache.

But.

There's a kind of...calm under all that ache. Like I'm looking at a really pretty painting that makes me feel sad and happy all at once. Because it's all here, right in front of me in my own handwriting.

My thoughts.

My heart.

My story.

My family.

Me.

I don't want to, but I love these poems. I loved writing them and I love reading them right now, even though they scare me. Even though they make me sad. Even though.

Because this is what it was all for.

All that patience and daring.

It was to...live.

And if there's one thing I've learned from knowing

Lena, from wanting to kiss Quinn, from having Margot stomp all over my heart, it's that living is messy.

But it's beautiful too. Like sitting on a surfboard in the calm water while the morning sun streaks the sky orange and pink. Like listening to Dave's super-whiny songs and eating butterscotch pudding. Like dreaming about kissing and love and best friends. Like Kate's hand on my back right now, sure and steady.

I'm not ready to give up the life I write all about. Even if it's messy and weird and even if I'm mad at Lena and even if Quinn doesn't like me. I don't want to go back to Old Life Sunny. Not one bit. This past week has been terrible. I've tried to bury myself in books and movies and hide myself in my little reef of a room, but my heart wants out.

My heart wants to live.

Kate sits quietly while I pick up the soda bottle from the coffee table. I pull out the cork and turn it upside down. It takes me a second to get the paper out, but finally I get hold of a corner and slide it free. Slowly I unroll it and read over the words. Then I read it again and again. I wrote this one so long ago, right after my surgery, I've almost forgotten what it said. And I shouldn't. I can't. I can't ever forget what this poem is all about.

I hand it to Kate. I want to send my poems out into the world, after all. I want someone to read them and love them as much as I do.

She takes the paper from me and spreads it out on top of her legs. I link my arm with hers and lean my head on her shoulder while she reads.

Because of you, I woke up this morning.
Every time it happens, I'm a little surprised.
I lie in bed and feel my heart
thrum-thrum-thrum.
I hear the ocean outside my window
slide across the sand.
I see my room get brighter and brighter
and feel my tiny self turn-turn-turn
with the earth in space.

I like this time of day,
when everything is new
and smells like lemons and salt.
Sometimes, I look at myself
in the mirror and wonder.
I wonder, wonder, wonder,
about all the pretty things my eyes will see
and all the people my mouth will talk to.
I wonder about the music my ears will hear
and the soft, rough, sharp, smooth things
my fingertips will touch.

I wonder about the way my heart
—your heart—
will skip and sing when I see someone I like.
How it will twist and turn when
I let someone read my words for the first
    time.
How it will slow down while I sleep,
steady like a lullaby,
and then gallop like a wild horse
when I run down the beach.

I think about the way my heart
—your heart—
will hurt sometimes.
It'll get scared and sad,
worried and angry,
tired and confused.
But it'll keep going
and I'll wake up the next morning.
When it turns dark and wants to hide,
when it forgets what you gave up
so it could keep me alive,
I'll take it to the ocean—
I'll take us to the ocean—
And I'll show us the sun.

I know when Kate's done reading it, because she lets out this big breath and starts wiping at her eyes, which are leaking all over the place. Then she really does yank me into her arms. I let her. It feels good and, hey, no shame in admitting I'm crying a little now too.

"I love you so much," she says, then pulls back to look at me. "You know that, right?"

"Yeah. I know. I love you too."

She smiles and wipes the tears off my cheeks. "I know you do."

After that, I let her read the poems Quinn found. She cries again. I do too. She squeezes my hand extra hard and then I tell her all about Quinn. About how I like her. About how I think I might like girls and boys and how Margot made me feel when she laughed at me and told all my secrets.

I don't know why I thought I needed to tell Lena first. Kate's my Kate and I'm her Sunny.

"I'm so, so proud of you," she says as she wipes away her tears and mine. "You're so brave and so beautiful. You're my hero."

I cry some more and let her hold me. I let her love me.

Later, when we're both all wrung out, she finds an eight-by-ten picture frame in the hall closet. It's really pretty, all distressed wood painted, of all things, aquamarine. Kate bought it from a local craftsperson at the Port

Hope farmers' market about a year ago, but she never had a picture big enough to fit.

Now she takes the back off and gently fits in my message-in-a-bottle poem. The poem isn't on regular notebook paper. No way. It's on a piece of stationery I got from Kate's desk. It's a light gold color and is textured to look like parchment from the 1700s or something.

When Kate flips the frame back around, my poem on that fancy paper—a little crinkled at the edges from the salty sea and being rolled up for so long—it looks like... art. Real, honest-to-god art.

"Can we hang it in my room?" I ask.

"We can hang it anywhere you want," Kate says.

She grabs a nail and the hammer from a toolbox in the laundry room and before I know it, my words are up on the wall by my window.

On display.

For the whole world to see.

Or maybe not the whole world.

Just my own little corner of it.

It feels weird, looking at my heart up on a wall. But weird is just doing things out of the ordinary. And if there's one thing I'm pretty sure my life is, it's the exact opposite of ordinary.

"What about this?" Kate says when she's put the tools away and I'm just standing in my doorway, looking at my poem. She holds out her hand and in her palm is a square of paper with a little yellow sun on it.

Quinn's letter.

I take it from her, but I don't open it. I already know what it says.

> I'm sorry.
> Can we still be friends?
> I just don't feel that way about you.

And you know, all that's okay. But I'm still not ready to read it.

But I am ready to talk about it. About that...and a whole lot more.

"Kate?" I ask as she curls the strand of white lights around the frame so it lights it up, all white and glow-y.

"Yeah, sweetie?"

I set Quinn's letter on my nightstand and take a deep breath. "Will you go with me to see Lena?"

CHAPTER

32

When we get to East Beach early the next morning, Kate slathers me in some SPF 40,000,000,000 and I let her. After she's done, we sit in the sand and wait. A week ago, I probably would've begged her to leave, but today I don't. I need her here. She's my Kate and I'm her Sunny and no new heart or Lena or wondering about kissing girls is ever going to change that.

"So, the other night…" I start, because now that I'm thinking about kissing girls, I'm thinking about Quinn, and then I start thinking about that little folded-up letter on my nightstand and I need to think of something else.

Something happy.

"Yeah?" Kate asks.

"I saw you kissing Dave."

She makes this weird choking sound in her throat. "You...you what?"

"The night I dyed my hair. You were kissing on the couch."

She covers her face with her hands. "Oh my god."

"It's okay. It's good. Isn't it?"

She peeks at me between her fingers and I can tell she's smiling. "I don't know."

"He loves you a lot."

She sighs and drops her hands. "He does."

"And you love him."

She doesn't say anything.

"Kate."

Nothing.

"Katie."

"Okay, fine, yes. I love him."

"So...keep on kissing, then."

She laughs and nudges me with her shoulder. "We'll see."

"What's to see? Is he a bad kisser?"

"What? No, I just..." She blows out a big breath and gazes out at the sea. The wind whips all over the place, stirring up the waves.

"I don't know, honey," she finally says. "It's just scary. Loving someone that much."

"But you love me that much."

"Yeah, I do. And it's scary sometimes."

"But you still do it. It's worth it, right?"

Tears fill her eyes. "Sunshine. You are worth every minute I've ever spent happy or worried or scared."

"Well...so are you," I say. "Maybe love isn't really love unless it's a little scary."

She wraps her arms around me and I lean my head on her shoulder. This. This right here. No matter what happens with Lena, Kate is my mom. I don't have to call her that for it to be true, and I'll never doubt it again.

We stay like that until I see Lena, her long hair flapping like a flag in the wind, heading toward us from the parking lot.

She brought her surfboard, just like I asked her to. My heart flips and flops in my chest. I'm scared, but maybe that just means that I love...something about being with Lena. Something about knowing this part of myself. And I'm not just scared either. I'm nervous. And super-mad, but it's all okay. I know my heart can take it.

I squeeze Kate's hand and stand up.

"I'll be right here, okay?" she says, and I nod. Then I grab my surfboard—which Kate and I barely managed to stuff into her car earlier—and meet Lena in the sand. She smiles at me, but she looks super-nervous too. She opens her mouth like she's about to say something, but I'm not ready for that, so I just turn and start walking toward the water.

She follows me. We splash into the surf and paddle out together. The sun is getting higher and higher, pushing out all the orange and red and filling the sky with blue. I paddle and paddle until we're deep enough that the waves are calm and we just bob on our boards and look at the sea.

"I'm really mad at you," I finally say.

"I know," she says back. "I'm so sorry, Sunshine. I know I haven't done much to earn your trust, so I can't even beg you to believe me, but I do want you to know that I was going to tell you about Janesh and Samaira. They're your family too. But I had to take things slow. For me. And for you and Samaira. And, yeah, I was really scared. I didn't want you to feel like—"

"Like you replaced me and didn't want me?"

Her shoulders droop and her sad eyes get even sadder. "Yeah."

"Well, I felt like that anyway."

Her bottom lip wobbles a little, but she keeps looking me right in the eye, amber to amber. "I know, baby. But that's not what happened."

"How do I know that? You left me and got a whole new family."

She swallows over and over. "I know that's how it

looks, but I never wanted her instead of you. I wanted you both."

My chest gets all tight, but my heart pushes me forward. "Then...why? Why can you be a mom to Samaira and not me?"

She sighs and rubs her forehead; then she looks out at the water, the sky. "I want to be. I want to be a mom to both of you. That's why I came here, honey. That's why Janesh agreed to move here too. To be a family. When I got pregnant with Samaira, I'd been sober for over two and half years. And as soon as I found out, I thought of you. You were my first thought."

"Really?"

"Really. I wanted you back so badly. I had for a long time, but I had to make sure I wouldn't ruin your life again. I had to make sure I was who you need me to be. And when I got here and you agreed to see me, part of me...well, part of me just wanted you to myself, honestly. It was selfish, but I'd missed everything, you know? Eight whole years, and I just wanted some time where it was just you and me getting to know each other. So I kept putting off telling you. Janesh said I shouldn't and I know he was right, but I was enjoying my time with you so much. I was scared to lose it."

I don't say anything for a few seconds, because my heart is all balled up in my throat. I swirl my legs in the water and feel the whole big sea underneath me and think about all that stuff I read in Lena's journal. Stuff she wrote months and months ago. She's a good writer—maybe that's where I get all these words packed into my head that just have to get on paper—and I can *feel* all of what she's saying in what she wrote. I could feel that she wanted to be with me. I could feel that she was scared. I could feel how much she loved S. And even though S wasn't me, Lena did write about me. She wrote about me all the time and I could feel that she loved me. That she was sorry. Journals don't lie. There's no reason to lie in something no one's supposed to see.

"I took your journal," I say, real, real quiet.

She doesn't say anything for a second and I can't look at her. Finally, I hear her exhale super-loud. "I wondered where that went."

"I'm sorry. I found it in your car and I...I just...I wanted to know who you were, I guess."

She sighs. "I get it. And I wasn't telling you the whole truth, so I can't really blame you for that."

I peek at her. She's watching me with soft, soft eyes. "I'll give it back."

"I'd appreciate that, thank you."

For some reason, it makes me sad, thinking about not having her journal to read.

"I used to pretend you were a mermaid," I say.

She tilts her head at me. "I remember that's what you called me that day in your hospital room. Your mermaid."

I nod. "I'd think about you and how, if you were a mermaid, I understood why I wasn't in your life. You were way far away and I kind of liked that, you know? That it was impossible for us to be together. I thought I didn't care that I couldn't talk to you or see you."

She sighs. "I'm sorry, baby girl. I don't think you can ever know how much. But I promise you that I'm here now. I'm not going anywhere. Janesh has a job teaching world history at Port Hope High School. I'm teaching music. I'm looking into preschools for Samaira when the time comes. I understand if you need time. I get it. But I want you to know that I love you more than anything and I am not going away this time. I won't. So you can be in my life, anytime you want. Or not. Whatever you want."

I think about all my poems sitting on my desk at home, about my poem in the frame up on my wall like a painting. My story. All the broken pieces, old heart and new. I know that's what I want. I want my family, as weird as it is.

"When's Samaira's birthday?" I ask.

Her eyes go a little wide for a second, and then she smiles. "January third. She turned six months yesterday."

"What's her name mean?"

Her smile gets bigger. "It's a Hindu name. Janesh's grandmother was named Samaira."

"It's pretty. She's pretty."

"She looks like you."

I try to fight a smile, but I think I fail. "A little."

"A lot. Janesh said he couldn't believe how much."

"Really?"

She nods.

"Is your last name different now?"

Her smile is soft. "No. I kept St. James when Janesh and I got married."

I can't keep the smile off my face when she says that. I was worried that her new family was totally separate from me, that I was the only mermaid in the whole sea. But really, we're all mixed up together, past and present and future.

"So, did you and Janesh have an epic first kiss?" I ask.

She throws her head back and laughs, then looks at me, her eyes crinkling. "It was actually very quiet and lovely. We'd been dating about a month and we were at a playground after dinner. He was pushing me on the swings and then he kissed me. Just like that."

"You'd been dating a whole month before you kissed?"

"I'm a slow mover."

"Not as slow as Kate."

She cracks up at that. "Poor Dave."

"Well, not so poor anymore."

She lifts her eyebrows and grins. "Really?"

"It's so happening."

She laughs and I laugh and this feels right. It doesn't feel easy. But it feels right, like this is exactly where I'm supposed to be right now. I'm still mad at her, I think. But she's still Lena. She's still a lady who I think is cool and brave and who makes me want to try awesome and amazing things. She's a lady who makes me really feel all that stuff I wrote in the poem I put in the bottle for my donor.

She makes me feel like I'm Sunny St. James. And part of being me is having Lena as my bio mom and Kate as my found mom. I'm a mess of Kates and Lenas. A good mess. A beautiful mess.

I smile at the water, thinking that'd be a really amazing poem.

Open me up and this is what you'll see:
A tangle of old hearts and new.
A mess of moms and daughters

and blood and water,
mermaid tails and flesh and bone.

"So, speaking of kissing..." I say, and then bite my lip, my chest aching. The water bobs me up and down, like it's trying to soothe me, but when it comes to Quinn, I'm a mess. And not the beautiful one from that poem either.

"Ah, the Kissing Quest," Lena says, paddling forward a little to fight the tide. "Please tell me you and Quinn finally kissed."

I nearly swallow my tongue. "What... why... wait, huh?"

She laughs long and loud. "Oh, honey. It's so obvious you like her so much."

I blink at her for a long time, trying to breathe normally. I've wanted to tell Lena that I like Quinn, and I've already told Kate, but now Lena's saying she already knew. I feel exposed, like my chest got cracked open all over again. She must notice that I'm freaking out a little because she reaches out and tucks a strand of wet hair behind my ear.

"Sunny, it's okay."

Her touch is soft and sweet and I feel myself relax. She smiles at me and tells me again that it's okay.

My heart slows down, calm and steady. "You could tell that I like her?"

Lena nods. "And that she likes you."

My eyes just about bust out of my face. "She doesn't, trust me."

"Did she tell you that?"

"No," I say. "But, wait, how did you know I like her?"

She shrugs, but her eyes get all shiny-looking. "I guess it was a feeling. The way you'd talk about her. The way you'd always blush a little and get all quiet after saying her name."

"I did not."

"You did. The same way she was always biting her lip and smiling this little smile whenever you talked to her that day we dyed your hair. She couldn't keep her eyes off you, you know."

"But... but I tried to... well, I tried to kiss her and she wouldn't."

Lena nods. "Well, I can't guarantee that I'm right, but there are a lot of reasons why she might've gotten scared. Two girls feeling like you do. The world isn't always kind, is it?"

My eyes sting and I look down at my board, swirling my hand in the water.

"But the world is wrong, Sunny," she says. "It's okay to like Quinn. To like anyone you want to. You know that, right?"

A few tears blur my vision. That night at Margot's slumber party fills my brain all over again. But after hearing Kate call me brave and listening to Lena say it's okay, after feeling for a while that maybe I was a little brave and that it was okay, that night doesn't fill my heart anymore.

Then I tell Lena everything I told Kate. I tell her about that slumber party and about the girls laughing at me. I tell her about me freaking out under the waterfall with Quinn. I tell her about the poems I wrote and how Quinn found them, almost every single one. And I tell her about that letter Quinn left me that I still haven't read.

By the time I finish, we've floated so far down the beach, I can barely see Kate in the distance, sitting on the beach reading a book.

"I think you should read her letter," Lena says. "Even if it hurts. Even if she says she can't like you like that. She's still your best friend, right?"

I nod and wipe at my face. "I just really, really like her."

"I know, honey. And if she doesn't like you back, it'll hurt for a while, but there will be other girls. Or boys. Or whoever. And if Quinn stays here on the island, I think she'd be a wonderful friend to go through all those crushes with, don't you think?"

"Better than Margot, that's for sure."

Lena smiles a sad smile but doesn't say anything. I take

a big breath and look behind us to where the waves are gathering and breaking.

"Can I meet Samaira later? I mean, officially?" I ask.

Lena reaches out and takes my hand. "I want that more than anything."

We smile at each other for a few long seconds, our hands dangling over the deep blue sea.

"But first," I say, "let's surf."

CHAPTER
33

On the way home. I stare at the pines and palms blurring out the window. I keep folding up my legs crisscross and then pulling my knees to my chest while I sigh a whole bunch. I'm tired from surfing, but I can't stop fidgeting.

"You okay?" Kate asks as she turns onto Juniper Island Road. The ocean blinks in and out of the trees, an aqua jewel in between all the green.

"Yeah," I say. And I am. Surfing was amazing. I rode two whole waves. I'm pretty sure Kate was freaking out the whole time, but she clapped her hands over her head, cheering my name as she watched me from the shore.

And Lena—well, I'm still mad at her. I'm still kind of hurt. But I think you can be all those things and still love someone a whole lot.

I let my feet flop back to the floor.

"Can you stop by Margot's?" I ask.

Kate slows the car and side-eyes me. "You sure?"

I bite my lip, really thinking through Kate's question. I don't really want to see Margot. I don't want to be in her house or in her room and I sure don't want to hear anything Margot might have to say to me.

But.

I've got some things to say to her and I think I've got the perfect way to say them.

"I'm sure," I say. Then I pop open Kate's glove box, which is full of tiny packs of tissues in neat stacks and cleaning wipes made especially for car interiors. There's also a little spiral-bound notebook, a pen hooked to its red cover.

Kate turns into Seaside Cove, the tiny subdivision filled with pastel beach houses where Margot lives. The street is so familiar, all palmettos and tabby driveways. I take a deep breath and open up the notebook. I slip the pen free, flip past some grocery lists Kate forgot to rip out, and start writing.

I don't remember a me without you.

I learned to swim
holding your hand,
the ocean wild and wide and scary.

We slept under the sky
and hid our wishes in the stars.
We built forts
with blankets and pillows,
a safe place for all our secrets.
Then my heart broke
and you couldn't
put it back together.
You blew out the stars
and tore down the fort
and scattered my secrets
into the sky.

I don't remember a me without you.

But I have learned
to swim on my own,
the ocean wild and wide and scary.

By the time I'm done, we're parked outside Margot's house. I look up, blinking into the bright sun, and Kate tucks a strand of blue hair behind my ear. I stare out the window for a second, taking in Margot's pale green house, the same big hammock in the front yard where we used to spend summer afternoons, loaded down with books and snacks.

In the front window, a curtain moves. I just about chicken out, but then I look down at my poem again. I reread it while Kate rubs my back. My words. My story.

My truth.

I rip my poem out of the notebook and unfasten my seat belt. Outside, a lawn mower hums across the street and the salty breeze rustles the palms. I jog up to Margot's porch and slip my poem through the brass mail slot in her front door.

I ring the doorbell.

I make sure I hear the sound of Margot's feet bounding down the stairs.

Then I turn and walk away.

CHAPTER
34

I cry the whole way home.

But it's an okay cry. The kind that means I'm finally good and empty of all that junk that made me feel so bad. The kind that means I've finally got room to make new memories, new friends.

After lunch, Kate suggests I take a nap. I don't fight her. I'm totally wrung out and I sleep most of the afternoon. When I wake up, though, I can't stop looking at Quinn's letter. I keep picking it up and turning it around in my hands. I take it in the bathroom with me when I take a shower, just to see if it's still there when I get out, if it's really real.

It is.

Right before dinner, Dave comes over. He hugs me for

a long time and I let him, Quinn's letter tucked into my palm. Then we sit down on the porch swing and rock back and forth while Kate gets ready for the Fourth of July bonfire. She and Dave are going as a date, which is pretty much the cutest thing ever.

Kate said I could go too, but I'm not sure I'm up for it. I don't have a best friend to go with, and sorry, but being Kate and Dave's third wheel on their first real date after it's taken them a bajillion years to get together? No thanks.

Plus, I'm meeting Samaira tomorrow, officially, which makes me all nervous and excited at the same time. I kind of just want to stay home and write her a poem. I want to write a bunch of poems about a bunch of things.

"Penny for your thoughts, kiddo," Dave says, kicking his feet on the porch so we keep swinging.

I shrug. Quinn's letter feels like a heavy stone in my hand. Dave doesn't push me to talk and I'm glad. I need all my brainpower to think. And what I keep thinking about is my New Life plan. How I've done lots of awesome amazing things since getting my new heart.

I think about how I found and lost a best friend.

I think about how my Kissing Quest has been one epic fail, but at least I tried.

I think about how it felt when I read that book with the girls kissing for the first time all those months ago and how it was scary to read that, but amazing too. I think about all that Quinn and I have done in just a couple of weeks and I...I...

I miss her.

I still want to kiss her, I think, but I want to be her friend even more.

"Will you sing me my favorite song?" I ask Dave.

He laughs. "Now? I don't even have my guitar."

"So? Your voice is nice enough to sing without it."

"Oh, well, thank you."

"Just make it super-whiny, please."

He cracks up again and puts his arm around my shoulders. "All the whine for you, Sunshine."

Then he starts to sing the kissing song, really soft and low, and I listen and get all achy in my chest, like I'm full of a bunch of sighs I need to let loose.

I turn Quinn's letter around and around in my hands, finally unfolding one corner of the paper. Then another. Then the third and then the fourth and soon the letter's wide open and I'm staring down at Quinn's curvy handwriting.

Dear Sunny,

There's a whole lot of stuff I want to say right now, but the most important thing is that I'm sorry. I'm so, so sorry. I don't know what happened that night in your room. I think I got scared. I think I freaked out that someone might actually like me back. I never knew that might be just as scary as having someone reject you, but I think it is. Because what if I move away? And what if you stop liking me one day? And what if you think you like girls but then meet some boy you like better? And what if people make fun of us when they see us hold hands?

But then I think about your poems and I wonder if we could be scared together? Maybe being scared is just part of liking someone, no matter who it is. And I want to be brave. I want to be brave and mighty and strong, just like Sunny St. James.

Will you meet me at the Fourth of July bonfire? If not, I understand. And if you just want to be friends, I get that too. You're my BFF no matter what.

I hope I see you soon.

Love,

Quinn

PS My mom's going to work at the aquarium!

Dave finishes the song and I finish the letter and my heart is a firework. It's a million sparklers lit at the same time and tossed into the air.

I peer up at the sky. It's already mostly dark, the last bits of sunset pink disappearing on the horizon. I sit up and fold the letter super-quick and super-messy.

"I've got to go," I say, stuffing the letter into my pocket.

"Everything okay?" Dave asks.

"Yeah, yeah, but I've got to go to the bonfire now." I yank the elastic out of my hair and run my fingers through all the blue knots. Did I put on deodorant after my shower? Did I brush my teeth this morning? I run back into the house and into my room to change, but then I see myself in the mirror. I've got on a plain navy tank top and cutoff shorts and you know what? That's me. That's been me the whole time. *Old Life* Sunny all mixed up with the new.

I pull on my black stomping boots and run back outside.

Kate's on the porch by then, slipping on her sandals while balancing with one hand on Dave's shoulder. "What's going on?"

"I've got to go to the bonfire," I say again, starting down the porch steps. Bike. Where's my bike?

"We're about to leave, honey," she says. "You can walk over with us."

"No, I need to go like *now*." I can't walk either. I need to run. Fly. Teleport.

I find Kate's bike leaning against the front porch. I had left it at Lena's house, of course, but she dropped it off this morning after we surfed. Now I toss my leg over it and start pedaling.

"Sunny, wait a second!" Kate says.

I skid to a stop and turn back to look at her. She's halfway down the porch steps, worry all over her face.

"I'll be at the bonfire," I say. "I'll be with Quinn, okay?"

Her brow wrinkles up, but only for a second. She and Dave share a look. He kisses her forehead and she nod-nod-nods before walking over to me and pulling me into her arms.

"I'm okay," I whisper into her shoulder.

"I know you are," she whispers back. "You're amazing."

Then she lets me go, her eyes all shiny. "Have fun, okay?"

Fun. Fun is such a little bitty tiny word.

Because if Quinn's letter is really real, if I didn't hallucinate it or something like that, I'm not going to have fun.

I'm going to change my whole world.

CHAPTER

35

I run across the sand in my boots. There are so many people here, all of them laughing and smiling while the sky goes from dark blue to black. I bump into a lot of them. Some yell out, annoyed, and some call my name, wanting me to stop, probably so they can marvel at the fact that I'm running across the sand in my boots like my life depends on it.

It's been a long time since Juniper Island saw Sunny St. James run.

I don't stop, though. I have a mission, the most important mission of my life, maybe.

Okay, not my life. I get that kissing the girl you like does not equal life. You don't die on an operating table, come back with a whole new heart, and get to know your long-lost mermaid mom without learning a little about what life and death really mean. Still, this is a big deal. Liking Quinn is a big, awesome, amazing deal and I sure am going to act like it.

It's getting darker and darker. Any minute, the fireworks will start, and I have to find Quinn before that.

There are a lot more people here than there were even a few minutes ago. The beach is packed, bodies everywhere, all of them loud and laughing, all of them with friends or girlfriends or boyfriends or partners.

Everyone but me.

Margot's here too, over by the volleyball net. She's with her swim team friends. When I catch her eyes, she lifts her hand to wave, but she doesn't smile. Right then, I know she read my poem. Not only read it, but *got* it.

For a few seconds, I let myself feel a little sad. Because there's no Margot and me anymore.

But then I count to three, take a deep breath, and move my feet through the sand. I keep moving, moving, moving, because my *New Life* is waiting.

At least, I hope she is.

I peer through all the people for purple anything, but all I see is a bunch of lavender bikini tops and lilac T-shirts and periwinkle cover-ups.

"Quinn?" I call out, but way too soft, because tears rise in my throat like a flood. I shove them back down, ready to go home and lick my wounds in private. Maybe call Lena and see if she wants to come over. Maybe she can bring Samaira and we can roast our own marshmallows in the fire pit out back. We can have a girls' night and talk about the woes of love. Of course, Samaira's too young to woe and Lena is all happy with Janesh, so really, I'll be the only one woe-ing. But that's okay. That's what you're supposed to be able to do with your family.

I'm already heading south when I finally, finally see her. Right there at the edge of the fire, sitting on a big piece of driftwood, is a girl with lavender hair and a white tank top dotted with a bunch of little—

I squint through the growing dark, just to make sure I'm seeing things right.

And I am. Quinn's tank top is covered in tiny yellow suns. She's looking down, trying to work a burnt-to-a-crisp marshmallow between a pair of graham crackers.

I walk over to her, my heart fluttering as fast as a hummingbird's wings.

"Hi," I say when I reach her. Or try to. My voice is suddenly all squeaky and, with all the partying going on, gets swallowed right up.

"Hi," I say louder.

Her head pops up and she drops her burnt marshmallow in the sand.

"Sorry," I say, bending down to pick it up, which gives me a second to catch my breath, my thoughts, my heart. I inspect the marshmallow and it's so charred, there's nothing sticky left for the sand to stick to, so I hand it back to her, totally edible.

Well, edible if you like lumps of coal in your S'mores.

"Hi," she says, standing up. "You're . . . you're here."

I press my fingertips to my heart, telling it to calm down. "You're here too."

"Did you come with Kate?"

I shake my head.

"Lena?"

I smile. "No. Although I have a *lot* to tell you about all that."

"You do?"

I nod again. "If you want to hear it, I mean."

"I do. Every word."

"And I want to hear about your mom's job. Does that mean you're staying?"

She grins and the fire dances in her eyes and she's so, so pretty.

"I'm staying," she says. "My mom's going part-time with *National Geographic*, so she'll still travel some, but only a few times a year and mostly in the summer. I get to go to your school. Maybe even high school. I get to . . . I don't know. See people so much I get sick of them."

"Except me. You'd never get sick of me."

"Never."

We smile at each other and the world feels soft and floaty, like I'm looking at everything from under the blue sea.

It's not a bad place to be.

"So you read my letter, huh?" she asks.

I take a step closer to her. "Yeah."

She presses her hand to her stomach and takes a deep breath. She's super-nervous. But so am I.

"We can be scared together," I say, taking another little step.

"We can?" Her voice sounds shaky.

"Yeah. I mean, if you want."

"I do. I really do."

I nod. Another step. "You know what I was thinking about earlier?"

"What?" She steps closer to me now. We're so close, our knees would bump together if I bent mine even a little.

"Our Kissing Quest."

She smiles and looks down at her feet. "Yeah. Me too."

"I mean, we wanted to find someone we liked, right?"

"Yeah."

"Have you . . . have you found someone?"

She glances at me. She knows I like her. I tried to kiss her. I really, really obviously tried to kiss her. But her letter didn't come right out and say she liked me. And call me a hopeless romantic—because I totally am one—but I really, really want to hear her say it.

"I totally have," she says.

My heart leaps, skips, and gallops, does a few cartwheels and somersaults. It's so happy right now.

"Want to go for a walk?" I ask.

Quinn's eyes go wide, but she nods. I hold out my hand. She looks at it for a moment, then glances over my shoulder. I know who she sees—a bunch of kids our age over by the volleyball net, including Margot and Eliza and all the swim team girls, who might definitely see us if we held hands.

The whole town might see us, for all I know. I think I might be shaking, because it is scary, but I keep my hand out and let her make the decision.

Finally, after what feels like a billion years of me holding my breath, she presses her palm to mine and tangles our fingers up, lacing them together super-tight. It's most definitely a girlfriend kind of handholding.

Quinn drops her S'more in the sand and we start walking next to the water. My heart pounds and we don't say much. Her palm is sweaty and I'm super-glad because that means she's nervous too. We're doing all this together.

Fireworks start to explode over the sky, blooming all sort of colors and shapes. The ocean rushes to meet our feet, then runs away, a gentle, happy dance. After a few minutes of silent, perfect walking, the finale starts up. Quinn and I stop, turning toward the water so we can watch the sky fill with color and light. She squeezes my hand and I squeeze back. Then she turns toward me and I turn toward her. It's just like I pictured it would be. She's so pretty and she's looking at me, smiling at me, and my heart is thrum-thrum-thrumming, strong and mighty and sure.

"Hey, Quinn?"

Her fingers tighten on mine. "Yeah?"

I swallow a whole bunch of times, my heart a sparkler in my chest.

"Can I kiss you?" I finally manage to ask.

She inhales a shaky breath and nods. So I take a step closer and she takes a step closer. I squeeze her hand and she swipes her thumb over my cheek and we both start giggling. But soon we stop giggling, and our foreheads touch and our noses bump, and then... well...

Step Three: Completed.

But really, I know my New Life is just beginning.

Acknowledgments

I know authors aren't supposed to pick favorites...and I'm not. But let's just say that Sunny swept in and stole my heart, and I'm forever grateful to those who helped me in the process of bringing her to life.

Infinite thanks to Rebecca Podos, who is my amazing, talented, empathetic, empowering agent. I could not have dreamed up a better champion.

Thanks to my editor Kheryn Callender, who loved Sunny just as much as I did and chipped away at this story with a beautifully deft hand. Thank you, Nikki Garcia, for reading early and checking in on Quinn, and for your excitement on seeing Sunny and me through to the end. Which I hope is only the beginning.

Thank you, Megan Tingley, Alvina Ling, Victoria Stapleton, Michelle Campbell, Christie Michel, Siena Koncsol, and everyone at Little, Brown Books for Young Readers, who not only created a warm, welcoming home for

Sunny (and Ivy), but poured their own hearts and souls into these girls, lifting them up so others could find them. Your support and confidence mean so much.

So many thanks to Sasha Illingworth and Angela Taldone for the breathtaking cover design and for bringing Sunny's very heart to life. And to Good Wives and Warriors for the stunning artwork. I think this cover is my favorite yet, and I honestly can't look at it without smiling.

Thank you, Jen Graham, for your careful and thorough copyediting. You're a miracle worker.

To my Nashville crew, I would not be who I am without you. Thank you, Lauren Thoman, Paige Crutcher, Courtney Stevens, Alisha Klapheke, Kristin O'Donnell Tubb, Erica Rodgers, Carla Schooler, Sarah Brown, and Christa Lafontaine, for all the miraculous ways you love.

As always, abundant thanks to everyone at Parnassus Books and Stephanie Appell, for your constant advocacy, excitement, and support for books for all ages.

Huge thanks to Katie, Kellie, Emily, Kay Kay, Jayme, and Hope for seeing me through my first full year of teaching while writing. You made me a better teacher and a better person, and this book wouldn't be half as coherent without your support during the school day.

Thanks to Craig, Benjamin, and William, who have

once again shown me patience, excitement, and love through another book.

Finally, thank you, dear reader, for entrusting me with your time, imagination, and heart. I hope Sunny helps you see just how mighty you really are.

Turn the page for a preview of

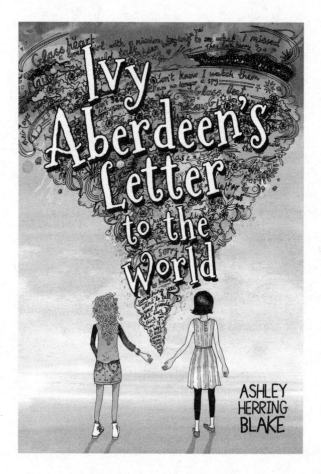

AVAILABLE NOW

⤙⤙◆⤚⤚

CHAPTER ONE

Stormy

A storm was coming, which was perfect.

Thunder rumbled through the night, rattling Ivy Aberdeen's bedroom windows and making a beautiful racket. She smiled and counted, only making it to two before lightning washed her room white. Ivy didn't know why people colored bolts of lightning yellow in drawings. They were silvery blue and made her think of whispers and magic, the perfect setting for what Ivy was about to do.

She adjusted the headlamp around her forehead, the thick elastic band pulling at her hair. On her nightstand, her clock glowed green, the numbers already inching toward the time she had to get up for school, but she had a good hour at least. She rubbed the sleep from her eyes, and the tiny headlamp shined a yellow circle onto the notebook in her lap. She called it a notebook because there wasn't a better word for it. She could call it a *journal*, but that didn't feel right either. The book was more like a portable, papery hope chest.

Mom stored Ivy's great-grandmother's hope chest up here in the attic, which became Ivy's room a few months ago so the twins could have their own space. It sat at the end of her bed and smelled like cedar and old stuff. Inside, ancient pictures and clothes and knick-knacks were tucked away like secrets. There was even an old wedding dress in there, which Ivy thought was sort of creepy. When she asked about it, her mom told her that way back when, a hope chest was where a girl collected things she would need when she got married, *hoping* for the right boy to come along so her real life could start. Then her mother went on and on about how marriage had nothing to do with a girl's real life and how Ivy should hope for lots of different things, not just a boy, which was a relief.

She kept her real dreams in a notebook, where everything was a complete secret. Her hope chest was securely hidden away and guarded.

Ivy aimed the headlamp's beam at the purple-and-white cover of her notebook. It was one of those Decom-position notebooks, and she got it from her language arts teacher at school. She liked thinking about her notebook like that—*decomposition*. That's what it felt like to her, anyway: taking things apart in her head and putting them down on paper so she could figure out how they worked.

Outside, the thunder and lightning snapped right alongside each other, perfect secret drawing weather. Ivy flipped through the crinkly pages and caught a glimpse of a drawing she'd abandoned a few months ago as a hopeless case. She narrowed her eyes and glared at her family sitting on the grass in a large field. The grass in this field wasn't green, it was sil-ver and pink with a border of blue-leafed trees. There were Mom and Dad, their eyes shining and their mouths happy, holding Ivy's new twin brothers, Aaron and Evan, in their arms. Her sixteen-year-old sister, Layla, was right where she should be—sitting between their parents, grinning at Evan while Aaron wrapped his tiny hand around her finger.

Ivy scanned the page for inspiration. There was one person missing from this family portrait, and she couldn't figure out where to put her.

Where to put *Ivy*.

She glowered at the picture and flicked the page over so hard, it tore right out of the notebook. She nearly balled it up and tossed it toward her garbage can, which was already overflowing with other drawings gone awry. But it felt weird to throw away a picture of her family, even if she wasn't in it. Instead, she folded it up and stuffed it into her swirly blue pillowcase.

It wasn't the picture for a night like this anyway. This night needed one of her stormy pictures, like the one she was so close to showing Layla just a couple of weeks ago. The one she wouldn't ever, ever show her now.

She found the most recent drawing she'd been working on. There were dozens just like it in her notebook. Each one had some sort of house snuggled up in the branches of blue trees, trees on fire, trees made of gold, trees under the ocean, and trees at the tippy top of the highest mountain.

All of them had a girl with curly hair inside the house...and she wasn't alone. Another girl was in there with her. Sometimes they were standing, looking out at flame-colored hills in the distance. Sometimes they were lying down, tucked into sleeping bags that glowed because they were covered with tiny fireflies, like a hundred little night-lights. Sometimes they were reading or, like this one, facing each other and smiling.

Ivy didn't know who the girl was, but she wasn't Layla, and she wasn't her best friend, Taryn, or any of the other girls at school, who lately only wanted to talk about boys. Ivy was twelve years old and had never had a crush on a boy before, but maybe she just hadn't met one she liked. Or maybe she couldn't even get crushes.

That was her: Uncrushable Ivy.

But that didn't feel right either, so really, Ivy had no idea what she thought about crushes at all.

Which was exactly why the thunder outside was perfect for this picture. When Ivy looked at it, she felt a storm in her stomach. She felt a storm in her head. She felt a storm fizzing into her fingertips and toes.

Because in every single picture Ivy drew, she and that girl were holding hands. And they weren't holding hands like she and Layla used to hold hands when they ran down the street to play in the park. It wasn't the way she and Taryn used to hold hands when they ran through the sprinkler in Ivy's backyard, before Taryn got too cool to run through sprinklers and Ivy told her she was too cool for sprinklers too.

Ivy stared at the picture, chewing on her lower lip. Maybe she should rip them all out, starting with this one. She liked storms, but storms could be dangerous. And if Ivy had shown one of her stormy pictures to Layla, maybe her sister would've looked at her like she was weird.

She should definitely rip them all out.

Her hands shook as she closed her fingers around the top edge of the paper, ready to tear.

But she couldn't do it. Her hand wouldn't move that way. Instead, she swallowed the giant balloon in her throat and picked up her indigo-blue brush pen. While the real rain lashed at her window, she slipped some inky rain in between the drawn branches and leaves. She used her arctic-blue pen to zigzag in some lightning. She filled the sky with rolling silver clouds.

Before she could change her mind, Ivy colored in the girls. She used her lightest pink marker for her own hair, the color of sweet and fluffy cotton candy. In real life, Ivy's hair was strawberry blond, with frizzy curls her mother used to braid into smooth plaits. Lately, Mom never had time to do that, and Ivy certainly didn't want Layla to do it, so now her hair was a coiling mane of wildness all the time. But in Ivy's notebook, her hair was a soft and pretty pink, her curls always silky.

Ivy gave the other girl dark hair, the color of a raven's sleek feathers. She had dark eyes too—so dark blue they nearly matched the chaos of the sky. Both girls were happy inside that treehouse, their secret small and safe. Ivy wished she was there right now. It sounded like a wild adventure, sitting in that treehouse while the sky fell down around them.

Color filled up the page, and when Ivy was done, she sat back against her pillows. Her heart galloped in her chest, and she was out of breath like she'd just finished the mile run at school. It felt like the whole sky was inside her body, but she liked her picture.

She might have even loved it.

That was when she noticed how quiet it was outside.

Not the storm-was-over kind of quiet. A creepy kind of quiet. The kind of quiet that made all the tiny hairs on her arms stick straight up.

Then a few things happened at once.

One: The storm sirens in town went off, slicing through the quiet like an angry ghost.

Two: Ivy's bedroom door flew open, and her dad stumbled in, his eyes the size of dinner plates as the beam from her headlamp hit him in the face. She slapped her notebook shut.

"Ivy, let's go, honey." He held out his hand, and his voice was calm like it was when he told her she had to get three teeth pulled at the dentist last year. Which is to say, not very calm at all. Fake calm.

"What—"

"There's a tornado nearby, sweetie, no time to talk. We need to get to the storm cellar."

She kicked off her comforter and stuffed her notebook into her pillowcase, hugging it to her chest. She yanked off her headlamp just as Dad crossed the tiny room in two strides and grabbed her by the arm. Not hard enough to hurt, but hard enough to scare her. He pulled her toward the door just as the freakiest sound Ivy had ever heard loomed over the siren.

It sounded like a train. It grew louder and louder, a locomotive that couldn't possibly exist out here in her family's little part of rural Georgia.

Just as Ivy and her dad reached the top of the narrow attic stairs, a third thing happened.

Ivy's window exploded, spraying glass all over her bed and bringing the sky with it.

~«‹•›»~

Chapter Two

Torn Away

Ivy's father never cursed, so when every bad word in the book flew out of his mouth, panic rose in Ivy's throat. She whimpered like a scared animal and nearly tripped over a pile of old clothes.

On her bed, her headlamp was still switched on, its light glinting off the glass scattered over her ruined sky-blue comforter. Her gauzy curtains were torn, wrapped around twigs and green-leafed branches. She got one last look at the mess before Dad yanked her in front of him and propelled her down the stairs to the second floor.

"Daniel!" Ivy's mother screamed her dad's name from the first floor. She sounded more scared than Ivy had ever heard her.

"Almost there, Elise!" Dad yelled.

Her dad was a big man, and he swooped Ivy into his arms, balancing her on his hip down the next flight of stairs.

Mom and Layla waited at the bottom of the staircase near the front door. Mom had Evan strapped to her chest in the baby carrier and Aaron wrapped in a soft yellow blanket in her arms. Layla gripped the baby bag, onesies and diapers overflowing. Everyone was breathing hard, and Aaron was wailing, his little three-month-old fingers grabbing at Mom's hair.

Pale pastels in blurry lines. That's how Ivy would draw all of them right now if she could.

The train outside got louder and louder.

Whoosh, whoosh, whoosh.

"Ivy," Mom gasped, reaching for Ivy with her free hand. Without a word, Layla stuffed red sneakers onto Ivy's feet.

"I can put on my own shoes," Ivy snapped.

"Not when Dad's carrying you, you can't," Layla said.

"All right, let's go," Dad said before Ivy could think of a good comeback. He nodded toward the door, and Layla threw it open.

Outside was a wild adventure, stuff full of wonder

and excitement when they were bright colors in a drawing, but not the kind Ivy had ever wanted to experience in real life.

The sound was painfully loud, that train huffing closer and closer. Underneath all that, there were *snaps* and *cracks* and *slams*. The air felt muggier than their normal southern Aprils. It was a choking kind of feeling, like the earth couldn't breathe.

They spilled out the front door, Ivy's arms and legs still wrapped around her dad like a koala.

"Go, go, go," Dad said, nudging a frozen Layla with Ivy's foot.

"But we can't see anything!" Layla yelled over the wind. "What if it's out there?"

"The storm cellar is just around the corner of the house," Dad yelled back. "We'll run. It'll be okay."

"What if what's out there?" Ivy asked. She squinted through the dark, hoping for a train. A train would be so much better than what she knew was actually waiting for them.

"A tornado, Ives," Layla said, like she thought Ivy really didn't know.

"Elise, let Layla take—" Dad started, but Mom cut him off.

"I've got them. We need to go now."

Dad pressed his mouth flat, but nodded. His arms tightened around Ivy, his eyes never leaving Mom. "On three, girls. One...two...three!"

They leaped off the porch. The world flew around them like something out of *The Wizard of Oz*. Tree limbs blew through the air as if they were nothing but tissue paper, while bits of dirt and pebbles stung Ivy's face. Her hair floated upward as though she were underwater. Layla's old bike was in the grass near their gray minivan, the handlebars twisted the wrong way. Ivy saw their mailbox, *The Aberdeens* written in curvy script, dented and on its side near the big oak tree. The trunk of a pear tree was broken in two, its bottom half like bony fingers reaching for the sky. Ivy had no idea where the top half was. She didn't think she wanted to know.

Dad ran, one hand cradling Ivy's head. The rain soaked through Ivy's T-shirt and plaid pajama pants. She squeezed her eyes shut, hoping that when she opened them again, she'd be in her bed, drawing secret pictures that scared her. That kind of scary was a lot better than this kind.

"Daddy!" Layla screamed from behind them. Ivy's dad whirled around so fast, she saw spots.

"Oh no," he said. Ivy could barely hear him over the wind's fierce roar, and he set her on her feet. "Keep running for the cellar, Ivy."

"But—"

"Go!"

He took off back toward the house. Ivy saw Layla hovering over their mom, who was on her knees in the yard, screaming and trying to wrap Aaron back in her arms. He flailed on the grass, but his cries were swallowed up by the storm. After months of wishing he'd be quiet, Ivy would give anything to hear him screaming right now.

Dad scooped Aaron up while Layla helped Mom. She was gripping Evan's bald head and crying. Layla was crying and Dad was crying and Ivy was crying. The whole world was crying as everything fell apart.

Dad pushed Layla forward, and she fought the wind to get to Ivy while Mom and Dad struggled behind. Ivy couldn't see anyone clearly. They were covered in whirling hair and earth and sky. Ivy knew she should move, dive into the shelter that would tuck her underground, but she couldn't go in there alone.

"Ivy, go!" Layla yelled, her chestnut hair sticking to her face. Hail the size of golf balls fell from the sky, and Layla screamed, covering her head. When her sister reached her, Ivy wrapped her arms around Layla's waist, her pillow sopping wet and smooshed between them. They dragged themselves to the cellar, which was nothing more than a dirt room underground, built a century ago to store canned goods and potatoes. The entrance was a wooden door in the grass, and it shook and rattled against Ivy's palm as she wrapped her fingers around the handle.

Before she could get it open, a horrible screeching sound exploded behind them. Layla and Ivy turned in time to see their van lifted off the ground. It spun and the metal crumpled and then the whole thing disappeared into... nothing.

There was nothing there. Ivy scrunched up her eyes, trying to see, but when she did, she wished she hadn't.

Because there *was* something there. It was dark and huge and swirling, and it wanted to eat Ivy's whole world. If she drew it, she'd use nothing but dark charcoals and twisting lines that fell off the page.

"Inside, girls!" Dad yelled as he and Mom rushed up next to them.

Ivy yanked on the door, and it yawned open, revealing a little staircase descending into the dark. She went down first, but her ankle twisted on the last step, sending her sprawling over the dirt floor. Through the pillowcase, the corner of her notebook dug into her ribs.

"Move over, Ivy!" Layla screeched. Ivy scrambled up, her ankle screaming at her as she scurried into a corner so Mom and Dad could get into the cellar.

Dad set Aaron into Layla's arms before he ran back to shut the door. Ivy hugged her pillow to her chest, catching one more glimpse of that huge *nothing* looming up in front of her father. Then the door slammed shut and everything went dark.

-‹‹‹◆›››-

CHAPTER THREE

Undone

I vy used to think this cellar was magical. Back when Layla was a person she could trust, they'd open the cellar door and stretch out on the grass near the opening and make up stories about what was hiding down there in the dark. They weren't allowed to go in. Mom was worried that the door would close on them and get stuck and that no one would know where they were for hours and hours. Ivy remembered arguing with her, telling her that being trapped in a dark dungeon would be an adventure.

Well, it wasn't. It was damp and smelled like dirt and rotten potatoes, and Ivy's clothes were soaked, and she couldn't stop seeing that *nothing* swirling closer and closer. Who knew adventures could be so terrifying?

Above them, the door rattled and the sky roared. It wasn't a beautiful sound. It was ugly and had teeth behind it as the train chugged on and on. Ivy didn't know what it was running over and crashing into and ripping apart. She didn't want to know. She just wanted to go back to bed. She wanted her treehouse on top of a mountain.

Next to her, she thought Dad was holding Aaron again. She couldn't really see anything, but she heard him singing softly to keep her baby brother calm. Somewhere in the dark, Mom probably had her nose smooshed against Evan's head. Her headlamp, abandoned on her glass-covered bed, sure would have come in handy right now.

Layla fumbled for Ivy's hand. Ivy grabbed on, and she was so relieved that tears stung her eyes.

"Ivy," her sister said, squeezing her hand even tighter.

"Yeah?" Ivy's voice sounded tiny, and she could barely hear herself over the noise outside.

"Should we make this a Harriet story? Maybe it's not really a tornado. Maybe it's really the magical north wind come to transform us into..."

Layla's words trailed off like she was waiting for

Ivy to fill in the next line. They used to make up stories all the time. Mom had written and illustrated the Harriet Honeywell books, a chapter book series, for the past four years. She would always brainstorm with Ivy and Layla, letting them spill all their ideas into her lap. The first book was even dedicated to "My brilliant girls, without whom Harriet would never have been born." Stories, written and drawn, were in the Aberdeen girls' blood.

But Ivy didn't want to make up stories with Layla anymore.

"This isn't some fairy tale," Ivy said after a few seconds. "This is serious." She pulled her hand away from her sister's, thinking she'd feel triumphant and grown up. Really, Ivy just felt lost. She laced her own fingers together and squeezed, but it wasn't the same as Layla's hand in hers.

"I know it's serious, Ives." Layla sounded exasperated and hurt, and it made Ivy's stomach feel sour. She never talked to Layla like that. She knew she sounded like Mom when they used to get in trouble for playing hangman during church. Ivy didn't know how to be around her older sister anymore. Not since Layla and Gigi stopped being friends.

"This will be over soon," Dad said. "Then we'll go back to—"

But he never got to say whatever they might have gone back to because the loudest sound Ivy had ever heard exploded outside.

A *crunch* and a *smash* and a *crumble* and a *boom*.

Ivy clapped her hands over her ears and colored the sounds in her head. Carbon black and clear glass, the deep russet of their front porch. Squeezing her eyes closed, she shook her head, her hair tickling her arms. Those colors were scary, so she brushed them over with fuchsia starbursts and flowers with cobalt stems and a house nestled among gold-and-emerald-striped branches. She made a whole new and beautiful world, even as she worried that her own world was coming undone.

-❮❮❮◆❯❯❯-

CHAPTER FOUR

Gone

It was over in a blink. All that noise turning into an eerie silence. Ivy's lungs seemed to have stopped working, and she knocked a fist against her chest to get them started again.

"Dad," Layla whispered. "What was all that?"

"I don't know," he said. His breathing must have just started up again too, because it sounded raspy and quick.

They sat for another few minutes, but it felt like five hours. Mom was totally silent, invisible in the dark. Ivy wanted to crawl into her lap, but her lap was pretty full with Ivy's baby brother right now, just like it always was.

"Is it over?" Ivy asked.

"I think so," Dad said. "Stay here. Let me check."

Ivy heard rustling as her dad stood up. Aaron squawked a little, and Layla shifted next to Ivy, so she knew her sister was holding him now. No one spoke, and Ivy was sure they all held their breath while the cellar door squeaked open. The storm siren got louder. It was barely any lighter outside, but Ivy made out Dad's silhouette against the greenish-black sky.

He climbed the steps, but stopped when his shoulders were out and pressed his fingers into the grass. His head turned this way and that. The storm siren wound down, like a balloon deflating on a slow leak. Ivy waited for a sigh of relief, a laugh, anything to tell them it was okay.

But none of that happened. In fact, a whole lot of nothing happened. Dad stood frozen on the third-to-top step, staring in the direction of their house.

"Dad?" Ivy asked. Mom shushed her. Dad stayed on the steps but tangled both his hands in his dark hair.

"Dad?" Layla asked. No one shushed her.

He didn't move, his hands still on top of his head.

"Daniel?"

Mom's voice seemed to snap him out of it. He released

a huge sigh and turned, his eyes roaming over Ivy and Layla until they landed on Mom.

Then he said a silly thing. A wild thing. An impossible thing.

"It's gone. Everything. It's all gone."

Craig Pope

Ashley Herring Blake

lives in St. Simons, Georgia, with her family. She is the author of the young adult novels *Suffer Love*, *How to Make a Wish*, and *Girl Made of Stars*, as well as the middle-grade novels *The Mighty Heart of Sunny St. James* and *Ivy Aberdeen's Letter to the World*.

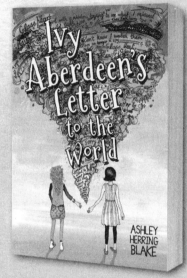
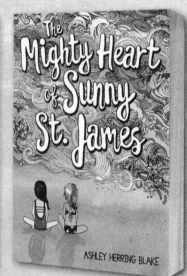